HEART BREAKER

REBELS OR RUSHMORE BOOK TWO

MICHELLE HERCULES

Heart Breaker © 2021 by Michelle Hercules

This book is a work of fiction. Names, characters, places, and incidents either are products of the author's imagination or are used fictitiously. Any resemblance to actual persons, living or dead, events, or locales is entirely coincidental.

Editor: Marginalia Editing
Proofreader: Hot Tree Editing
Photography: Michelle Lancaster
Cover Model: Andy Murray

Paperback ISBN: 978-1-950991-44-0

1

JANE

I'VE LOST count of how many times I nearly convinced myself to forget my plan and go home. But I've come this far, and if I chicken out now, I'll spend the rest of my life wondering what could have been.

I'm tired of pining for Andreas from afar. I was fifteen when we met. He was a freshman at Rushmore and my brother's new teammate.

Charming, attentive, and so beautiful it was impossible not to develop a crush on him instantly. I didn't know then about his reputation, but it wouldn't have changed what I did. An impulsive and foolish act that has left me mortified ever since. After that, he simply kept me at arm's length. I was nothing more than his best friend's kid sister.

Everyone says he's a player. It's the reason Troy pretty much forbade me to even glance in his direction. But I need to see it with my own eyes, which brings me to my current situation. I'm standing in front of Andreas's building in the chilly night air dressed as Harley Quinn, an outfit that offers zero protection against the cold, and I can't move.

For fuck's sake, Jane. Seize the moment. It's now or never.

I'm a ball of nerves. There are a lot of people coming and going, all ready to celebrate Halloween. I keep my gaze down, afraid someone will be able to tell I'm a high schooler and don't belong here.

I adjust my Harley Quinn cap to make sure it's hiding my blonde hair. My face is covered by makeup thanks to Charlie, my brother's girlfriend. I'm not even wearing perfume to be safe. I feel bad that I had to lie to her. She thinks I'm going to a party with my high school friends. I hope that with my outfit, she won't recognize her handiwork.

As I get near the party, my heartbeat accelerates, and then it pumps to the rhythm of the loud music coming from Andreas's apartment. No sooner do I step foot inside than someone shoves a red Solo cup in my hand. I hold on to it for a while, trying to blend in, but there's no chance in hell I'm drinking from it.

At first, I search for Troy and Charlie. Wherever they are, I have to keep my distance. Andreas's apartment has four bedrooms and an open living room and kitchen space. For a college pad, it's rather large. With the number of people here, I should be able to fit in and remain incognito.

Andreas has only one roommate, Danny Hudson, who I spot first, and only because of his blond curls. He, like Troy, is dressed as one of the Horsemen of the Apocalypse, and has full skull makeup on. He's chatting with a pretty girl dressed as Gamora from *The Guardians of the Galaxy*. It seems everyone got the painted face memo tonight.

A few other people are familiar, like the guys from the football team. But so far, no sign of my brother, Charlie, or Andreas. I realize then that I might have waited too long to come. A lot of people are already super drunk. If Andreas is nowhere in sight, it's possible he's already hooked up with someone. My heart sinks at the probability.

I berate myself for the idiotic feeling. I don't know what I was expecting. No one gets a reputation for being the biggest manwhore on campus for nothing. Someone bumps into me from behind, sloshing the liquid inside my cup all over the front of my costume. It has a red tinge to it, but for the love of God, I can't figure out what it is. All I know is that I have to clean up before it stains. I whirl on the spot, and fight my way through the throng of people until I reach the hallway leading to the bedrooms.

I've been here once with Troy as soon as Andreas moved in, so I know which one of those closed doors leads to his bedroom. I should use the bathroom in the hallway, but my feet take me to the end of the corridor. My hand reaches for the doorknob, and then I freeze. *What if he's with a girl in there?* My stomach ties into knots. It will probably destroy me, but on the other hand, it would force me to get over him once and for all.

I take a deep breath and brace for the worst, but before I can actually turn on the knob, the door opens inwards, dragging me forward with it. I stumble on my high heels, and crash against Andreas's solid chest. He grabs my arms, stabilizing me.

"Whoa, careful there, girlie." He chuckles.

My heart leaps up to my throat and gets stuck there. I look up, terrified he's going to recognize me. Immediately, I know that's not going to happen. His eyes are a little glazed, and the sexy smile on his lips is not something he ever bestowed upon me. It sends tingles down my spine.

"Were you looking for me?" he asks when I don't say a word.

My tongue feels thick in my mouth. *Come on, Jane, don't fuck it up now. This is your chance.*

"Yes," I croak.

His smile broadens. "You found me, babe. Would you like to come in?"

"I guess."

I guess? Good grief, girl. You're dying to go in.

He opens the door wider and lets me through. I stop in the middle of the room, trying not to show how nervous I am. My heart is pounding furiously inside of my chest, and all I can hear is my pulse drumming in my ears. *Oh my God. I'm in Andreas's bedroom.*

"I dig your outfit," he says, stopping next to me.

I turn to him. His skull makeup is a little smeared and his hair is messier than usual. For a second, I wonder if I'm the second girl to come through his bedroom door, but his bed is immaculate.

"Thanks. I like yours too."

He smiles again, and then reaches for my face, cupping my cheek. "What's your name?"

"Harley," I blurt out.

Andreas chuckles. "For real? Sweet."

He steps closer, invading my personal space. I'm shaking so hard, I don't know how I haven't fallen to the floor yet. He brushes his thumb over my lips, sending shivers of pleasure throughout my body. My breathing catches.

"You're beautiful," he says, leaning down.

He's going to kiss me and I'm seized by overwhelming panic. *What if he remembers?*

"How can you tell?" I ask through a parched throat.

"Trust me, babe. I know."

He closes the final distance between us, pressing his lips against mine, tentatively at first. I thought I'd be ready for it, but I forgot what kissing him was like. It's fireworks in July. It melts my body; it scrambles all the thoughts in my mind.

I reach for his biceps, needing an anchor to remain standing. He pries my lips open with his tongue, deepening the kiss. I taste alcohol, something sweet and potent, but I can't distinguish what. A heady feeling takes over me, like an ice-cold fever. I let go of his arms in order to link my hands behind his neck. A distinctly possessive groan comes from deep his throat, which acts like gasoline poured over my churning fire.

He pulls back suddenly, leaving me lightheaded and unsteady.

"What's wrong?" I ask stupidly.

"Nothing is wrong, babe. I just want to ask if this is okay."

My brain is fuzzy; I'm too lost in him to be able to form a coherent thought.

"I wouldn't be here if I had a problem with it," I say, faking confidence.

He reaches for the back of my head and kisses me again. It's hungry, greedy, and nuclear. It sets me ablaze; it ignites a fire deep in my core that won't be extinguished by anything besides him.

This is completely insane. I came here to finally put to rest my obsession with him. And now all I want is for him to take my clothes off and make me his, even if it's only for one night. There's no getting over him.

He breaks the kiss again to whisper against my lips, "I want to fuck you. Tell me it's what you want too."

I try not to wince at his crude admission. In all the times I fantasized about this moment, in none of them Andreas was drunk and without a clue of who I was. But he's also my weakness, a drug I can't let go of. I want him with every fiber of my body. None of the boys I kissed after him made me feel this way.

"Yes. More than anything," I murmur.

Relief shines in his green eyes right before he pounces. His mouth slams against mine, fiery and intense. His hands make quick work of the invisible zipper on my back. Before I know it, he's peeling off my catsuit, leaving me exposed in only my underwear. Goose bumps spread all over my skin when it meets the cold air. Without breaking the kiss, Andreas continues his eager exploration. He runs his fingers down my arms, and then he moves along to my breasts, squeezing both through my bra.

A moan escapes my lips, followed by his approving chuckle. Dropping his hands to his sides, he steps back to glance at my body.

"Damn, you're more beautiful than I imagined."

I cross my arms over my chest, feeling insecure under his scrutiny.

"What are you doing? Don't cover those lovely tits, babe." He pulls my arms down, and then he steers me to his bed.

I'm shaking so much that it's a relief to sit down. Andreas remains standing as he stares at me with eyebrows slightly furrowed.

Oh God. He finally figured out it's me.

"What?"

He shakes his head. "Nothing."

Grabbing the back of his shirt, he pulls it off and tosses it aside, revealing abs so perfect, they look photoshopped. He's the definition of male perfection. My mouth waters. I've never wanted to lick something as much in my life as I want to lick his taut skin. I'm surprised by my train of thought. I didn't think I had it in me to have such naughty inclinations.

The corners of his lips twitch up, but he doesn't make any comment about my ogling. Instead, he proceeds to get rid of his pants and boxers. My jaw drops to the floor when I take in the sight of his erection. I'm not a prude. I've watched porn before. But this is the first time I'm in front of the real deal. Panic begins to take hold of me. I don't know what to do now. He's going to know this is my first time. *Ugh.*

While I'm freaking out, he steps forward. His cock is right in front of me. Maybe he wants me to suck him. I don't move though, just keep staring at it like a moron. This is a disaster.

Maybe I should have drank something before attempting to seduce Andreas. Not that I had any idea this would happen.

"You can touch it if you want, babe," he says in the huskiest voice I've ever heard.

It makes my pussy throb. *Gee, if he can do that with only words, imagine what he could do with his mouth there.*

Before I lose my nerve, I reach for his shaft, curling my fingers around his girth. He hisses, and then reaches for my cap. *Shit.* He can't take it off. He'll figure who I am if he sees my hair.

"I want to stay in character," I tell him.

"That's fine by me." He caresses my cheek and I'm surprised by the tenderness.

My heart overflows with emotion, but I have to remember his gesture doesn't mean anything. To him, I'm nothing more than a hookup.

I return my attention to his cock. The skin is smooth and warm, and when I begin to pump him up and down, he seems to grow larger.

"That's it, babe," he says gruffly.

Encouraged by his words, I bring the head to my mouth, licking it first to get a taste. He grunts loudly, motivating me to continue my exploration. At first, I think I'm doing it all wrong. I don't know if I should keep using my hand while I suck. The silver lining is that if I'm awful at it, he won't know it was me. But soon I find my groove, and my worries take a back seat.

When Andreas makes a guttural sound and pulls back suddenly, it alarms me. I worry that I accidentally bit him.

"What did I do?" I ask, wide-eyed.

"I don't want to come in your mouth. I said I was going to fuck you and I meant it."

He walks over to his nightstand, and takes a condom packet from the drawer. The jitters return stronger than before. This is really happening. *Oh God.*

He turns to me and frowns. "We don't have to continue if you don't want to."

I shake my head. "I haven't changed my mind."

Then why are you staring at him like deer caught in headlights? To prove my point, I reach behind my bra and release the clasp. The fabric drops onto my lap, but Andreas's eyes remain glued to my breasts. My nipples are as hard as pebbles, and I'm not sure if it's because of the temperature in the room or his heated gaze.

"Jesus, are you trying to kill me?" he asks.

"No, not really," I answer, and then realize his question was rhetorical.

Heat creeps up to my cheeks.

He looks into my eyes and smiles, revealing his adorable dimples. Butterflies take flight in my stomach. His dimples were my undoing when we first met three years ago, and they still have the same power over me. Without breaking eye contact, he brings the foil packet to his mouth and tears it open with his teeth.

I swallow the huge lump in my throat when he rolls the condom down his shaft. This is it. No going back now—not that I want to stop what's about to happen. Andreas has awakened something primal in me. He's ignited a rebellion in my heart, in my soul. I'm tired of being the good girl, the obedient daughter. Being with him tonight is not only about sleeping with the man I've pined after for years; it's about me breaking my shackles.

Condom in place, he joins me in bed, sitting next to me. His eyes drop to my lips as he reaches for my face and cups my cheek. The gentle touch is at odds with his callused hand, and yet it sends chills down my spine. Silently, he brings his lips to mine. I expected a gentle kiss, but his tongue is possessive now.

We fall onto the mattress together side by side. While Andreas devours my mouth, his hand plays with my breasts, kneading and teasing them. Then he draws his fingers down my stomach, pebbling my skin in their wake. Right before his hand disappears underneath my panties, I gasp and freeze.

He pulls back, looking into my eyes. "Do you want me to stop?"

My pulse is thundering in my ears, my blood is rushing through my veins. There's only one possible answer.

"No."

I want his lips back on mine, but he maintains eye contact while his fingers slowly continue their travel south. He parts my folds, and then sweeps his index finger back and forth over my clit. I arch my back, closing my eyes as the most amazing sensation quickly spreads through my core. I've played with myself before, but this feels ten thousand times better.

"Damn it, you're so ready for me already, babe."

He keeps playing with my bundle of nerves, but when he teases my entrance, I open my eyes and grab his wrist.

"I don't want your fingers there. I want your cock."

God, did I really say that out loud? My face is burning up. Thank fuck for the makeup.

"As you wish, beautiful."

He takes my panties off and then rolls on top of me. The head of his erection is pressing against me now, slowly nudging in. I kiss Andreas hard to hide the fact I'm shaking like a tree in the path of a hurricane. He matches my enthusiasm with his tongue and with his hips. The first thrust is agony. He's so big that I don't even know how he can fit inside of me. But as he begins to move in and out, the pain morphs into something bearable, and then it becomes really, really good.

"Oh my God. You're so fucking tight," he murmurs against my lips.

On instinct, I raise my knees and hook my ankles behind his ass. He seems to like this new position if I'm to judge by how his grunts become louder and his thrusts faster. A familiar sensation begins to build below. I feel like I'm floating on air.

But when the orgasm hits me, I'm unprepared for it. I scream against his mouth, I bite his lower lip, I scratch his back. I've never felt anything remotely similar when I've masturbated.

Andreas's climax follows mine in the next moment. He doesn't scream like I did, but he lets out a string of curses, only stopping when the tremors in his body cease. With his face pressed against the crook of my neck, he collapses on top of me, breathing hard.

My heart is beating so fast, I'm afraid it will burst out of my chest. l did it. I fucked Andreas's brains out like I'd dreamed a thousand times before. I should feel terribly guilty that I concealed my identity from him, but right now, I'm too happy to care.

2

ANDREAS – Two months later

ONE OF MY timers is beeping, and I can't find which one. I turn around too fast and end up bumping my elbow against the flour bag, sending it to the floor in a cloud of white dust.

"Motherfucker!"

Danny comes into the kitchen then, rubbing sleep from his eyes. "What happened?" he asks through a yawn.

"I can't find my damn timer."

He raises an eyebrow. "And you decided to get your revenge on the bag of flour?"

"Yeah, that's what I did, smartass."

He circles around the mess and pulls the timer from under a recipe book. "Is this what you're looking for?"

I yank the gadget from his hand. "Yes. Ah, my sponge is done."

Danny eyes the mess over the counter—I'm not a tidy baker —and then reaches for another timer tucked between the sugar and the cart of eggs. "Why do you need more than one?"

"Different things need different times in the oven."

"Makes sense. What are you making today, anyway?"

"Lorenzo's birthday cake."

"Oh, I didn't know it was coming up. What kind of decoration are you doing?" Danny grabs my set of measuring spoons and begins to twirl them around his finger.

With a jerky movement, I retrieve them. He knows I don't like anyone messing with my stuff. "Nothing crazy."

"What? No *Paw Patrol*?" He smirks, earning a droll look from me.

"He's twelve, not five."

Danny shrugs and heads to the living room. "I'd love a *Paw Patrol* cake for my birthday."

"I'll keep that in mind," I grumble.

"The question is: why are you baking a cake? Isn't that your stepmom's department?"

The mention of that snake turns my mood sour. It's bad enough that I have to suffer her presence during special occasions. I don't need my roommate reminding me she exists.

"Probably. But I want Lorenzo to have something from me. Plus, he loves my cakes."

Danny looks at me from the couch. "Dude, do you want me to come with you to his party?"

His question makes me pause. Danny knows why I hate going to my father's. I blabbered my ugly secret to him in a moment of drunken stupidity.

"Don't you have a date or something?"

"I can cancel. It's not like I'm really into this chick." He shrugs.

As tempting as his offer is, I don't want to subject Danny to my personal nightmare. "Nah, it's okay. I'm just going to stay for the cake and then bail. I'm taking Lorenzo out for a proper birthday celebration another day."

"Okay. But do me a favor and quit stressing about baking. It's just cake." He turns the TV on.

"I'm not stressed," I grit out.

"Sure, sure."

"I just don't like to suck at things."

"Dude, you don't suck. Your cakes are better than my mother's. Just don't tell her I said that."

He can't possibly understand where I'm coming from. His mother idolizes him and thinks he can do no wrong. My father, on the other hand, believes I'm always screwing up. No matter how hard I play on the field or how many games I win, he's never satisfied. He's always pushing me to play harder, be better, through any means necessary.

Fuck. My mood is definitely rotten.

If he knew I have a hobby, I'd have to face his wrath. That prospect used to terrify me when I was younger. Not anymore. He wants me to dedicate all my free time to training. He's been pushing me to go pro, even used his connections and got scouts to come see me play. I'm a good player, but not good enough to be drafted to the NFL. That doesn't deter him and his delusional ideas though.

Playing professional football was never my dream. Baking, on the other hand, has always fascinated me. I used to watch my mother in the kitchen when I was younger, and sometimes she let me be her assistant. After she died, I relegated those sweet moments to a far corner in my mind. The memories were too painful. But reality TV, of all things, reminded me of my interest in the craft. I watched *The Great British Baking Show* one day and got hooked.

Now I know what I want to pursue. I'm switching my major from business to hotel management since they don't offer culinary arts as a degree at Rushmore—and my asshole father wouldn't pay for it. I want to own a baking company someday, and a degree in hotel management will offer me more tools than a simple business degree. He's not going to approve, so I'm not asking for his permission.

The man is a NASCAR legend. He was big in the nineties and made a lot of money. Since he was the shit back then, he won't tolerate his offspring being less than what he was. The fact his oldest son won't go pro will be a big hit to his ego.

I push thoughts of him to the back of my mind and focus on finishing Lorenzo's cake. This will be the only good part of my day, and I don't want to spoil it by worrying about my dad and his awful wife.

I ARRIVE at my brother's party late on purpose. I simply couldn't stomach being in my father's house for hours until they cut the cake. My father's mansion is in Malibu. He and Troy's father are almost neighbors.

Not surprisingly, there's valet, but I opt out of it, parking my Bronco on the side of the road. I plan on making a quick exit. Cake in hand, I circle back and enter the house through the staff's entrance. It's the quickest way to the kitchen and the path most likely to be devoid of obnoxious obstacles, such as Crystal's phony friends. They're as bad as she is.

There's a flurry of movement in the kitchen, making it resemble a restaurant and not a home. Immediately, I spot the cake Crystal ordered for Lorenzo. It's weird as shit, more like an abstract sculpture than an actual cake. I bet it cost a pretty penny. I feel like an idiot for bringing my own. Whatever, I'll eat it, and I know Lorenzo will too.

"Who are you?" a man wearing a chef hat asks me in a French accent.

"The birthday boy's big brother." I set my cake in a corner on the counter.

"Oh, you're not supposed to be here. Mrs. Rossi will be most displeased."

"Pardon my French, but I don't give a flying fuck about Mrs.

Rossi." My answer drips with venom, and it's a surprise I don't choke on it.

Jesus, Andreas. Get your act together.

"Andy!" Lorenzo's voice pulls me out of my funk immediately. "You made it."

He walks over and aims for a cool handshake, but I'm having none of it. He's my baby brother and he's getting a proper bear hug.

"Happy birthday, squirt." I rub his head for good measure, messing up his hair.

"Dude, cut it out." He tries to break free from my hold, but I have pounds of muscle against him. He'll get there though. He's almost as tall as me already.

I finally let him go, laughing when he tries to fix his hairdo.

"So, what's all this?" I point at the fancy food I know he won't touch.

He shrugs. "All Crystal's idea. This is more a party to show off to her friends than to celebrate my birthday."

"Did you get to invite any of *your* friends?"

"Yeah, a few."

"Any hot babes?" I elbow his arm playfully.

"Hot babes?" He chuckles. "You've been watching *Cobra Kai*, haven't you?"

"You got me there. It's a good show."

"Told ya."

I love my brother. He has the gift to pull me out of my crappiest moods. When our mother died eight years ago, it felt like we had nothing left in the world besides each other. Our father had been absent our entire lives save when he wanted to put the fear of God in me through punches and threats. That didn't change once Mom was gone. It only got worse.

"Don't worry about this party. We'll do something cool this week."

"Okay. You're coming to my race tomorrow, right?"

"Yeah, of course." I fake enthusiasm.

It's not that I don't want to support my brother, but going to his kart race means rubbing shoulders with our father. It's his first time racing in the junior class, so I have to be there.

"Pierre, I'm still waiting for the—Andy, when did you get here?" Crystal sets her soulless eyes on me, and just like that, my cheer is gone.

She walks over in a skintight outfit that's definitely not appropriate for a kid's party. Her fake tits don't even bounce when she moves, not that I'm staring at them. I have too much hatred toward the bitch to ogle her body.

Lorenzo sidesteps quickly, leaving me wide open to be engulfed by her unwanted hug. The scent of her overly sweet perfume mixes with all the vodka she's had already, making me nauseated. I don't return the hug. Instead, I suffer the unwanted proximity stiff as a board.

When she steps back, I'm sporting a glower. She runs a hand over the front of her dress, smoothing invisible lines, and pulling the neckline down to reveal her cleavage. She's trying to use the same tricks as before, only I'm no longer a gullible four-teen-year-old virgin.

"I thought this was supposed to be Lorenzo's party. I don't remember when he acquired a taste for French cuisine," I say.

"It's never too early to learn to appreciate the good things in life," she replies with an air of smug arrogance.

One would think she was born with a silver spoon in her hand by the way she talks. In reality, she's just a generic gold digger.

"Where's my cake?" Lorenzo asks me, interrupting our conversation.

I turn around and point at the white box in the corner. "There. I hope you like it."

"You got him a cake? What for?" Crystal asks in a high-pitched voice. "I spent a fortune ordering from the best bakery in LA."

"Don't care. Have your cake and eat it too," Lorenzo replies with a chuckle.

"Oh, you're a brat. Wait until your father hears about this."

She turns on her heels and walks out of the kitchen, almost colliding with a server who was coming in. I expect her to lash out at the guy, but she strides forward without a glance in his direction.

Lorenzo makes a face. "Oh, shit. If she tells Dad we were picking on her, he'll probably ground me."

Dad never laid a hand on Lorenzo, at least never in front of me, but my brother's comment makes my blood boil nonetheless. Crystal used to pull that shit every time when I was still living with them, but it was only with me. I was stupid to believe she wouldn't continue her manipulative ways after I moved out.

I don't want her to mess up Lorenzo's party more than she already did, so I follow her, hoping I can convince the viper to forget my brother's quip. He's the only person in the world who could make me seek her of my own accord.

I catch up with her as she's veering toward the main powder room. "Crystal, wait up."

She turns around on her heels, and in her drunken state, almost falls on her ass. She's too shitfaced to appear embarrassed.

"Andy, are you ready to apologize?"

"For what? We did nothing wrong."

Shit. The wrong thing to say. I came to try to smooth things over. But I can't play nice with her.

"Oh?" She raises an eyebrow, and her dark eyes seem to shine with mischief.

She opens the door to the powder room and drags me inside with her. It takes me by surprise, and it's the only reason

I don't resist right away. The door is not even closed and she's all over me.

"Oh Andy, I've missed you." She flattens her body against mine, making me sick to my stomach.

I push her off me in disgust, making her stagger back. "What the fuck are you doing?"

"Giving you what you want. What's your problem?" she retorts angrily.

"I didn't come here for this. I want you to leave Lorenzo alone. It's his fucking birthday, for God's sake."

"Oh, Andy. You were always so concerned about your brother. But that didn't stop you from screwing his nanny, did it?"

I'd never punch a woman, but if Crystal were a man, I'd pound her face flat. "Fuck you."

I walk out of the powder room, seething, and make a beeline to the front door. From the corner of my eye, I catch a glimpse of my father, chatting with a guest. I'm sure he wants to grill me about something, probably offer criticism about my last game's performance. *No, thank you.*

I hear him call my name as I walk out the door, but I don't stop. I keep moving, mighty glad that I parked my car outside. Jesus, I was expecting an ambush from my father, not from his deranged wife. I can't believe I ever felt anything for the woman. She's a despicable human being, I can see that clearly now. But to a naïve fourteen-year-old, she was a fucking angel.

3

JANE

My head is about to explode. Against my will, my mother dragged me to one of her boring ladies' luncheons and so far, all she and her obnoxious friends have talked about is the upcoming debutante ball they help organize. Mom is the head of the committee, which means this year, I must take part in it.

Debutante balls are not super common in California, but the affair involves planning an uber exclusive and ostentatious party, plus all the pre-event mixers, and those are right up my mother's alley. But if I hear the info sheet of another possible escort candidate, I'm going to hurl.

My stomach twists into knots and the desire to puke the salad I just ate is real. *Shit.* I *am* going to be sick. I excuse myself and make a hasty exit out of the ballroom. The sign for the restroom looms ahead, but when I see a group of girls my age veer toward it, I change course. If they hear me puking my guts out in that bathroom, the gossip will spread like wildfire throughout my mother's circle. The last thing I need is Mom

Dearest thinking I'm knocked up. That's what she would do instead of believing I had an eating disorder.

Hell. What if I am pregnant? Come to think of it, I haven't had my period since my hookup with Andreas. It's been almost two months. *Oh my God.*

I break into a run in the hotel lobby, hoping to find another restroom not currently occupied by anyone I know. A twist in my guts warns me I might not have enough time. On instinct, I follow someone from the reception desk through a door that says "Employees Only". It opens to a narrow corridor with several doors lining each side. One of them says "Restroom". *Thank heavens.*

I make it to a stall a second before my salad comes up my throat. My grotesque noises echo loudly in the tiled room, and I'm glad there's no one here to witness my humiliation. I hug the toilet until I'm dry heaving. There's a film of sweat on my forehead now, and my headache is as acute as ever.

Major disaster was avoided, but my heart is constricted painfully inside my chest. I can't believe I didn't stop to consider the possibility I might be pregnant until now. On the night I slept with Andreas, we used a condom, and I saw him discard it afterward. But what if there was some leakage?

I pass a hand over my face, feeling incredibly lost all of a sudden. I can't tell any of my friends about it because inevitably someone is going to blab to a parent and my mother will find out. I also can't go to Andreas. He doesn't even know it was me at his Halloween party. This is so messed up.

In a daze, I get out of the stall, and wash my face and mouth. My mother must be wondering where I am. I'm still lost in thought when I bump into someone coming into the restroom in a hurry. Her bag slips off her shoulder, falling to the floor and spewing a stack of flyers in the process.

"I'm so sorry," I say, even though the collision wasn't really my fault.

"Don't sweat it. I'm always bumping into people because I'm always running places. Story of my life."

She drops into a crouch to collect the flyers that are spread around her bag. I do the same to help her out. The bright colors and the group of girls wearing tight clothes, helmets, and roller skates catch my attention. I hold on to one and read the text, intrigued.

"Do you like roller derby?" she asks.

"I've never been to one." I keep my eyes glued to the flyer.

"It's so much fun. You should come next Saturday. I'm playing." She taps her index finger over one of the girl's faces. "That's me. I'm a jammer."

I look up, finding her smiling brightly at me.

"Cool. I'll try to make it. What's your team called?" We both unfurl from our lowered positions.

"Second Time Around Divas. I know, it's a mouthful, but it fits us."

"I like the name. I'd better get going before my mother sends a search party for me."

"You're a guest at the hotel?" She raises an eyebrow.

"Not exactly. I'm attending a luncheon."

"Why are you using the staff's restroom? Did you get lost?"

I shake my head. "It's a long story. Thanks for the flyer."

"No problem. I hope to see you at the game so you can tell me your long story." She winks at me.

I nod before slipping out of the bathroom. It's only when I hit the fancy hotel lobby again that I realize I didn't ask her name. I glance at the flyer one more time before I fold the paper neatly into a small square and tuck it inside my bra. *Classy, Jane, so classy.* I can't let Mom see this under any circumstances. She'll criticize my interest. But something about the girls on the picture called to me, and I want to find out what it is.

When I approach the table, I see that the second course has

already been served. It's soup, and it's probably cold. It's not likely I can eat anything now. I don't want to risk another bout of nausea.

No sooner do I sit back down than my mother asks, "Where have you been?"

"I had to use the restroom." I give her a meaningful glance, hoping she'll drop the subject. Let her think I was taking a shit. Better than the truth.

"Well, you'd better not eat anything else then."

"Yeah, I probably shouldn't." I slouch against the chair, relieved that I don't have to force any more food down, but worried sick about the possible reason why I can't keep it in my stomach in the first place.

Mom and her friends resume their conversation about the debutante ball, and I tune them out. As soon as we're out of here, I have to slip out of the house and get a home pregnancy test at the pharmacy. I can't have this doubt hanging over my head, but I also know I'm too chicken to face taking the test alone. There's only one person who I trust won't say a thing. Charlie, my brother's girlfriend.

I'M BOUNCING on the balls of my feet as I wait outside Troy and Charlie's house. They started as roommates, but now they live together as a couple. I've never met two people more perfect for each other than them.

Charlie finally opens the door and lets me through. I called ahead to let her know I was coming, but I made sure to ask if Troy wouldn't be around. If he finds out I might be pregnant, he's going to lose his shit. And if he ever learns Andreas could be the baby daddy, he might actually kill him. Not really, I'm being dramatic, but for sure their friendship will be over.

I greet Charlie with a hug, and then she stares at me with a question in her gaze. "What's up, Jane?"

Knitting my fingers together, I ask, "Troy is not home, right?"

"No, he's running errands for your grandmother. What's going on?"

I take a deep breath. Here goes nothing. "I'm in big trouble. I think I might be pregnant."

Charlie's eyebrows shoot to the heavens. "What? When did that happen?"

I pull my hair back, yanking at the strands. "You're going to be so mad at me."

"Jane, whatever is it, I promise I won't get angry."

I swallow the huge lump in my throat. "It happened on Halloween night."

She stares at me without speaking for several beats, making me even more anxious. "So, the possible father is someone from your high school?"

I shake my head. "No. This is the part you won't like. I lied to you. I didn't go to a party with my friends. I went to Andy's party."

Her jaw slackens. That evening was a disaster for her and Troy, and now I'm adding another sour note to it.

"Troy and I left the party early," she murmurs.

"I don't think you were there when I arrived."

She touches my arm. "Please tell me that whatever happened there was with your consent."

Crap. Why would she think someone assaulted me? Has Troy's insane protectiveness rubbed off on her already?

"Oh yeah. I wanted it to happen. Very much so," I reply with vehemence.

It takes a moment for my words to make sense to her. Her eyes widen a fraction when she connects the dots. She's a smart girl; she must have noticed how hopelessly in love with Andreas I am.

"Oh my God. It was Andy."

"Yep." I stick my hands in my pockets, feeling foolish now that the truth is out in the open.

"Troy is going to flip."

"You can't tell him. Promise me, Charlie," I beg.

I'm putting her in an awful position, but I can't think of a better alternative.

"Does Andy know?"

I scoff. "He doesn't even know he slept with me that night."

She furrows her eyebrows together. "What do you mean?"

"He didn't recognize me. That was my plan all along, remain incognito. I didn't expect to hook up with him—that wasn't my original intent. I just wanted to see firsthand if the rumors about him were true."

Crossing her arms over her chest, she watches me through slits. "Jane, that was wrong on so many levels. You know Andy would never cross that line with you."

"I know, okay?" I snap. "But you don't know what's like to pine for someone for years, knowing it can never happen." Tears gather in my eyes, so I turn around, ashamed of my outburst.

Charlie walks over and pulls me into a hug. "It's going to be okay, hon."

"I'm not sure it will. Like you said, Troy will lose his mind, and my mother.... Oh my God. She's going to flay me alive."

"For what's worth, I think Andy likes you."

I ease off her embrace, shaking my head. "He finds me attractive. That's all. He's a player. I know that now without a shred of doubt."

She lets out a sigh. "Okay, one issue at a time. We need to find out if you're indeed pregnant. Then we'll go from there."

I pull the plastic pharmacy bag from my purse. "I got all the pregnancy tests they had."

"I would have done the same." She smiles. "You can use my bathroom upstairs. Do you want me to come with you? I'll wait outside."

"No, I think it's better if you stay here. I'd be too self-conscious to pee on a stick knowing you're just on the other side of the door."

"All right. I was going to make some tea. Would you like some?"

"Yeah, that's probably all I can handle right now."

ANDREAS

It took me a good couple of hours to get rid of the anger from my system. I can't believe Crystal tried to get with me at Lorenzo's birthday party. That's the lowest of bitch moves. But it's not a surprise coming from her. She's vile and disgusting.

I went straight to the gym from the party. I had to get rid of all my aggression. Usually, I like to work out with a partner, but I wasn't in the right frame of mind to be near any of my friends. When I got home, I baked a batch of cupcakes, and after their sweet smell permeated my apartment, I felt a little better.

Now I'm heading to Troy and Charlie's place to drop off a box of treats. As usual, I made too many and if I don't get rid of them quickly, Danny and I will eat them all. Coach Clarkson will definitely frown if we turn into two round piglets.

It took me a while to warm up to Charlie, mostly because she acted like a total bitch when I first met her. She and Troy were like cats and dogs, and I don't tolerate anyone messing with my friends. In the end, I realized all their hate was nothing more than foreplay. I know now Charlie is crazy about my best friend, so she's cool in my book.

I don't knock before I let myself in. They never lock the house no matter how many times Danny and I tell them it's not safe. My plan is to simply drop off the goods and head out. I know Troy is not home, and since I didn't call in advance, I have no idea what Charlie is up to. She's usually super busy.

The coast is clear downstairs. There's a kettle on the stove, but it's not on. Charlie must be in her room since her car is parked outside. I'm about to set the box on the counter when I hear a toilet flush. A moment later, Charlie emerges from the bathroom near the stairs.

"Andy? What are you doing here?" she asks in a high-pitched voice.

"Uh, sorry to barge in. I came to drop off some baked goods. I'm not staying."

A girlie screech comes from the second floor, followed by the footsteps of someone running. I don't even have time to ask who is upstairs before Jane yells, "I'm not pregnant!"

A second later, she appears at the top of the stairs, holding a home pregnancy test. My blood runs cold. Our eyes lock, and immediately, her ecstasy morphs into horror. She tries to hide the test behind her back, but it's too late. My shock is quickly replaced by fury. Someone touched Jane, almost got her knocked up, which means he's dead meat.

"Andy, wh-what are you doing here?" she stammers.

Flaring my nostrils, I say, "I want a name."

4

ANDREAS

I'M SO FUCKING JEALOUS, I can't see straight. I tried to be a good friend, stayed away from Jane, and now, some douche almost got her pregnant. When she doesn't give me the answer I want, I repeat, "What's his name, Jane?"

"Andy, calm down," Charlie pipes up.

"No, I won't calm down." I turn to her. "Do you know who he is?"

Her round eyes look guilty as hell. She knows.

"It's none of your business, Andy," Jane finally replies.

She comes down the stairs, but the damned pregnancy test is nowhere in sight. She must have tucked it in her back pocket.

"The hell it's not my business. You're my best friend's kid sister. If someone took advantage of you, I have every right to know."

Her face turns beet red. "Oh my God. What makes you think was I taken advantage of?"

"Come on, Jane. You're barely eighteen. Who was it? Is it a guy from your high school?"

She crosses her arms over chest. "You can huff and puff all you want. I'm not telling you jack. You're not my keeper."

I clench my jaw tight to avoid saying something regrettable, and count to ten in my head. "Fine. Don't tell me. I can't wait to let Troy know the wonderful news." I whirl around and veer for the front door.

"Andy, you wouldn't dare." She comes after me.

"Oh, Jane. I would." I walk out of the house, fuming and ready to break things.

She grabs my arm, making me stop. "Please, Andy. I'm begging you. Don't tell Troy. He's going to go ballistic."

Her beautiful green eyes are bright with unshed tears. God, the sight of her desperation breaks my heart. I don't actually want to tell Troy. I just want to protect her at all costs, even if she's not mine to do so.

"Then tell me his name, Jane. Please?"

"I can't tell you."

"Why not? Is he someone I know?" My mind immediately thinks it's a guy on the team, which doesn't help matters.

"Why can't you let it go, Andy? I had sex; it was consensual. End of story."

I notice she doesn't answer my question, which means it *is* someone I know. *Fuck me.* If it's one of my teammates, I'm going to go savage on his ass. Jane is barely legal.

"I can't, Jane. Whoever he is wasn't careful enough and almost got you pregnant."

"You don't know anything," she grits out. "Condoms aren't one hundred percent foolproof."

I wince hearing her talk about condoms so openly. I've always known the day would come when she would start dating, I just didn't expect it to happen so soon or to feel like someone carved my heart out with a saw.

"I'm glad to hear you weren't completely stupid and used one," I retort angrily, regretting my outburst immediately.

Her lower lip quivers. She's fighting to not cry, making me feel ten times worse than I already do. One rogue tear rolls down her cheek, which she wipes away hastily.

"You're such a jerk," she says in a broken voice. "Fine. Go ahead and tell my brother. I don't fucking care."

She walks away with her chin raised high. I should stop her, say I'm sorry, but I don't move from the spot. I'm too caught up in my turbulent emotions. Plus, there's a high chance that if I stop her from leaving, I might do something even more stupid, such as kiss her senseless like I did three years ago.

Three Years Before

I can't thank Troy enough for inviting me to spend Thanksgiving with his family. I couldn't bear the thought of being in the same room with my father and Crystal and pretending I am grateful. I feel guilty for abandoning my brother, but he never experienced our stepmom's toxic ways like I did. Or our father's fists. I've only been free of them for a few months. I need more time before I can face that vipers' nest again.

Troy's mother's house is in the Hills. It's not as big as my father's mansion in Malibu, but she and my father share the same taste for modern and cold things. I hate the minimalist shit. It makes me feel like I'm in a spaceship waiting to be probed by aliens.

He warned me that his mother might be a bit prickly. She doesn't like last-minute changes. I told him not to worry about it. She can't be worse than Crystal.

True to his word, the woman is cold to me when Troy introduces us. She warms up a bit when I give her a bottle of expensive champagne. It cost five hundred dollars, a small price to pay for some peace of mind.

I meet the rest of the guests—two of his mother's friends, and his grandmother, Ophelia Holland. I quickly understand why he won't stop praising the old lady. She's a hoot and a half, completely different from her stuck-up daughter.

"Troy, can you find your sister and tell her dinner is almost ready?" his mother asks in a testy tone.

"I'm here, Mom," a pretty blonde answers from the other side of the room.

My eyes widen in surprise, and my heart skips a beat. I knew Troy had a younger sister. I didn't know she was a knock-out. Tall and curvy in all the right places, she's exactly the type of girl I gravitate to. Her hair is blonde like Troy's, but that's the only similarity they share. Her eyes are big and almond-shaped in the most beautiful green shade I've ever seen. High cheek-bones and bee-stung cherry lips complete the look that seems to have been designed to bring me to my knees.

"Jane, come meet my friend Andy." Troy's voice wakes me from my daze.

Shame immediately takes hold of me. His sister is only fifteen, for crying out loud. I'm such a perv for ogling her like that. I try to hide my reaction as I watch her come over.

"Hi, Andy. Nice to meet you." She extends her hand, and it takes me a second to snap out of my paralysis and shake it.

"Same," I reply, dropping her hand quickly, as if the contact burned me.

I'm acting like a complete idiot. It's not like I don't meet beautiful girls all the time. *So what's my problem?*

"Jane, what in the world are you wearing?" her mother says, making her wince.

"Elaine, leave the poor girl alone," Ophelia intervenes, but the damage is already done. I can see how deflated Jane is now.

"For what's worth, I like your clothes," I say.

She glances down at the flannel shirt-style dress she's wear-ing, and then she looks at me again from under her eyelashes.

My chest takes another hit. *Fuck me. Why am I having such visceral reactions to her?*

"You do?" she asks.

"I like it, too. Don't let Mom get into your head." Troy throws his arm around her shoulders. "Let's head outside. It's getting too stuffy in here."

I follow behind them, purposely keeping my eyes glued to the back of Troy's head. I barely noticed what Jane was wearing. I was too stunned by her pretty face. But I refuse to check her out. I have to remain in control here. My body betrayed me once, and it led to nothing good. I can't go down that path again, especially with Troy's sister.

We hang out on the terrace for as long as we can, but eventually we have to go back inside to eat. The dinner runs smoothly, and I dare to believe Troy's mother's obnoxious behavior was only a fluke.

I'm stuffed like a pig, ready for a nap or some serious caffeine intake, when my phone vibrates in my pocket. A quick check tells me it's Lorenzo calling. Guilt once again pierces my chest. I excuse myself from the table and take his call on the terrace.

I'm relieved he's not calling to complain I didn't come. On the contrary. He's ecstatic about the gift Dad got him. A kart. Lorenzo, unlike me, is obsessed with racing, which obviously pleases our father to no end. We talk for about five minutes before I tell him I'm being rude to my hosts. On my way back, I make a pit stop at the restroom.

I wonder when Troy wants to leave. As Thanksgiving dinners go, this wasn't bad. But I'm tired of keeping my inappropriate reaction to his sister concealed. My eyes kept wandering in her direction throughout the meal. I hope no one noticed. I need some strong liquor and maybe a hookup to set my head straight.

It's just my luck that when I step out in the hallway, I bump into the girl.

"I'm sorry," she blurts out and then dashes down the corridor.

Troy's loud voice warns me something changed while I was taking a piss. He's arguing with his mother about something she said to Jane. I remain in my spot, not knowing what to do. In the end, I go after Jane, justifying to myself that someone needs to check on her.

I expect to find her in her room, but I didn't hear a door banging shut. To my surprise, she's in the laundry room, sorting out clothes.

"Hey, are you okay?" I ask.

"Yeah, I'm fine," she replies in a choked voice.

"What are you doing?" I walk over even though my senses are warning me I should leave her alone.

"Folding laundry."

"Why?"

"Because it's menial work and it helps me calm down."

I look closely at her face and notice the tear streaks. *Ah, man.* Whatever her mother said made her cry.

"It's not worth it, you know."

"What isn't?"

"Trying to please a parent no matter what."

"It sounds like you speak from experience. Is your mother a bitch too?"

A sharp pang in my chest robs me of words for a second. "My mother is dead."

Jane stops her maniacal folding and glances at me with round eyes. "I'm so sorry. I had no idea."

"It's okay. She passed away a long time ago."

"But you still miss her very much, don't you?"

"Every day. Missing her is a constant ache. It will never go away."

"At least she was a good mother to you, even if briefly."

The pain I see shining in Jane's eyes echoes with my own. My mother died, leaving Lorenzo and me alone with an egomaniac. Unable to restrain myself, I reach for Jane's face and wipe off the moisture from her cheek. She gasps out loud, making me drop my hand in an instant.

"I'm sorry. I shouldn't have done that," I say.

She doesn't say a word as she stares at me with those beguiling eyes. I expect her initial shock will give way to revulsion in the next moment. Instead, she grabs me by the shirt and seals her lips to mine. I'm frozen, completely astonished by what's happening. But soon my body wakes up and seizes control. I grab her by the hips and deepen the kiss. Her lips taste like cherry, her tongue is sweet and demanding, and it's wreaking havoc on my mind.

I devour her mouth like I'm a starved man and she's the only sustenance I need. But when she steps closer, pressing her belly against my erection, it serves as a wake-up call. I break the kiss suddenly, pushing her back. *She's fifteen, damn it! What am I doing?*

"We can't do this," I say.

A blush spreads through her cheeks. She steps away from me, covering her mouth. "I'm so sorry."

"Andy?" Troy's voice echoes in the hallway.

Jane walks around me and runs away, going in the opposite direction of where Troy's voice is coming from. I'm still stunned by what happened when he finds me.

"I was looking for you. How did you wind up in the laundry room?"

I pass a hand over my face. "I got lost."

He chuckles. "Only you, man. I'm ready to bail. Have you seen Jane?"

"Why would I have seen her?" I ask defensively.

Shit. Get your act together, Andreas. You're acting hella guilty.

"She must be hiding from Mom. Oh well. I'll call her later. Come on, let's get out of here before more shit hits the fan."

I follow him silently, hating myself already for lusting after his sister, and for kissing her back. I'm a fucking scumbag. There's no denying it.

5

ANDREAS

I'M NOT proud to say I'm stalking Jane online. We've been friends for a while, but I've never paid much attention to what she posts—or to what anyone posts, for that matter. Social media is a waste of time. There are a few photos of her with friends from school, and also of her in several different kinds of volunteering work. There's only one picture where she's standing next to a guy in Disney character scrubs. He's much older than her—around thirty would be my guess. Immediately, my perverted brain marks him as a suspect even though I know the guy is probably a doctor at the children's hospital where she volunteers.

I shut my laptop and then go make myself some coffee. I'm tired as fuck thanks to a sleepless night. My mind was partially obsessing about Jane and also agonizing about what I must endure today. I blew off Dad yesterday, which means he's going to make me pay today, and at the tracks, there aren't a lot of places to hide.

What I need is a buffer. I veer toward Danny's room. The door is partially open.

"Danny?" I call out as I stick my head in.

There's no answer, and his bed is made. It takes me a moment to remember he went to visit his mother today. *Damn it.*

I pass a hand over my face. Troy would come with me in a heartbeat. That is, if he doesn't already have plans with Charlie. I'm not keen on seeing him face-to-face, knowing about Jane's secret, but I can't hide from my best friend forever.

"Ah, screw it."

It's only ten past nine, he may not be up already. I call him before I change my mind. It rings a few times before he answers with a groggy voice.

"Hello?"

"Yo, dude. Don't tell me you're still in bed."

"What time is it?"

"Not as early as you think."

In the background, I hear sheets rubbing together and then Charlie's faint voice asking who is on the phone. Sometimes I forget they're still in the honeymoon phase, so they're probably not getting much sleep either. A strange tightness forms in my chest and I can't make sense of it. *I'm not jealous of Troy's relationship bliss, am I?*

"It's Andy," Troy tells her.

"Oh, what does he want?" she asks in a tense tone.

Shit, she must think I'm calling to tell Troy about what happened yesterday.

"Lorenzo has a kart race today," I say. "Do you guys want to come?"

My original idea was to invite only Troy, but there's no reason to not extend the invite to Charlie as well. The more the merrier. Fewer chances for Dad to corner me. Plus, it might also give me an opportunity to grill Charlie about Jane's secret hookup.

Troy asks Charlie, and a moment later, he replies that they're game.

"Do you want me to pick you up?" I ask.

"It's easier if we meet you there."

"Sounds good. See you in an hour."

TROY AND CHARLIE are ten minutes late, but one glance at their faces tells me why. With a smirk, I say, "I'm surprised you two can still walk."

Charlie's cheeks turn a shade pinker while Troy widens his eyes innocently. "I have no idea what you're talking about, bro."

He hits me on the shoulder playfully while trying to hide his own grin.

"Have you been waiting long?" Charlie asks.

"Not long. Don't worry about it."

"I've never been to a kart race before. Thanks for inviting me."

I smile to hide my guilt. She doesn't know I had ulterior motives when I invited her here and that makes me feel bad. I don't know why the sentiment persists every time I do something shady. It shouldn't affect me anymore, considering my asshole ways.

"No problem, dudette."

"Dudette?" Charlie and Troy ask at the same time, making me laugh.

I shove my hands in my pockets. "It's what I call all my friends' girlfriends."

"Since when?" Troy arches both eyebrows.

"Well, since now. You're the first of my buddies who got serious about a girl."

"Don't Paris and Puck have girlfriends? Do you call them dudettes too?" Charlie asks.

"Uh... Puck would kill me if I even said hello to his girl, and I don't think I was ever officially introduced to Paris's jailer."

Charlie looks at Troy with an eyebrow raised. "Jailer? I hope that's not a word used to describe all your teammates' significant others."

Troy sighs heavily. "No, only Geneva has claimed that title. I'll tell you about it later."

"Yeah, let's not sour the mood with tales of Geneva, the Ball Buster," I pipe up.

"There'd better be a pretty good reason for calling her all those names." Charlie crosses her arms over her chest, sobering me up.

"There is, babe. You'll see." Troy tosses his arm over her shoulders.

I shouldn't have said anything about Geneva. Charlie would eventually pick up on the weirdness of Paris's relationship with his girlfriend. But now she clearly thinks I'm the jackass calling an innocent chick names. She's still not sure about me, all thanks to my horrible behavior last year.

"Let's get inside. The race will start soon."

We head to the pit where conversation will be difficult once the race starts. I immediately spot my father speaking with one of the crew members. Lorenzo is standing apart from everyone else, staring at the tracks. He's shifting his body weight from foot to foot while chewing on his thumbnail. He's nervous.

I sense my father's stare when I walk past him, but I don't stop until I'm standing next to my brother.

"Jitters getting to you, little brother?"

He turns to me, dropping his hand from his mouth. "No."

The furrow on his eyebrows worries me. I know how my father gets when the Rossi name is on the line.

"You're going to kill out there."

"I can't mess up," he says, then switches his attention to Troy and Charlie before I can get another word in.

While Troy introduces his girl to Lorenzo, I search for my father. He's still talking to the crew member, but maybe sensing my stare, he lifts his eyes to mine. I catch the slight narrowing of his gaze, which tells me a storm is coming my way. I lift my chin in response. *Bring it on.*

"I can't believe you're already competing at junior level. Time flies," Troy tells my brother.

I turn around in time to see the simple nod Lorenzo gives in response. *Shit.* I've never seen him act like this before a race. Something is definitely eating at him. I lock gazes with Troy. He seems to have caught on the how weird Lorenzo is acting. Wordlessly, he steers Charlie away so I can have a private moment with my brother.

"What's going on, buddy?" I ask.

"Nothing. I'm trying to get in the zone."

"It's our old man, isn't it?"

He glances at me with wide eyes, and then looks over my shoulder. Like someone flipped a switch, his green eyes turn darker, and the muscles around his mouth tense. He's too fucking young to be sporting such a somber expression.

"It's nothing, Andy. Drop it, okay?" He walks off before I can get another word in.

Seething, I stride toward my father. The asshole must have said something to Lorenzo to make him act like that. He used me as his punching bag for years. I won't let him do the same to my brother. I didn't have anyone to protect me from his evil ways, but my brother has me.

"What did you do to Lorenzo?" I ask loudly, not caring about who hears it.

"Watch your tone, Andreas. You're not talking to one of your friends."

I step into his personal space. "You'd better not pull the same crap with him as you did with me."

A shrill horn announces the race is about to start. My father glances at the track for a second, and then back at me. "I don't have time for your bullshit right now."

He walks away, leaving me choking on my anger. My breathing is coming out in bursts when Troy and Charlie join me again.

"Are you okay?" he asks.

"I'll be fine in a moment," I grit out.

"Let's find a good spot to watch the race. It's the reason we came, right?" Charlie links her arm with mine, and without hesitation, steers me closer to the tracks but far away from my father.

To say I'm shocked by her initiative is an understatement. I'm pretty sure she only puts up with me because Troy is my best friend. And after my caveman display at their house yesterday, she has even more reason to be leery of me.

Troy is sporting a satisfied grin when I glance at him. His reaction serves to dissipate my fury a little. I force my mind to stay in the present so I can cheer my brother on properly. But the worry won't stop gnawing at my insides. If I discover Dad is hurting Lorenzo in any way, there'll be hell to pay.

6

JANE

I SPEND the entire week pretending nothing happened last Saturday, but I kept waiting for Troy to come over and demand the name of the guy who took my virginity. But he never did, which means Andreas kept his mouth shut. It's so fucking ironic that he went crazy over it when he's the culprit. One more reason to take this secret to my grave. He's never going to forgive me if he finds out I tricked him. I hope Charlie doesn't cave and tell Troy.

With the fiasco of Mom's love life a couple of months ago, she spent too much of her spare time focused on me. She has eased off a little now that's she dating again, but still, the entire week was all about the stupid debutante ball. She has narrowed down my potential escorts to three candidates, and they all sound like complete toads. I'm supposed to meet them at another luncheon where the girls get to meet and pick their dates. It's like *The Bachelor* on steroids since there are only a few candidates who are considered top prizes. *Gag me.*

This weekend I manage to keep my calendar free so I can

check out the roller derby game. Getting out of the house without Mom grilling me to the umpteenth degree will require deception. My go-to person would have been Troy, but I was afraid he'd offer to tag along. I don't need a chaperone.

Without options, I have to involve Sheila, my closest friend at school. She's a nice girl, but she stresses way too easily, especially when she needs to lie. It takes a lot of cajoling to convince her to cover for me tonight. I tell her I'm going to the movies on a date. She asks the name of the guy, which forces me to make one up. He can't be someone she knows.

The game doesn't start late, so I'm hoping it's over at a decent hour. Mom has a date, which means she might come home super late, but I can't be too careful. I definitely don't want to get grounded.

The game is being held at a gymnasium thirty minutes from my house. The parking lot is full, which surprises me. I didn't know there were so many roller derby fans. It feels weird to be going in alone when everyone around me is in groups. I shove my hands in my jacket pockets and try to become smaller. Years of public reprimands by my mother made me dislike crowds.

I take a seat on the row farthest from the banked track and wait. Slowly, the place begins to fill up, but everyone is trying to find a spot closest to where the action is, so my row remains empty. To keep busy, I pull out my phone and read more about the rules. I did some research before, but I haven't memorized all of them yet.

"Jane?" Someone taps me on the shoulder.

I turn toward the voice, completely surprised when I find Fred Johnson, Charlie's friend, standing there with the biggest smile on his face. I haven't seen him in over a month. His hair is back to blond. When we met, it was bright green.

I jump to my feet. "Oh my God, Fred. What are you doing here?"

"I could ask you the same thing. I didn't peg you for a roller derby fan."

A short brunette with curly brown hair walks up to him holding a large popcorn bucket. "Hey, I found us seats closer."

"Hold on, Sylv. Do you know who this is?" Fred asks.

She glances at me. "Haven't the faintest clue."

"I'm Jane, Troy's sister."

"Ah, you're the famous Jane." She smirks, then looks meaningfully at Fred.

Did I miss something here?

He rubs the back of his neck, looking sheepish. "Yeah, this is Jane."

"I'm Sylvana, Fred's cousin. Are you waiting for someone?"

"Oh, no. I'm solo tonight."

"Oh, then you must sit with us. Come, there are better seats down a few rows."

Not wanting to be rude, I follow them. To be honest, I feel better now that I'm not alone anymore. Sylvana enters the row first, and then Fred tells me to follow her. Now I'm sandwiched between them.

When I first met Fred, he was a bit of a flirt, but I didn't think much of it. It was actually nice to be on the receiving end of his attention. He's funny, cute, and smart. But then Andreas showed up and ruined the evening with his antics. He acted like a jealous boyfriend, annoying me, and also giving me hope something had changed between us. It was all just in my head.

"Never in a million years would I have pictured you as someone who enjoys roller derby," Fred comments.

"Why?"

He shrugs. "I don't know. You seemed like the type of girl who does ballet or plays the piano."

"Dude, stereotyping much?" Sylvana butts in before I can reply. "Don't listen to him, Jane."

"That's okay. I've done both things actually, at my mother's insistence. I didn't care for either."

"What do you like to do?" Fred asks.

"I'm a horror movie fanatic, but I think you already know that." I smirk, remembering the severed head he got made in my likeness.

"Oh yeah." He chuckles. "Man, that prank was epic. Did you see the video?"

My heart squeezes in my chest. The night of the prank was when I seduced Andreas and kicked off my current problem.

"Yeah, Charlie sent it to me. So, what brings you here tonight?" I ask to change the subject.

"My girlfriend is a jammer on one of the teams," Sylvana replies.

"Oh really? Which one?"

"Second Time Around Divas."

"Shut up!" I say enthusiastically. "I've met her. That's why I'm here."

Sylvana frowns. "You've met Katja? When?"

"I bumped into her in a restroom at the Magnolia Hotel last weekend. More like collided with her, actually, and sent her roller derby flyers flying."

She chuckles. "Ah, that makes sense. She's always running somewhere."

I turn to Fred. "What about you?"

"Sylvana didn't want to come alone."

She snorts. "Like it's a hardship for you to be here."

"I never said it was. What's not to like about a bunch of badass chicks wearing skimpy outfits and playing for dominance on skates?"

"This is my first time watching a live game. I've seen *Whip It* though. It looked fun."

"Well, it's not as dramatic as in fiction, but it's pretty entertaining to watch. I'd join the team if I didn't have the coordination of a giraffe on stilts." Sylvana laughs.

"Can you skate, Jane?" Fred asks.

"Yeah. I used to do it all the time when I was younger."

There's a sudden rush in the crowd, and a moment later, the game starts. Sylvana yells when her girlfriend enters the track with her teammates, almost making me deaf.

Fred leans closer. "Do you want to trade seats with me? Sylv will be obnoxiously loud the entire time."

"It's okay." I force a smile.

He's so nice and adorable. I should be flattered that he seems to be into me. But I can't even entertain the idea of dating anyone when my heart is still bleeding over Andreas. There's not a day that I don't relive my evening with him. I'm constantly craving the taste of his lips, and the feel of his arms around me.

I shove the memory to a dark corner of my mind. One of the reasons I came here tonight was to take my mind off Andreas, my mother, and the clusterfuck that is my life right now. And don't get me started on my father pushing me to attend Stanford, his alma matter.

It doesn't take long for the game to capture my full attention. I'm enthralled by the rules, the ferocity of all the girls on the track. It's clear both teams have a tight bond among their members, and I find myself wanting that too.

I never had strong female friendships growing up. Most of the girls in my private school are phony bitches. Half of them only wanted to be my friends so they could get closer to Troy. Sheila is the exception, but it's because she's pathologically shy, and her parents are even more controlling than mine.

The game goes by in a blur. Katja's team wins, which sends Sylvana into a fit of cheers and shouts. We wait until the crowd begins to walk out, and then I follow her down to the track.

After Sylvana congratulates her girlfriend for the win, she steers the redhead to where Fred and I are.

Katja recognizes me immediately. "Hey, you made it."

"Yeah. Awesome game."

"Thanks."

Fred steps forward and hugs the girl before returning to my side.

"How do you know Syl and Fred?" she asks.

"Jane's brother is Charlie's boyfriend," Fred answers.

"And we just met," Sylvana adds.

"Wow. Small world. What did you think, Jane?"

"It was incredible. I wish I knew about roller derby when I was younger. I'd totally beg my parents to let me join a team."

Katja's blue eyes light up. "Are you a good skater?"

"I think so."

"You should come to our Fresh Meat tryouts next Saturday."

"What's that?"

"It's tryouts for our league's bootcamp program. If you're good, you might make it to our team. We're losing a teammate to the East Coast."

"I haven't used my skates in ages."

"You have a week to shake off the dust," Fred pipes up. "You have to try. It will be epic."

The insecure little girl inside of me wants to say no, but I'm tired of feeling small and unworthy. Maybe I've been obsessing about Andreas because he's the only person besides Troy and Grandma who actually saw something in me.

"Okay. Tell me where and what time, and I'll be there."

7

ANDREAS

I'M HALF ASLEEP, rubbing the tiredness from my eyes as I make
my way to the kitchen when I find my father sitting on the sofa
as if he owns the place. Technically, he does, but that doesn't
give him the right to barge in whenever he feels like it. Oh, wait.
It does. He's such an asshole.

"What are you doing here?" I grumble, aiming for the state-
of-the-art espresso machine.

I can't deal with the man without caffeine in my system. I
haven't forgotten about our little interaction at Lorenzo's race.
My brother ended in third place. Considering it was his first
time racing in that class, it was a pretty good result, even for
Giancarlo Rossi.

"You've been avoiding my calls."

"Yeah. On purpose. Take the hint."

My back is to him, but the rise of the small hairs on the
back of my neck warn me he's walking over. My spine becomes
tense, an involuntary reaction thanks to the many years of
abuse. I turn around, bracing for what's to come. He hasn't laid

a hand on me since I got strong enough to fight back, but that doesn't mean I can let my guard down around him.

"You changed your major without my consent."

"I fail to see how my degree choice is any of your damn business."

He narrows his eyes while a muscle in his jaw twitches. Faster than a cobra, he grabs me by the T-shirt and pulls me close to his furious face. "You seem to be forgetting who pays for your tuition and all this luxury. I can take it all away with a snap of my fingers."

"Do it then. I don't care."

He shoves me away, and I hit my lower back on the edge of the granite counter. Pain shoots up my spine, but I ride it in silence. I won't give him the satisfaction of knowing he hurt me again.

"Yo, Andy, what's up with the no—Mr. Rossi, I didn't know you were here." Danny walks into the kitchen wearing nothing but his boxer shorts.

My father's murderous expression vanishes. When he glances at my roommate, he has his friendly and approachable persona on—the one he uses on a daily basis to fool strangers into believing he's a nice guy.

"Hi, Danny. I had an urgent matter to discuss with Andy. I never got the chance to congratulate you on your game performances this past season."

"Thanks." He shrugs. "I couldn't have done it without the rest of the team."

"Nonsense. Let me tell you something, son. This whole team mentality is bullshit. If you're a star, you should flaunt it. I expect great things from you next year."

Fuck him. He's only praising Danny like that to rub in that I'm not good enough. Not that Danny doesn't deserve praise, but I know how my father operates.

Danny glances at me as if he's looking for a clue for how he should behave. He knows I don't get along with my father, but he doesn't know the man used me for his punching bag while I was growing up. Thankfully, the only dirty secret Danny knows about me is the Crystal deal.

"Thanks, sir," Danny replies.

Dad knocks once on the island counter with his knuckles, looking pointedly at me. "This conversation isn't over. You *will* reverse your idiotic decision."

I cross my arms over my chest. "My decision is final. Don't force me to involve Coach Clarkson in this matter. You don't want to tarnish your reputation, do you?"

I'm bluffing. My father could very well stop his financial support and I'd have no choice but to drop out. It's too late to apply for a scholarship, and I wouldn't qualify anyway. I come from money.

If looks could kill, I'd be dead on the spot. But I no longer tremble under my father's cruel gaze. I lift my chin in defiance. Wordlessly, he turns around and walks out of the apartment.

"Whoa, that was intense," Danny pipes up as soon as the front door shuts.

"You don't know the half of it." I focus on making another espresso. The first one has gone cold already.

"What happened?" He pulls up a stool and rests his forearms on the counter.

"He found out I switched majors. He wasn't happy about it."

Danny whistles. "Yeah, I definitely noticed that. I don't see what's the big deal. Hotel management is almost the same as business, but focused more on what you want to do. Why is he angry?"

"He thinks it's beneath the Rossi name," I reply bitterly.

"I'm sorry, man. I don't envy you, and this is coming from a guy who has always wanted to have a dad around."

Danny was raised by a single mom. I don't know what the situation is with his biological father, but he's never been in the picture. Like me, Danny is private about his life, only telling Troy and me the bare minimum. We all have skeletons in the closet. Maybe that's why we bonded as friends.

"Yeah, you definitely have nothing to be envious about my fucked-up family. The only saving grace is Lorenzo."

"He's a cool kid." Danny smiles. "Hey, want to make me a cappuccino?"

I chug the hot espresso, not caring that I burn my tongue and throat in the process.

"What's wrong with your hands?" I ask after I set the cup down.

"You know yours is better than mine."

I roll my eyes. He always gives me the same excuse. I'm not fooled, but Danny is the perfect roommate. He never makes any messes, he doesn't complain about all the parties I throw here, or the noise I make when I have company. Sure, I charge him ridiculously cheap rent, but he could be a jackass.

"Fine, but this is the last time," I tell him.

He grins from ear to ear. "Thank you. Are we hitting the gym before class?"

"Yeah. Today more than ever I need a good workout."

It's not a surprise I couldn't get into a better mood even after pumping iron at the gym. I barely paid any attention during my morning classes. After lunch, I have to escape campus. There's only one place I can think of going that will probably ease some of the heaviness in my chest. I head to Jane's high school. I've done that more times than I can count in the past. It's something utterly absurd. I come at the most bizarre hours and never get to see her leave the building. Just the fact that I know she's somewhere inside is enough for me.

But today of all days, she leaves early. I'm instantly suspicious. Why is she leaving school before everyone else? Jealousy erupts in my chest like a churning volcano. She must be skipping class to meet with the asshole who almost got her pregnant.

I sink in my seat, hiding from view, and wait until she gets into her car. Then I follow her. I have to know who she's seeing in secret. *Fuck.* If it's someone I know, I'm going nuclear on his ass.

She heads to the mall, and I think that makes perfect sense. What better place to have a clandestine meetup than in a busy location where you can easily blend in with the crowd?

I keep my distance. My Bronco is too recognizable. Lucky for me, an upscale store in the mall offers valet. I don't have to waste time finding a parking spot. If I lose sight of her, it's game over. I shove a fifty-dollar bill in the valet's hand along with my car key and then run across the parking lot. I didn't want him to give me shit for not entering the mall through the fancy store.

I pull my hoodie over my head as I follow Jane. She speed-walks ahead, as if she's in a hurry. Maybe she's late for her date. My anger increases at the thought, making me grind my teeth hard until my jaw hurts. When she stops suddenly, I'm forced to duck behind a column, afraid she sensed someone was following her. I wait a couple of seconds to peer around my hiding spot. Her head is down; she's looking at her phone. A moment later, she veers inside a small boutique that has colorful and racy outfits on display. *What the hell is she doing there?*

Like a stalker, I linger nearby. Maybe she's meeting her guy there. I wait ten minutes and not a single dude goes inside the store. *Fuck it.* I'm going in. Patience is not a virtue I possess.

As soon as I step foot inside, two salesgirls smile at me, and the closest asks in a flirtatious tone if she can assist me. I shake my head, and wordlessly head toward Jane. She's far in the back, distracted as she peruses a rack of clothes.

"Hey," I say when I'm standing next to her.

I shouldn't have done that. Her sweet perfume reaches my nose, bringing back forbidden memories.

She whips her face to mine, widening her eyes. "Andy, what are you doing here?"

"I was in the mall when I saw you come in here." My eyes drop to the clothes draped over her arm. "What are those?"

Cagey, she steps back, attempting to hide them from view. "Workout clothes."

I reach over and pull one pair of flimsy spandex shorts from the stack. It's small enough to pass for underwear.

"You're joking, right? You can't work out in these."

She pulls the scrap of fabric from my hand with a jerky movement. "My God. When did you become Troy's second-in-command? I told you, I don't need another overprotective brother."

Her remark makes me wince. I don't want to be her brother. Not now, not ever.

"These clothes aren't you, Jane. Please tell me you're not buying them to please your fuckboy."

Her face turns beet red, right before she shoves all the clothes in her hands at me. "You're unbelievable. Stay out of my life!"

She walks around me and strides to the door. When did she develop a temper like that? My astonishment lasts a couple seconds before I snap out of it. The stupid clothes she tossed at me meet the floor, and then I run after her.

"Jane, wait."

"Leave me alone, Andy. Don't make me call mall security on you."

I grab her arm, forcing her to halt. "Will you just stop for a second?"

She whirls around still trapped by my steely hold. "Why?

So you can keep pestering me with your misplaced protective attitude?"

"I care about you. I don't want you to get hurt."

Her green eyes become brighter. "Well, it's too late for that."

Her admission feels like a punch to my stomach. Some asshole did hurt her, like I suspected, and now he has to pay.

"Jane, babe. Just tell me his name, please."

"*Babe?*" Her eyebrows arch.

Shit. I can't believe I called her that.

"Sorry, slip of the tongue."

My answer seems to add fuel to the fire. Incensed, she pulls her arm free from my grasp, and then pokes me in the chest.

"I'm not your *babe*, asshole. Don't insult me by putting me in the same league as the girls you fuck."

I'm taken aback by her remark. Jane has always been shy and soft-spoken. This new side of her is terrifying and exciting at the same time.

"I'd never do that. You're high above them, Jane. They're nothing, barely a hazy memory."

She recoils, almost if I physically hurt her.

"Whatever. Just stop harassing me about my love life."

She turns around and speaks over her shoulder. "If you follow me again, I *will* scream for help. Don't try me."

8

JANE

I'M STILL FUMING when I cross through the gates of my mother's house. I can't believe Andreas cornered me in that store and started pestering me. I'm pretty sure that encounter wasn't a coincidence, which means he followed me there. What was he trying to achieve? I do not need a bloodhound on my case, especially him.

I decided to skip art class to get to the mall and buy clothes for the roller derby tryout. I was totally going to buy regular gym clothes until Katja told me to check out the store with the inappropriate attire—according to Andreas.

Jackass. Even when he's annoying me, he makes my pulse skyrocket with yearning. I don't know what I have to do to eradicate him from my heart once and for all. *You shouldn't have lost your virginity to him, Jane. Now there's no forgetting him.* Ugh! Am I doomed to be forever in love with Andreas?

All I want is to hide in my room and not come back until dinner. That is, if Mom is around. I'm hoping she has a date.

But that idea flies right out of the window when I find her and two other guests in the living room, and a plethora of evening gowns on hangers and draped over her furniture.

"What in the world?" I mumble.

Mom lifts her gaze to mine. "Jane, I'm glad you're home early. Come see all these beauties."

Leery, I walk closer. "What's all this?"

"Dresses for your debutante ball!" she replies in a high-pitched squeal.

Lorena Meester, one of her closest friends, walks over holding a flute of champagne. "When Elaine told me you hadn't picked your dress yet, I knew I had to intervene."

Mom rolls her eyes, a reaction I rarely see on her. "Please. You just wanted an excuse to hit up all your favorite designers."

"Why do you need an excuse?" I ask.

Lorena is married to one of the wealthiest men in the country. He's also ancient, but she doesn't seem to mind that as long as he keeps showering her with jewelry and fancy trips.

"Pete claims I don't need more gowns." She pouts, glancing at my mother.

"He clearly doesn't know his wife." Mom laughs, reaching for her own glass of champagne.

My jaw drops. I can't remember the last time I've seen her in such a good mood.

A tall man with bleached white hair and pale complexion to match comes over holding an ethereally beautiful gown in his hand. "I think this will look phenomenal on you, darling."

"Oh, Jane. This is Caz, the best stylist in Hollywood," Lorena pipes up.

The man smiles a little. "You're making me blush, dear."

There's literally no change in his skin color, so I guess he's being fake modest.

"I guess I can try that," I say.

"Oh for heaven's sake, Jane. Can you stop being such a Debbie Downer for a moment? How about showing some excitement?" Mom retorts.

Ah, there's the criticism. I was beginning to suspect I had walked into *The Twilight Zone.*

I clap my hands together and force a phony smile on my face. "Oh my God. I can't wait to try that on!" My squeaky tone is fake as hell too, which only makes Mom glower more.

"Don't be a brat."

I shake my head and then take the dress from Caz's hand. "I'll be right back."

He twists his brows into a frown. "Uh, I have to help you with that. It's a piece of art, very delicate. We can't risk getting it ruined."

Wait. Does he want me to undress in front of him? Not a chance.

"I'll be careful. Besides, if I snag the fabric, Mom has to buy the dress. So it's a win for everyone." I smirk at her.

"Ha ha. You're hilarious today, Jane. No one is asking you to get naked in the middle of the living room. Go behind the partition Caz brought and get the dress on already. He'll help you zip up."

Grumbling, I do as she says. The quicker I pick a gown, the quicker I can disappear for a while. Behind the partition, I undress fast, grimacing when I look at the underwear I'm wearing today. It's hot pink with black skulls all over it. It will totally show through the thin fabric of the dress. *Oh well.*

Caz was right though. The dress is so fine that I fear any tiny movement will cause the fabric to rip. As beautiful as it is, I'd be terrified to wear it, but I'd like to see how I look in it. I step into it and then pull the bodice up until it covers my breasts. It's a corset draped with the most beautiful lace I've ever seen. It even has tiny crystals woven through it.

Holding the top part in place, I step from behind the partition, and immediately Lorena and Caz gasp.

"Oh my. Look at you, Jane. You're a vision." Lorena presses her hand over her chest.

"That dress was made for you. That's it, no need to try anything else." Caz waves his hand.

I turn to Mom, waiting for her to tear me down. "Hmm, I don't know. Maybe if Jane ever learns to stand straight without slouching. A dress can only do so much."

My spine goes rigid, and I hate how she can manipulate me like a puppet. I don't have bad posture. In fact, my ballet teacher couldn't praise me enough for my stance.

"I don't like this dress anyway. It's too flimsy."

"Pity. You look like an angel in it," Lorena declares.

"Who is your escort?" Caz asks out of the blue.

"Undecided," I say.

"You haven't secured an escort yet?" Lorena screeches, and then turns to Mom. "How come, Elaine?"

"Jane has been most uncooperative. If she had followed my guidance, she would have already made headway with Hanson van Buuren."

The name doesn't ring a bell. But again, I only pretended to listen when Mom prattled on about escorts. He must be one of the top three candidates she'd already pre-selected.

"Who? It's the first time I've heard of him," I ask out of spite, knowing very well she must have said his name a hundred times.

Mom narrows her eyes to slits. "That goes to show how little effort you're putting in all this. It's *your* debutante ball, Jane. Not mine."

"Are sure? I never said I wanted to take part in this archaic ritual."

Lorena widens her eyes. "Jane, dear. Don't say that. It's a rite of passage and so much fun. Many girls even find their future husbands at the ball."

"How is that not an ancient mentality?"

"Don't waste your breath on her, Lorena. Jane is determined to make me suffer. She's going through a rebellious phase."

"Oh, you think I'm rebellious? Watch this."

I drop the gown to the floor, not caring that I'm standing now in the middle of the living room in my underwear. Lorena and Caz stare at me with mouths agape, but Mom maintains her bitchy face.

"How mature, Jane. Keep acting like that and you'll have to attend the ball with some idiot with bad skin."

"Why can't I find my own date?"

Mom snorts. "Oh, that's rich."

"Your escort can't be just anyone," Lorena chimes in. "Hanson's mother owes me a favor. I'll set up a date for you two to meet."

Shit. I don't want to go on a blind date set up by anyone. It's bad enough that I have to attend the stupid ball with a guy who's probably a snob.

"I thought that's what the bachelorette luncheon was for."

Lorena furrows her brows. "I don't follow. What bachelorette luncheon?"

"Jane is being a smart-mouth. She's referring to the luncheon at the marina."

"Oh, no. That's just a formality. You can't wait to snag an escort there. All the good ones will have made commitments by then."

"You'll need a dress for your meet-cute," Caz chimes in. He turns to the rack of cocktail attire. "What are you thinking, Lorena? Will it be a lunch date or dinner?"

"Definitely lunch," Mom replies. "Dinner implies other things. Saturday will be best."

Oh my God. Is she for real? Not that I want to have dinner with a complete stranger. But I don't want to have lunch either. Besides, the Fresh Meat tryouts is this Saturday. I can't miss that.

"I already have plans for Saturday," I reply.

"Cancel them. Nothing you have on your schedule can be more important than a date with Hanson van Buuren."

I curl my hands into fists. "I have a meeting to work on a school project," I grit out.

"I'm sure you can reschedule that," she replies dismissively. "Lorena is right, I've slacked off. You do need to secure the best bachelor available to make up for your lack of polish."

Heat spreads through my cheeks. Why does she have to bring me down all the time? Now I regret dropping the gown to the floor. Exposed like this, her insults seem to hurt more.

"And Hanson goes to Stanford. I'm sure he can answer all your questions about your future school," Lorena pipes up.

"I'm not going to Stanford," I declare.

Up until this moment, I have pretended to follow along with my parents' plan to send me to my Dad's alma matter. I never said out loud I have no intention of going there.

Mom's eyes narrow. "We'll see about that. I'm sure once you meet Hanson, you'll change your mind. He's quite the looker."

"Like that ever mattered to me."

Yeah, right. I never cared about all the pretty boys in my school because I was already head-over-heels in love with Andreas.

"I've had enough of this nonsense. You're going on this date, Jane, even if I have to drag you by your hair."

Her comment makes me see red. I'm done being her punching bag. She wants me to meet this Hanson guy? Fine. I will. But I can't promise I'll behave or that I will stay past starters.

I glance at the rack and spot a rich sapphire blue dress. "How about that one?"

Caz pulls the dress from the rack and holds it up for my inspection. "The Versace?"

"Too over the top for a lunch date." Mom wrinkles her nose.

Ignoring her remark, I say. "Sold."

Good girl Jane is gone.

9

ANDREAS

I WATCH Jane walk away from me in a daze. I can't fucking believe the sweet girl I used to know turned into a hurricane. And the worst of all is that I'm so onboard with this new version it's not even funny. My heart is pumping like a machine, and it feels like it's going to pierce through my chest. Not to mention what's going on in my pants. I'm sporting wood in the middle of the mall, lusting after my best friend's little sister. I'm despicable.

It's no use. I have to accept that this obsession with Jane is no longer only a matter of wanting what I can't have. Something has changed, and now I'm so screwed. Even if by some miracle Jane gave me the time of day now, there's no chance in hell Troy would ever accept me dating his sister. He knows too much about my heathen ways. He'll never believe I could give up all the women and partying for Jane. To be honest, I don't know if that's something I can do either. I'm broken and there's no fixing it.

I pass a hand over my face, at loss about to what to do. I

can't keep going on this path, following Jane everywhere like a fucking psycho with murder intent in my mind. If I see her with the motherfucker who almost got her pregnant, I won't be able restrain myself. I'm going to teach him a lesson he'll never forget.

My phone vibrates in my pocket, pulling my mind from turbulent thoughts. It's a message from Troy asking if I want to hang out later. *Fuck.* Now I feel even worse than before. I don't reply, needing time to think of an excuse. I can't hang out with him now after my epiphany.

I call Danny, the only friend I can trust with this shit. He answers on the second ring.

"Hey, you home?" I ask.

"I'm just about to walk through the door. Why?"

"Wanna meet me at Goldsboro Mall?"

"What the hell are you doing there?"

"It's a long story. They have an Irish pub somewhere here. I think it's called O'Shea's."

"Yeah, sure. I'll be there in twenty minutes.

DANNY TAKES AT LEAST HALF an hour before he walks into the pub. I'm already on my third pint and trying my best to ignore the big-titted server who keeps giving me come-hither glances. The old Andreas would be all over her like a hobo on a hot dog. Now her obvious interest makes me uncomfortable. It's like I've traded places with someone else.

"About time," I grumble.

"Sorry, I had a delay." He sits across from me and flags the waitress.

She stops next to our table, all smiles. Now she has two of us to try her luck. She'd probably be down for a threesome. The idea is depressing. Another side effect of the new me.

"What can I get you, hon?" she asks Danny.

"Same as him." He turns to me. "Need another round?"

I chug the rest of my beer, and then reply, "Sure."

When she's gone, Danny levels me with a serious gaze. "What's going on, Andy? Is this about your dad's visit earlier?"

"No. And don't remind me of that. I'm fucked, bro."

"How so?"

I lean back and run a hand through my hair. "It's Jane."

His eyebrows arch, but his surprise only lasts a split second. "So, you're finally ready to admit you have feelings for her."

"What the hell are you talking about?" I'm on edge in an instant.

"Dude, only a blind man couldn't see that you have a major crush on little Jane."

"Don't call her that," I snap.

"Sorry. But I'm right, aren't I?"

"Fuck. I don't know. Truth be told, I've been obsessing about her since we kissed."

"Wait. You kissed?" His eyebrows shoot up. He leans forward and asks, "When did that happen?"

I sigh, forgetting that I never told anyone about my lapse in judgment. "The first time Troy brought me over to his mother's house, three years ago."

"Jesus, she was only fifteen then." Danny stares at me like I'm the biggest perv on the planet.

He's not wrong.

The waitress returns with our drinks, interrupting the conversation for a moment. As soon as she leaves, I continue. "I didn't plan to kiss her, all right? She was upset about something her mother had said. I was just consoling her when she attacked me."

"She kissed you?" His tone is incredulous.

I don't blame him. I wouldn't believe it either if I were in his shoes.

"Yeah. It caught me completely by surprise. But I'm not guiltless. I didn't end the kiss right away as I should have. I kissed her back and enjoyed every second of it." I pinch the bridge of my nose and close my eyes for a second. "I'm fucking scum."

"Just because you were weak once doesn't make you scum. Please don't rip my nut sack off for saying this, but Jane is hot."

I glower at him. "Watch it."

He leans back, raising his hands. "I'm just making an observation. You haven't done anything else with her since then, have you?"

I take a large sip of my drink, needing to dull my guilt somehow, before I answer. "No. I haven't crossed that line yet, but I want to."

"Man, Troy's going to flip."

"I know. That's the problem. He's one of my best friends. I don't want to ruin our friendship."

"There's only one solution. You have to tell him."

I rest my elbows on the table and then yank my hair back. "I can't. He's never going to forgive me for even thinking about Jane in that way."

"Bro, you don't think he already suspects? Like I said, it's pretty fucking obvious."

I shake my head. "No. There has to be another way."

"If you're thinking about sleeping around, that won't work. You do that plenty." He chuckles, earning a glare from me.

"Thanks, jackass."

His amusement vanishes as he sits straighter. "Do you think Jane is into you as well?"

Danny's question makes me pause. She did kiss me first, but that could have been just a teenage impulse, a way to get back at her mother.

"I don't know. We've always been friendly, but never flirtatious or anything. She's pretty mad at me at the moment."

"Why? What did you do?"

The answer is on the tip of my tongue, but I stop just in time. I can't betray Jane's secret, not even to Danny, who I know won't tell a soul.

"I bumped into her earlier. She was in the mall buying provocative workout clothes. I gave her a piece of my mind."

Danny rolls his eyes. "Translation: you acted like a caveman."

"Kind of. I was jealous as fuck. The last time I felt this way was... you know when."

Bitterness pools in my mouth. I can't even speak about the past without feeling the need to puke. After what happened to me in my teen years, I swore to never let myself be vulnerable like that again, and here I am, desiring the impossible.

"You can't compare the two situations. That piece of shit used you to get to your father. Whatever you thought you felt for her wasn't love. With Jane, you might actually experience the feeling."

He takes a large sip of his beer while I stare at him with mouth agape. "Are you sure you're only eighteen?"

"Shh. Do you want to get me kicked out?"

I give him a droll stare. "Like that waitress will ever do that to you."

"One can't be too cautious. But seriously, man. I think you should tell Jane how you feel. If she reciprocates, then you tell Troy."

A humorless laugh escapes my lips. "You clearly don't know Troy very well. Or me."

Danny's brows furrow. "What do you mean?"

"Even if I fall head-over-heels in love with Jane, I *will* hurt her. It's unavoidable, and Troy knows that."

"Bullshit, Andy. I don't believe it."

I snort. "I appreciate the trust, but it's misplaced. I'll never be able to fully commit to anyone. That's who I am. A broken, heartless asshole."

My phone rings on the table. Troy's name is boldly displayed. "Shit."

"Aren't you going to get that?" Danny asks.

"He wants to hang out, but I've been avoiding him."

Danny reaches for my phone and answers before I can stop him. "Yo, Troy. What's up?"

"Why are you answering Andy's phone?" he asks.

The jackass gives me a pointed look. "Andy is in the restroom. Wanna meet us at—"

I yank the phone from his hand. I don't want Troy to come here. "Hey, Troy."

"Where have you been? I haven't talked to you since Lorenzo's race."

"Busy with school and family stuff."

"And pussy," he adds, making me grimace.

I haven't been with anyone since I found out about Jane's secret. She's all I can think about—her and the asshole she's been seeing.

"Actually, no girls."

Danny seems surprised for a second, but then understanding shines in his eyes. I feel like punching his knowing face.

"Jesus, are you sick or something?" Troy asks.

"I guess something," I grumble. "So, do you wanna hang out?"

I might as well face the music. I can't avoid Troy forever.

"Can't now. I've made plans with Charlie. The reason I'm calling is to ask for your help with something."

"All right. I'm listening."

"Jane has this silly ass debutante ball next month and Mom is pestering her to find an escort."

For a split second, I fear Troy is going to ask me, but then I remember he'd never steer Jane in my direction.

"She's going on a blind date with someone called Hanson van Buuren. Wanna help me dig up intel on the guy?"

Immediately, my pulse skyrockets and my vision becomes tinged in red. I don't want Jane going out with anyone, especially a douchecanoe with that name.

"When is the date?"

"Saturday, I think."

I hear Charlie's voice in the background, but it's muffled so I can't make out what she's saying.

A moment later, Troy continues in a lower tone. "Charlie is unhappy with my attitude right now. I had to promise her I won't do anything. But it doesn't mean you can't. I'm counting on you, buddy."

"Don't worry. I'll get all the dirt on this schmuck."

When I end the call, Danny is watching me through slits. He must have heard every word Troy said.

"What if that guy doesn't have any skeletons in the closet?" he asks.

"No one is perfect. And if I can't find anything before Saturday, then I guess I'll have to crash Jane's date."

10

ANDREAS

I'M HUNCHED over my laptop, distracted, when Danny comes into the kitchen. He covers his mouth, trying to suppress a yawn, and then says, "You're up early."

"I haven't been to bed." I reach for the cup of coffee next to me.

It's empty. I don't even remember drinking from it. I'm definitely going to need ten more if I'm to survive the day.

"Why? Please don't tell me you spent the night looking up the dude Jane is supposed to meet Saturday."

I groan. "No, I didn't. I couldn't find anything on the guy yet. As far as his social media profiles are concerned, he's clean. But that doesn't mean anything."

"Then why didn't you sleep?" He opens the fridge and grabs a jug of orange juice from it.

"Today is my first class in my new major track, Introduction to Food Service Management. I spent the night studying the syllabus."

"Was that necessary?" He raises an eyebrow.

"I don't want to be unprepared. I'm already behind thanks to switching majors this late in the game."

"But falling asleep in class because you're too fucking tired is okay?" He chuckles.

I peel my eyes from the laptop to glower at him. "Don't you have some place to be?"

"I'm going soon. What are you going to do about that Hanson guy? You're not really going to crash Jane's date if you can't find anything compromising, are you?"

As tempting as the idea is, I can't cross that line. Jane is already furious with me. If I show up at her date, she might not ever talk to me again.

"No, but maybe I can convince her not to go on the stupid date, period."

Danny leans against the fridge, crossing his arms over his chest. "Oh, and how do you plan to do that?"

"I don't know. I'll think of something."

"I have an idea. Why don't you just offer to be her escort? And maybe, I don't know, tell her how you feel?" His grin becomes wider.

"Quit trying to turn me into a Nicholas Sparks hero."

"The fact you know who the guy is, is telling."

I close my laptop and glare at him. "Are you trying to get your ass kicked, buddy? Because I *will* if you keep pestering me about confessions of love."

"Yeah, yeah." He chugs his orange juice, and then says, "Just don't do something crazy like lock her in the house."

"That's the stupidest shit you've said today. I'd never do that to Jane or anyone else for that matter."

"I was joking. Jesus, I'd better get out of here before you do kick my ass."

"Yeah, you do that," I say. Then I look at the time and let out a string of curses. I stand in a rush. "Shit! I'm going to be late."

CURSE DANNY for distracting me with his ideas on romance. I had to race to get to class in time. I can't make a bad first impression today. I was so damn lucky to snag a last-minute spot, and I want the teacher to know it wasn't wasted. Out of all of the classes that are now available to me thanks to switching majors, Food Management is key in order to run a successful business in my chosen area. I plan to take specialized cooking classes too, now that football season is over.

I'm not the first to arrive like I had planned, but I'm not late either, which is a miracle. I take a seat in the middle row next to a wiry guy who looks as nervous as I feel. I notice his legs are bouncing up and down. Freshman jitters, I guess.

"Hi, I'm Andy," I greet him.

"Taiyo. Nice to meet you."

"Are you from LA?"

"Yeah. And you?"

"Same."

Could this conversation be any stiffer? Gee, it's like I've forgotten how to socialize.

The classroom begins to fill, and I pay attention to the newcomers. I don't recognize any of their faces, but it's no surprise. This is an introduction class, after all. A minute later, the professor comes in. He's sporting a serious countenance that immediately reminds me of Coach Clarkson.

The rattling coming from Taiyo's desk increases. I cut him a look. "Are you that nervous?"

"Yeah. I heard Professor Norman is pretty tough. He rarely gives his students an A, but I can't let my average go down. My parents would kill me."

"I'm sure you'll be fine."

"You don't know them. They're strict as hell."

I bet they don't punish you with punches and kicks when you don't meet their expectations.

"My father is strict too, but I've learned that the only person I have to please is myself."

Taiyo stares at me with his jaw slack. I sense he wants to comment, but Professor Norman begins his lecture. I face forward and ignore my neighbor for the time being.

In the first ten minutes, he explains what he expects from us, and then goes over the required work assignment at the Rushmore Hotel we all must complete for the class. My father will love that. A Rossi doing manual labor is going to severely abuse his ego. Too fucking bad.

After Professor Norman finishes his introduction, he asks each of us to introduce ourselves and explain in a short sentence why we choose hotel management as a major. When it's my turn, I try not to squirm when all eyes turn in my direction. I should be used to attention, but this is different than when I'm on the field, dressed in my uniform and surrounded by my teammates.

"Hi, I'm Andy Rossi. I want to own a bakery business someday, so I figured a degree in hotel management would be the smart course of action for me."

"You're on the football team," someone pipes up.

"Yep," I reply curtly.

I don't know why it matters that I play sports.

"You switched majors late in the game, something that doesn't happen often," Professor Norman says. "I hope you didn't make that decision on a whim."

"No, sir."

"I'm sure you're used to receiving special treatment from my colleagues, but let me warn you, it won't happen in my class. I won't tolerate diva-like behavior here."

My entire body becomes rigid in an instant. I never acted like an ass in class because of my status as a football player or expected to be treated differently by my professors. I'm royally pissed now for Professor Norman to assume so.

"Don't worry, Professor. I won't pull a Kanye West move on you," I reply through a fake smile.

He narrows his eyes for a brief moment, and then turns his attention to Taiyo who stutters through his answer. I get lost in my head throughout the rest of the student introductions, still riding the anger. But eventually, my thoughts wander to Jane and what I'm going to do about the stupid feelings swirling in my chest. I vowed I'd never let them take control of me again, but it seems I'm losing the battle.

When the class actually starts, I have to force myself to pay attention. Professor Norman has already taken my measure and found me lacking. I wanted to do well in this class before—I'm already too far behind—but now I have the extra motivation of proving him wrong.

11

JANE

I HAD to look for an hour until I found my old roller skates. The Hello Kitty print is faded—thankfully—and they're a bit snug, but they'll have to do until I can get to the store and buy a new pair. I was planning on doing that the last time I went to the mall, but Andreas's sudden appearance derailed my plans.

A spike of anger surges within me. I can't believe he followed me there. He'd better not pull that crap again. The worst of this situation is that a part of me—the idiotic, in-love part—is gleeful that Andreas was watching me.

The house is silent. Either Mom is still sleeping, or she didn't come home last night. I tiptoe in the dark anyway until I'm outside. Then I put my skates on and try a few laps on the driveway first. I'm not wearing knee or elbow pads, so I'd better not fall. It takes me a minute to get used to being on wheels again, but once I get my groove, happy memories trickle back. The rush of excitement makes me giddy and for a moment, I forget my problems.

Okay, Jane. Now that you know you still remember how to skate, it's time for the real test.

I press the code to open the gate, and then venture out on the street. The issue is that my mother lives in the Hills. I have to be extra careful not to break my neck going down. My bravado vanishes when I begin to pick up speed and see my death flashing in front of my eyes. I swerve to the side, reaching for the neighbor's gate. My heart is hammering loudly inside of my chest while I try to get air into my lungs.

"Holy shit. That was dumb."

I sit on my ass and remove the skates before I trudge back to the house. I'm so glad the sun isn't up yet, and no one saw my humiliating moment. I have to practice skating on a flat surface. I hurry inside the house to grab my purse and shoes, and then I'm off to the beach. There's no better place to practice than the boardwalk.

Traffic is still relatively light at this time and thus, I arrive at my final destination in no time. School starts in a couple of hours, which means I have at least an hour to practice. Surprisingly, there are quite a few people out already either jogging or exercising on the beach.

I get on with it, and it's like I've been doing this for years. But soon my breathing becomes labored and sweat dots my forehead. I might feel like I'm a pro, but I'm clearly out of shape.

I stop next to a popular cafe to catch my breath and berate myself for not bringing a bottle of water with me. My throat is parched. I don't think they'll mind if I go in with my skates on. I turn to the entrance and then spot a familiar face approaching the cafe from the opposite direction.

"Fred?" I call out since his gaze is down, glued to his phone.

He looks up and a second later, a wide smile blossoms on his face. "Jane. What in the world are you doing here?"

"I could ask you the same question."

He drops his eyes to my skates and slowly looks up. "I see you're practicing for tryouts. Nice."

"Yeah. I have to. I've been skating for less than ten minutes and I'm already winded."

"You'll be fine." He pockets his phone, but the easygoing smile stays in place.

He's an attractive guy. More so now that his hair is no longer an unnatural color. And he's so nice. Why can't I get butterflies when I'm in his presence? Why did I have to meet Andreas first?

"Have you ever been to a tryout?" I ask to keep my thoughts from wandering where they shouldn't.

"A couple of times. They're fun. I could probably give you some pointers."

"Really? That would be awesome."

"Do you have time now? I was going to grab a quick breakfast before heading to work."

"Yeah, I could use a break."

"All right then."

We head to the cafe side by side, but then I remember I don't have any money. "Shit. I forgot my wallet in the car."

"Don't stress about it. It's my treat." He points at a table outside and waits for me to go first, but I'm too self-conscious already.

"No, go ahead. I feel like a giraffe on stilts wearing my skates here."

He laughs. "Trust me, you look nothing like that."

I know he's being flirtatious and it's a nice stroke to my ego, but I feel guilty for enjoying it when my heart is pining for someone who doesn't care.

As soon as we sit down, an energetic waiter comes to take our order. I select the first thing I see on the menu, plus water.

Once he leaves, Fred asks, "Aren't you a little far from home?"

"I felt like coming to the beach to train."

"Hermosa Beach is a good spot. I love living here."

"It's definitely a different vibe than the Hills."

"Don't you have school today?"

"Yeah, but I still have time before first period. Plus, it's not a big deal if I'm late. I'm always on time. Getting a tardy won't kill me."

"Oh, I like this rebellious side of yours. But then again, I always knew you had sass in you."

My cheeks become warmer and I end up lowering my gaze. As much as I want to pretend that I'm a bad girl, I feel like an impostor.

"Thanks? I guess." I shrug.

"So, what do you want to know about the tryouts?"

"How good is the competition? I mean, do I even have a chance?"

"No one expects you to know the rules. If you're a good skater, then you have a strong chance. How fast are you?"

"I don't know. I've never timed myself."

"If you're fast, you'll increase your chances even more. Teams are always looking for potential jammers. And since you're on the slim side, I think that's probably what they'd want you to be."

"What? Are you saying I'm not tough enough to be a blocker?" I fake being offended.

"No, not all. I mean, I don't know. I suppose you're tough since you have an older brother."

"I don't know what having an older brother has anything to do with being tough."

"You remember my cousin Sylvana, right? She has two older brothers, and they were pests to her growing up. She had to toughen up or she wouldn't survive their antics. Even I had to get some brawl in me to deal with them." He chuckles.

"They sound like a fun bunch," I joke. "Troy never picked on me. On the contrary, he was super protective—still is."

"Yeah, I got that vibe from him. What else you want to know about the tryouts?"

"What are they going to ask me to do?"

"Run a few laps on the banked track, see how you do when there are obstacles, etc. Nothing crazy."

The waiter returns with our food and drinks, interrupting our conversation. I dig in, surprised how hungry I am. I'm too busy shoveling food in my mouth to speak. When I'm done, I find Fred looking at me with glee.

"What?" I ask.

"If you skate with the same ferocity you eat your food, then I think you have nothing to worry about."

My cheeks turn as hot as lava. "Oh my God. I wasn't eating like a wild animal, was I?"

He shoves a piece of muffin in his mouth and grins in answer.

I watch him through slits. "Shut up. I wasn't."

"Did I say you were?"

"You implied. But whatever. I don't care. Mother Dearest is not here to chastise me."

His amusement seems to vanish. "Does she give you a hard time often?"

I shouldn't have mentioned her. It's not like me to complain about my mother to anyone. Suffer in silence is my motto. "She has expectations for my future that I don't agree with."

"Let me guess, roller derby isn't something she'd approve of."

"Nope. Hence the appeal."

"See? You're a rebel girl. I can't wait to see you rock on that track."

I cover my face with my hands. "Oh, the pressure. I hope I don't screw up."

12

JANE

I PRACTICED for the tryouts in any free time I had during the week. I was lucky that Mom was super busy with her business and didn't check on me often. But I still don't think I'm prepared enough for today. I couldn't sleep last night because I was worried about the tryouts.

Restless, I go to the boardwalk again at the crack of dawn for one final practice. I don't return home until eleven, and when I walk through the door, my mother is home and in a tizzy.

"Where the hell have you been?"

"I went to the beach for some exercise."

She looks me up and down, furrowing her brows in a disapproving manner. "You look dreadful. Get in the shower immediately. Your date with Hanson is in less than two hours."

I turn around, and head to my room. She misses my eye roll, not that she'd care. I lost track of time at the beach. I do actually want to look my best today, but not because I want to snag the most eligible bachelor. I don't plan to pick him as my date for the debutante ball anyway, no matter how the lunch goes. This is a test for me to see if I can actually shed the good girl persona. Fred said I was a rebel, and I'm ready to see if it's true.

You've been bad once already, Jane.

My inner voice can be such a bitch sometimes. Yeah, I tricked Andreas into sleeping with me, and look where that led me. Now I have another pain in the ass on my case, as if Troy wasn't bad enough.

I rush through the shower so I can have enough time to blow dry my hair and put my makeup on. I wish Charlie lived closer. She did such a good job with my Harley Quinn makeup. But alas, that's not the case, and anyway, she's probably busy today.

An hour later, I'm satisfied with the way I look. The royal blue dress is stunning and brings out the color in my eyes. It is a bit much for a lunch date, but fuck it, no regrets now. To finish up, I choose strappy sandals that make my legs seem longer. It's a pity that my ensemble is wasted on a date I don't want to go on. But at least I won't be staying long. The tryouts start at two, which gives me just enough time for an appetizer before I have to bail.

Looking in the mirror, I practice my confident posture. If I can get past the dragon—aka Mom—without crumbling under her criticism, then I'll be fine. I need to find my inner strength more than ever today.

She screams my name, telling me I'm going to be late. I glance at my phone and wince. For once, she's not wrong. I'd better hurry or I won't make it on time. I had the foresight to leave my duffle bag and roller skates in the trunk of my car, so I just grab a light jacket and blast past Mom in the living room, going straight for the front door.

"Jane!" she calls me, but I don't stop.

"I'm late," I yell over my shoulder and keep striding toward the front of the house where I parked my car.

My heart is already hammering inside of my chest, but when I see who is waiting for me outside, it stops beating for a second. My steps falter.

"Andy, what are you doing here?"

ANDREAS

It didn't take much to find out the time of Jane's date. I just casually asked Troy when the deadline was to find intel on the guy, and he told me everything I needed to know. On the drive to his mother's house, I agonized over what I was going to tell Jane. Danny wants me to confess, but how can I when I don't even know what the hell is going on inside my heart?

To be sure I wouldn't miss Jane, I arrived early. I've been waiting fifteen minutes when I finally spot her coming down the driveway. I get out of my car, and as she comes near, it seems like a burning fever takes over me. My throat is suddenly dry, and my tongue is stuck in my mouth. There's a crazy commotion in the pit of my stomach, which unfortunately reminds me of what I used to feel for the viper when I was a teen.

Jane stops in her tracks when she notices me. "Andy, what are you doing here?"

I step forward as my mind races at the speed of light. Trying to remain calm is impossible when Jane is wearing a dress that's meant to give men wet dreams. It's a miracle—and a blessing—I'm not sporting a boner right now.

"I heard you were being forced to go on a date with some preppy boy from Stanford."

She snorts. "Let me guess. Troy told you that. Did he send you here to be my chaperone?"

"Actually, he doesn't know that I'm here."

Her eyebrows shoot to the heavens. "Why did you come?"

Here it is, the opening I need to tell her something meaningful, something true. But I can't get the words out. I'm unable to tell her that I don't want her going on any dates or to balls with another guy because I'm jealous as fuck even thinking about it.

"Listen, you don't have to attend that debutante ball with a stranger. I'll gladly be your escort."

Her mouth makes a perfect O, drawing my eyes to her deliciously plump lips. I feel a stirring in my pants and curse my cock for not behaving. She doesn't answer for a moment, but when she does, it's not the answer I was hoping for.

She shakes her head, laughing without humor. "My God, Andy. You are one conceited prick. I'd rather go to the stupid ball with some random guy than suffer your presence for another minute."

Her barb feels like I've been hit by a cannonball. Words shouldn't hurt me so much, but the fact hers did means I've let my guard down again. I should be mad at myself for being weak, for breaking the promise I made years ago. But I don't care that Jane managed to pierce through my barriers.

"Come on, Jane. You can't still be mad about the incident at the mall."

She walks around the front of her car and opens the door. "I'm not. I'm just done with overprotective men in my life. Tell Troy to mind his own business."

"I told you he didn't send me here."

"Whatever. I don't have time for this crap. Bye, Andreas."

She disappears inside the vehicle and takes off in the blink of an eye. I don't move from my spot, processing what just happened.

"Fuck!"

What did I expect? I gave her nothing, not even an apology. Of course she wouldn't accept my offer. Clearly, she's still pissed at me.

I get behind the wheel, but don't drive off right away. There's a good chance that if I catch up with Jane's car, I might end up following her. What I need to do is get Jane alone for more than five minutes so I can plead my case. Maybe I won't choke next time.

13

JANE

I'M STILL FUMING when my phone pings, warning me of an incoming message. I glance briefly at the screen, expecting to see Andreas's name on it, but the text is from Hanson. At a traffic light, I read the message.

SORRY, Jane. Something came up and I won't be able to meet you today. Let's reschedule. I AM looking forward to meeting you.

I CAN'T BELIEVE IT. *This fucker is canceling on me?* Ugh, all the time I wasted getting ready I could have spent practicing for the tryouts.

Fuming, I make a U-turn and head to the gymnasium. I'll be early, but it's better if no one sees me wearing a cocktail dress. I don't want them thinking I'm a pampered girl from the Hills. My annoyance quickly vanishes when I encounter more traffic than I expected. What I thought would be a thirty-minute drive ends up taking an hour. When I arrive, I'm not the first one there. Great.

I put on my jacket, but it's short and you can still see the bottom half of my dress. My windows are tinted, so I could change in the car. *Ah, fuck it. I'm doing it.* I fumble with the zipper at the back, but eventually I managed to get the dress off. No one comes near the car, but I'm still uber self-aware that I'm half naked. *You're a rebel girl, Jane. Stop worrying.*

I never went back to the funky store at the mall after Andreas ruined my shopping trip that day. I did go back to buy a new pair of roller skates, but I opted for getting regular workout clothes.

There's a mix of everything today. Girls who are clearly into the culture and went all out with fishnet tights, tiny, colorful shorts, and rock-and-roll makeup. Others, like me, chose the blend-in style. Fred said being a good skater is what's important, not theatrics. I hope he's right.

I follow the herd toward the registration desk. I'm happily surprised to see Katja there, even though the knot in my stomach is tighter than ever.

"Jane! I'm so glad you came. I've heard you've been practicing." She hands me a form to fill out.

"Yeah. Not sure if it will be enough though."

"Don't stress about it. Just try to have fun."

"Oh, stressing is my middle name."

"I'm the same," a girl to my right says.

She's a head shorter than me, and stocky. Her hair is curly and short, dyed hot pink at the tips. But it's her crazy T-shirt that draws my attention the most. It's a pattern print of her face sporting different expressions.

"Nice shirt," I say.

She stretches the fabric down proudly. "I know! I'm Alicia Jackson, by the way."

"Jane Alexander. Nice to meet you."

We get out of line and find a place to sit in the crowded room. It's crazy how popular the sport is. I had no idea. We manage to snag two chairs and for a minute, neither of us speaks, busy filling out the registration form. When I have to list a contact person in case of an emergency, I freeze. *Shit. Who am I going to list?* No one knows I'm doing this.

I nibble on my lower lip and then finally decide to write down Troy's information. I'll tell him if I join a team. I don't want to live a secret life.

"Are you all done?" Alicia asks me.

"Yeah."

"Come on then. Let's pay the registration fee and then check out the competition."

I follow her back to the front of the registration desk. After we pay, Katja hands over blank name tags. Alicia quickly scribbles "Thunder Rose" on hers and places the tag over her chest. *Ah crap, I don't have a moniker.*

"I didn't realize I was supposed to have thought of a nickname," I say.

Katja laughs. "You don't need to pick a name now."

"Thunder Rose is what my grandma used to call me when I was little because I was such menace and my middle name is Rose," Alicia explains.

I follow her to where a cluster of girls are facing the banked track. Alicia butts in the conversation, introducing herself as if she owns the room. Some of them give her a haughty look, others offer names but quickly ignore us. Alicia gives me a what-can-you-do shrug and continues on her recon mission.

"This is so wild. I can't believe I'm here." She leans over the railing, smiling from ear to ear.

"When did you become interested in the sport?" I ask.

"Oh, since I was maybe five. My mother introduced me to it. She was a jammer."

"Oh, how cool. She must have taught you everything."

The happiness vanishes from her face. "Not really. She died when I was young. Breast cancer. I went to live with my aunt after that and she has zero interest in roller derby, or anything extreme for that matter."

"I'm so sorry."

She shrugs. "Don't be. Everyone always gets a look when they learn about my mother. Playing roller derby is a way to keep her memory alive, that's why I'm stoked to finally have turned eighteen so I can participate."

I notice she doesn't mention a father, so I don't ask.

"I just recently learned about roller derby."

She gives me a surprised look. "Shut up. You didn't know about this awesome sport?"

"Well, I knew about it, but I never gave it a second thought. It wasn't until a couple weeks ago that I came to a game and became fascinated by it."

"How do you know Katja? She's a badass jammer. I hope to join her team."

"I collided with her in a hotel restroom. She had flyers for a game and invited me to come."

"There you are," a male voice says from nearby.

Alicia and I turn. Fred is walking in our direction holding a big cup of soda in his hand.

"Hi, Fred. You weren't kidding when you said you'd be there."

"I never joke about roller derby." He turns to Alicia. "Who is your friend?"

"This Alicia Jackson. She's a roller derby legacy."

"Nice." Fred raises his hand up for a high five, which Alicia immediately reciprocates.

"Are you Jane's boyfriend?" she asks.

A blush creeps up my cheeks. "Noooo, Fred is just a friend."

"Damn, girl. Way to put emphasis on that no." He laughs.

"Oh God. I didn't mean it like that. I'm sorry."

"Don't stress." He looks over the gymnasium and whistles. "Wow, there are more girls here today than the last time I came."

"Fantastic," I mumble.

A guy wearing a tracksuit and holding a clipboard begins to steer all the hopefuls to the center of the banked track.

"We'd better get ready," Alicia pipes up.

My pulse accelerates as anticipation shoots up through my veins. I try to remain calm, or project a serene expression, but my hands are shaking as I put my skates on.

"Good luck, girls." Fred waves from his spot near the railing.

I'm too nervous now to respond, so I just follow Alicia and then sit on the floor among the other girls.

The guy with the clipboard proceeds to separate us in groups of five. He does it by alphabetical order, which separates Alicia and me. I'm in the first group, which doesn't help with the nerves.

We run laps on the banked track first, which is harder than it looks. I fall behind on the first loop and when I'm finally getting the hang of it, a girl collides with me and we both fall down in the most ungraceful manner. Laughter echoes in the room. Mortified, I don't make eye contact with anyone as I get up. The girl who bumped into me got back on her feet faster and is already speeding ahead.

It takes another full loop for me to regain my confidence and then it's time for the next group on the track. My face is still in flames when I skate back to where Alicia is sitting.

"That wasn't so bad," she says as sit down.

"It was horrible. God, I fucked up already."

"No, you didn't."

"Didn't you see? I fell."

"So what? Falling is part of the game. Getting up is what matters."

Despite her words of encouragement, I sulk throughout the rest of the first trial. Alicia does extremely well when it's her turn, which doesn't surprise me. She must have been practicing her entire life.

My group is called back on the tracks, and this time, there are cones on it. We must skate in a zigzag while they time us. I put my game face on and try to forget everyone else. My goal is to remain standing and not finish last. Pumping my legs and swinging my arms, I take off, glad that Fred told me about the obstacles so I could practice. I'm so focused on the course that when I approach another girl from behind, I wonder when I fell behind her. I zoom past her, and another. It's not until I pass the fourth girl that I hear Fred shout, "Go, Jane, go!"

I don't slow down until the whistle sounds, and even then, I need another moment to skate off the track. When I return to my spot, Alicia is smiling from ear to ear.

"Jane, that was amazing! I have to step up my game."

"Well, I didn't fall this time." I remove my helmet to cool off my head.

"Not only that. You skated so fast; you were a blur."

"Really? I didn't notice. I was too focused on not falling."

"If you don't make it on a team, I'll be shocked."

I don't want to jinx things by getting my hopes up. After everyone goes through the obstacle course, we practice playing the actual game with some of the team members. I'm first positioned as a blocker. Katja is a jammer for the opposing team. Trying to block her is impossible. She speeds past me before I can move into her path. After a while, it's clear that I'm not cut out to be a blocker. Fred was correct in his earlier assessment. That means I have to do my best as a jammer.

My chance comes up after an hour. The teams switch again, and this time I'm a jammer and Alicia is a blocker on my team. A mean-looking chick with long jet-black hair is my opposing jammer.

"Are you ready to eat dirt?" she asks me with a sneer.

I can't think of a comeback, so I don't say anything.

"That's what I thought," she adds.

The whistles blares and off we go. She takes the lead easily, but I can't let that discourage me. I have to give my all. Adrenaline and motivation fill me with energy. I pump my legs, keeping my gaze sharp to find openings to breach through. And when I can't find them, I make them. Alicia sees me coming hot on her heels, and without a second thought, body slams against the blocker in my path. I blast through and finally score a point for our team.

In the end, we lose, but not by much. I run a lap over the track to catch my breath, and finally search for Fred. He's clapping enthusiastically with a proud smile on his face. I feel a slight tug in my chest. I don't know if it's the high of the game or if I'm actually beginning to see Fred as something other than a friend.

Maybe I'm ready to let go of Andreas once and for all.

14

ANDREAS

"HOW DID IT GO?" Danny asks the minute I walk into the apartment.

I throw him a glower in response.

"That bad, huh?" His eyes drop to my crotch. "Well, you still have your nuts attached. That's a good sign."

"Ha ha. You're such a comedian." I fall on the couch like a sack of defeated potatoes.

"What happened?" He joins me in the living room, still holding a can of Pringles, but sits as far away from me as possible.

"I offered to be Jane's escort, and she shot me down."

"Did you apologize first?"

"No. And before you say I told you so, I know I messed up, okay?"

He pops a couple of chips in his mouth, chewing loudly as he observes me. I reach for the remote control and pretend to watch whatever game is on TV.

"What's your next move?" he finally asks.

"I don't fucking know. I have to get Jane alone for more than a minute to figure shit out."

"I have an idea."

As annoyed as I am with this whole situation and with the fact that Danny knows too much about my inner turmoil, I still turn to him, showing clear interest in whatever he has to say.

"I'm all ears."

"Two words: barbecue party. The weather is supposed to be nice tomorrow, so let's have a barbecue at Troy's and invite some guys on the team, plus Jane, naturally."

I give him a droll look. "I said I need time alone with Jane. How do you think I'm going to get that in a full house and with Troy watching her every move?"

He grins, his eyes gleaming with mischief. "Simple. It's all a matter of giving Jane the wrong time and creating a reason to get Troy and Charlie out of the house."

I shake my head. "Jesus, where do you get those convoluted ideas? This is real life, not a soap opera."

He shrugs, popping another chip in his mouth. "Make fun of me all you want. My plan will work. Do you want to get Jane alone or not?"

There's no point denying the obvious. I'm desperate. "Fuck yeah."

"Okay then. Don't worry. I'll take care of everything. All you have to do is not muck things up on your end."

I grumble, sinking further into the couch as I cross my arms. "That, my friend, is the biggest challenge."

JANE

I'm on pins and needles as the organizer reads from this clipboard, announcing the names of those who have been selected for the league's bootcamp and what teams they will join after the four weeks of intensive training. When he says Alicia's name, she lets out a squeal and squeezes my arm so hard, I know it will leave a mark. I don't mind the pain. I'm sore in so many places already, what difference does one more spot make?

My heart is racing; there are only two spots left. The second-to-last name he calls is not mine. My heart sinks. That's it. I didn't make it. Alicia laces her fingers with mine and holds my hand in a death grip. *Gee, she's strong.*

"And last, but not least, Jane Alexander, for Second Time Around Divas," the organizer calls.

"Yes!" Alicia throws her arm over my shoulders. "I knew you would make it!"

"Oh my God. I can't believe it," I murmur, still stunned.

She helps me to my feet, and in a daze, I let her steer me toward the railings where Fred is waiting for us. No sooner am I within reach than he hugs me enthusiastically, almost sending us both to the floor.

"Easy there. I can't fall now in front of the organizers. They might realize they made a mistake."

He pulls away. "No way, Jose. You were the fastest skater today. They'd be crazy if they didn't snatch you."

Katja approaches us, grinning from ear to ear. "Congrats, Jane. I'm so stoked we got you on our team. And Alicia, wow. Your mother would have been so proud."

"Thanks," she beams.

"What happened to your voice, Katja?" Fred asks, noticing how rough it sounds.

"Oh my God. You have no idea how hard it was to snatch Alicia and Jane for Second Time Around Divas. It ended in a screaming match."

"More than one team wanted us?" I ask, unable to hide the surprise from my tone.

"Oh yeah. The Bay Hurricane team wanted you badly. But in the end, Scary Samantha made our case for us."

"Scary Samantha? Who is that?" I ask.

"The jammer who gave you a hard time," Alicia replies.

"Oh. The brunette?"

"Yup." Katja nods.

"How did she make the case for you?"

"She didn't want you on her team. She doesn't like competition. So in the end, her refusal to accept the obvious worked in our favor."

"Accept the obvious? I don't follow."

"You're way faster than she is. She's afraid you'll dethrone her," Alicia pipes up.

"Aren't you worried that will happen to you?" I ask Katja, even though I really don't think that's possible. She was so good in the game I watched.

"Of course not. I don't care who is the lead jammer on our team. I care about winning, and with you two on board, damn, there's no stopping us next season."

"When do we start bootcamp?" Alicia asks eagerly.

"Next weekend, bitches. We train Saturday and Sunday from eight to four, so you'd better clear all your weekend plans for the next four weeks."

Ah, crap. I have the stupid luncheon at the marina and the debutante ball is in six weeks, which means more long and boring social events until then. How am I going to get out of them?

"That sounds great," I say through a fake smile.

Fred lingers while I remove my skates, and then walks out with Alicia and me. She asks for my phone number and we make plans to meet up next week to practice. Once she leaves, Fred turns to me.

"You did really well out there. I even recorded some of it if you would like to see."

I twist my face into a grimace. "Ugh, better not. I probably look awful."

"Not at all. Anyway, I feel like such an achievement needs to be celebrated. Do you want to go somewhere grab a bite to eat?"

Now that I'm coming down from the high, my body remembers that I've been running on fumes. I never ate lunch, thanks to Hanson canceling our date. But looking at Fred's open and expectant face makes me hesitant to accept his invitation. I know he likes me, but I'm not sure yet if I'm ready to see where this will lead. He's not a rebound guy, that's for sure. I need more time.

"Gosh, I wish I could, but my mother is expecting me, and I don't want to push my luck."

Disappointment washes over his face, but he quickly buries it under a smile. "That's okay. Raincheck?"

"Yeah, sure. Thanks for coming today to cheer me on."

"You're welcome. I can't wait to watch your debut."

"Four weeks. Boy, that's going to fly by." I hug my middle when a sudden tension forms in the pit of my stomach again.

I thought surviving the tryouts would be the hardest part and that once it was over, I wouldn't have this ball of dread in my belly. I was obviously wrong. First, I have to find a way to come to bootcamp without my mother finding out. And then I actually have to get out there, and be part of a team of badass chicks.

Did I bite off more than I can chew?

I say goodbye to Fred and once inside my car, I check my messages. Mom texted me a few times to ask how the date went. I ignore her for now. There's also a missed call from Troy. Did he call to apologize for sending Andreas over to do his dirty work? I still don't buy that he came of his own accord.

Curious, I call my brother back. He answers on the second ring.

"Hey, Jane. How's it going?"

"What's up, Troy?" I reply coldly.

"Do you have any plans tomorrow? I'm throwing a last-minute barbecue party at my place since the weather will be nice. Wanna come?"

I consider his invitation for a second. My body is too sore after today, so there's no practicing tomorrow. And if I come, Mom won't have much opportunity to pester me about the debutante ball or how I still don't have an escort. The only issue is that Andreas will probably be there.

"Who's coming?"

"Danny, Andy, Puck, I think Paris too, and a few other people you don't know. It's not a big party or anything. It will be chill. That's what I told Danny, anyway, when he made the suggestion."

"Oh, so this barbecue was Danny's idea, not yours?"

"Yeah. Does it matter?"

Considering Danny is Andreas's roommate, I have reason to be suspicious. On the other hand, Andy wouldn't be crazy enough to pull a stunt in front of Troy.

"No, not really," I say. "What time?"

"Eleven."

"Okay, I'll be there."

15

ANDREAS

Danny and I arrive at Troy's a little before ten to have enough time to setup for the barbecue. I still don't know how he plans to get them out of the house for at least an hour so I can a have chance to speak to Jane alone. He told me not to worry about it, so we'll see what he comes up with.

I'm in the backyard getting everything ready when Troy sticks his head out and shouts. "Yo, Andy. We have to run to the store. Charlie needs something and I forgot to buy the veggie burgers for Paris's fancy ass."

I'm about to ask why Paris can't buy his own damn burgers when my brain catches up with my mouth. That's the excuse to get Troy out of the house. How he fell for it will remain a mystery until I can grill Danny later.

"Okay. I'll keep working here."

I wait a couple of minutes before I head back in to make sure the coast is truly clear. I also don't want to miss when Jane arrives. My stomach is tied in knots, a sensation I never thought a girl would make me feel again. I pass a hand over my face, fighting the urge to grab a cold beer from the fridge to take the edge off. But alcohol won't help me now. I have to be stone-cold sober for this. The likelihood I'll say something wrong is already high enough as it is.

Whenever I'm nervous, keeping my hands busy helps. I search Troy's pantry, hoping he has the basic ingredients for something simple. Surprisingly, I find everything I need— thank you, Charlie—and that alone already calms me down. I spot a few bananas that are turning brown and decide to make a banana cake. As I measure the ingredients, I keep an eye on my phone. Jane was told to get here at eleven, and it's already ten to.

A minute later, I hear a car door slam outside. My heartbeat kicks up a notch. Another moment passes before Jane walks in, carrying two grocery bags. We both freeze as our stares connect.

"Hi Jane," I croak.

"Where is everyone?" she walks over slowly, her eyes shining with apprehension. Any wrong word will send her into flight mode. I have to be careful here.

"They had to make a quick run to the store."

She sets her groceries bags on the counter and glances at the mixture bowl in front of me. "What are you making?"

"Banana cake. I was bored."

"I never knew you baked."

"There are many things you don't know about me."

She doesn't reply, but she also doesn't break eye contact. There's something different about her today. She seems more confident and I wonder if it has anything to do with her date yesterday. I become blind with jealousy, but fight to appear unaffected.

"How was your date?" I ask, making an effort to keep my tone normal.

Her eyes narrow. "Don't start."

I widen my eyes innocently. "What? It was just a question. Can't a friend ask?"

"We were never friends." She crosses her arms over her chest. "You're my brother's annoying sidekick."

Ouch. Jane one, Andy zero. I walk over the counter, needing to get closer to her. She seems leery of my approach, but at least she doesn't step back.

"My mistake. I thought we were more than that." My voice drops to a low timbre, giving my words a double meaning.

Satisfaction rushes through me when I catch Jane swallow hard. She noticed it too and is not unaffected.

"That's because you think the world revolves around you," she retorts.

I stop in front of her, an inch away from invading her personal space. My heart is beating savagely inside of my chest, almost as if it wants to burst out. *Jesus fucking Christ. What's happening to me?*

"You didn't answer my question," I press.

"God, you can't drop anything, can you? You're like a dog with a bone."

"You have no idea how much that statement is true."

"Fine, if you must know, the douchecanoe canceled the date."

Yes! I shout in my head, punching the air.

"Try not to look so smug about it," she continues.

"I'm not." I grin.

"Ugh. You're insufferable." She slams her open palm over my chest as she tries to sidestep me, but I grab her arm, stopping her.

She whimpers, causing me alarm. I let go of her at once. "I'm sorry. Did I hurt you?"

Without making eye contact, she steps back, massaging the place I held her. "No, don't be silly."

I watch her carefully. She's hiding something. "Let me see your arm, Jane."

"What for? I told you I'm fine." Her voice rises an octave.

She's definitely lying. *Why?*

"Let me see your arm, Jane." I stalk her, not caring if I invade her personal space now.

"No," she replies stubbornly.

I reach for her again, grabbing her arm and squeezing a bit tighter this time.

"Ouch! Let go of me, you brute."

"I'm not pressing that hard. You're hurt."

Done with her bullshit, I yank her hoodie's sleeve off her shoulder, and see then the massive bruise on her arm. She pulls away from my grasp, face red with fury, and adjusts the sleeve.

"What the hell, Andy!"

"I could say the same thing, Jane. What the hell? Who did this to you?"

Her eyebrows shoot to the heavens. "No one."

"Don't lie to me. You're protecting that fuckboy who almost got you pregnant, aren't you?"

Her mouth opens, but no sound comes from it.

"That's it, isn't it?" I whirl around, pressing my knuckle against my forehead. I'm so furious that I could break something. "Fuck! I'm going to kill him."

"For fuck's sake, Andreas! No one hurt me," she shouts, frustrated.

I look at her again. "Then what happened?"

She takes a deep breath, dropping her gaze to the floor for a second before meeting my eyes again. "I got hurt during roller derby tryouts yesterday."

"What?"

"You heard me." She lifts her chin higher.

"Roller derby? For real?"

Her green eyes darken. "Yeah, for real. What's with the surprised tone? You don't think I can handle roller derby?"

I shake my head. "It's not that. I just didn't know you were into extreme sports."

"It's a new interest."

I'm relieved her injury wasn't caused by an asshole. But now I have so many questions.

"Fair enough, but why are you keeping it a secret?"

She runs her hand through her hair. "Well, my mother will never approve, for starters. And I don't know yet what Troy will say. I'm tired of having people dictate what I can and cannot do. It's my life, damn it."

Shit. I'm one of the assholes who was trying to keep Jane in a cage. I feel wretched, worse than the lowest scum.

"I'm sorry."

"For which part? Acting like a deranged caveman, or calling me a liar?"

"For everything. I lost my mind when I learned you were no longer...." *Ah, fuck, I can't go there.*

"I was no longer what? A virgin?" She raises an eyebrow in challenge.

I shake my head, not meeting her eyes. "Forget I said anything."

"Oh my God. That's what you were going to say. Why do you care? I'm nothing to you, just your best friend's little sister who stole a kiss from you a million years ago."

Her reminder of that day forces me to look at her. Her cheeks are red from anger, but it's her eyes that are my undoing. They're so open and vulnerable. This is it. It's now or never.

"You have no idea how wrong you are. There hasn't been a day that I haven't thought about that kiss. It might be a distant memory to you, but to me, it's like it happened yesterday."

She snorts. "That's rich. Do you want me to believe that the kiss of a clumsy fifteen-year-old is imprinted in your mind? Maybe as a horrifying memory."

"Horrifying? Are you insane? It's one of the best memories I have."

"What are you trying to say, Andy? Do you have a thing for me now? Is that it?"

I yank my hair at the strands. "I have no other explanation."

Disappointment washes over her face and it's clear I said the wrong thing.

"No other explanation, huh? I have one for you. How about you're a player, and I'm just something new that caught your eye?"

"No, you're not just another plaything. I care about you." I step closer. "More than I should."

She laughs with derision. "You know, if you had told me that a few months ago, I might have believed you. But I've seen you in action. I know you don't mean a word you say."

"You've seen me action? What's that supposed to mean?"

Her face turns ashen as guilt shines in her eyes. "Never mind."

"Don't 'never mind me'. Tell me, Jane. Where and when did you see me in action?"

"I don't have to answer anything." She turns around and veers for the door.

"Oh no. You're not going to run away from me without answering the question." I run past her and block the exit.

"Get out of my way, Andy. I'm serious."

"I will if you tell me when you got proof that I'm too much of a player to possibly develop feelings for you."

This is going all wrong. I'm confessing, but not exactly how I planned in my head.

"You don't have feelings for me. Stop saying that!" she snaps.

"You want proof that what I'm saying is true?" I step closer, but this time, Jane steps back.

I don't stop though; I keep going until she has nowhere to go. I back her against the wall, caging her in.

"How about I've been going crazy out of my mind imagining you with someone else? It kills me that you slept with another guy. And do you want to know why? Because I don't want you with anyone else but me. I tried to fight it, Jane. By God, I did. You've always been off-limits for more reasons than one."

Tears gather in her eyes, confusing the hell out of me. I reach for her face to wipe the first tear that rolls down her smooth cheek. "Why are you crying?"

A storm of dark emotions forms in her eyes. She bats my hand away. "Because you're saying everything I've always wanted to hear, but it doesn't matter now. It's too late."

The truth hits me like a steely punch. Jane might have had feelings for me before, but I waited too long and now she's in love with someone else.

I step back, not wanting to prolong this awkward moment any further. My whole life, I've always fought for what I wanted, but with Jane, I can't force my will. She should run far away from me.

"You're not going to ask me why it's too late?" she asks in a tight voice.

"No need. I get it now. I lost my chance. Don't worry. I won't bother you anymore. I'll try to rein in my jealousy. I hope this dude is worthy of you."

Speaking those words out loud is like stabbing myself in the chest. It seems now that I've confessed my feelings for her, everything hurts ten thousand times more. I've lowered my shields. There's no protection from the blows.

She watches me with round, bright eyes, and when more tears streak her face, she doesn't bother to dry them off. She should be relieved that I'm backing off without a fight. So why is she staring at me like I broke her heart?

"It was you," she blurts out.

"It was me what?"

"You were my first and you don't even remember."

The floor seems to vanish beneath my feet. My pulse skyrockets, blowing my head off its orbit, making my ears ring. How could I have done something so careless and not remember? Fear grips my insides. I'm terrified to find out the truth, but I have to know how low I managed to go.

"Jane, what did I do?"

16

JANE

WHAT HAVE I DONE? I swore to take my dirty secret to the grave, and I just go and blurt out the truth to Andreas?

"Jane, what did I do?" he asks in a pitiful voice.

Hell, he must think he did something horrible to me, when in reality, I'm the one who did the despicable act. I can't backtrack now. I have to tell him everything and risk him hating me forever.

"I went to your Halloween party."

He furrows his eyebrows together, probably trying to fish out his drunken memory from a forgotten corner of his brain. Suddenly, his eyes widen.

"You were Harley Quinn?"

I close my eyes for a second, fighting a new wave of tears. "Yes."

"I was drunk out of my mind that night, Jane. You knew I hadn't recognized you. How could you?"

"I'm sorry."

"You're sorry? You're sorry!" he yells, making me wince.

"You tricked me into crossing the line with you, something I tried so hard not to do."

"I know! And that's why I did it. It was wrong, no denying that. You weren't ever supposed to know."

"Oh, that makes it so much better." He throws his hands up in the air. "Why would you want your first time to be with someone so wasted he wouldn't recognize the girl he had been pining after for years?"

I hastily wipe the tears from my eyes. "Because it was *you!* I've been in love with you since I stole that kiss."

There's no point keeping that part a secret anymore. I'm already in a pit of despair, might as well get all the truth out.

His face contorts as if he's in pain. "You lied to me. I've been going crazy, hating the asshole who almost got you pregnant. Little did I know that jerk was me."

Dropping my chin, I glance at the floor. "You weren't supposed to know," I repeat weakly.

"I can't be here. I have to go."

I look up and watch Andreas stride out of the house. As soon as he closes the door with a loud bang, I cover my face with my hands and let the ugly tears fall. The torrential stream gets worse when I hear the loud rumble of his Bronco. He's never going to forgive me. If only I had known that he had feelings for me. *God, what a mess.*

A moment later, the door bursts open again. My breath catches. Andreas is back and he's coming for me.

"Andy, I—"

He captures my face in his large hands and crashes his lips against mine. His possessive tongue invades my mouth with fury and passion. I can taste the anger in his savage kiss, but also all the suppressed feelings he hid from everyone, even me.

When I don't think I can remain standing any longer, he pulls away, leaving me confused and lightheaded.

"You're coming with me." He takes my hand and steers me out of the house.

I'm too dazed to question him, so I just let him take me wherever he wants.

"Where's your car?" he asks.

"I had to park it a block away."

"Good."

He opens the door of his Bronco for me, waits until I slide inside, and then shuts it again. I don't take my eyes off him, trying to decipher what's going on in his head. The intensity in his eyes is still there, but I can't read the emotion.

Silently, he takes his seat behind the steering wheel. He left the engine running when he went back into the house to get me. But he doesn't drive off immediately.

He turns to me. "Buckle up."

With shaking hands, I do as he says. It's only then that he puts the car in Drive.

"Where are we going?"

"Back to my place."

"Why?"

"Because I need to make things right."

I have no idea what that means, but there are excited butterflies and a knot of dread in my stomach competing for space.

"What about Troy? The barbecue?"

"Don't worry about that."

Andreas's jaw is locked tight, and I can't see his eyes anymore since he's wearing sunglasses now. He kissed me, but now he's acting like he didn't set my body ablaze a minute ago.

I face the road ahead, but I couldn't recall the color of the car in front of us if asked. My mind is racing, going at hundred miles an hour. My heartbeat is not far behind. The thumping inside my chest is as loud as the car's engine.

The drive is shorter than I remember, maybe because

Andreas broke the speed limit to get us here faster. I force my body to move and get out of the car before he can circle around to open the door for me. I feel like I'm inside a vortex and I need to regain some control.

The corners of his lips twitch upward as he steps in front of me, then he takes my hand again and together we enter the building. We bump into two sorority girls in the lobby. They both greet Andreas in a sugary tone, completely ignoring me. But he doesn't acknowledge them, and despite my nervousness, I smirk, pleased beyond measure.

We ignore the elevator and head for the stairs. Andreas's apartment is on the top floor, but it's only four flights up. Whatever is on his mind, he's in a hurry to get to it. We race up the stairs, taking two steps at a time. My leg muscles protest; I'm still sore from yesterday. I suck it up though. I'm eager to reach his place too, because the suspense is killing me.

Andreas doesn't let go of my hand, not even to fish his key out of his pocket or open the door. When I step foot in his apartment, all the memories come rushing back. I haven't been here since the Halloween party.

The sound of the door slamming shut again makes me jolt, but I don't have time to recover from it before Andreas spins me around and kisses me again. He drops my hand to capture my face once more, almost as if he's afraid I'm going to run away. He obviously doesn't know how intoxicating his kiss is. I wouldn't be able to move from this spot even if his apartment were on fire.

He moves one hand to the back of my head, tangling his fingers with my hair, while his other hand runs down my side, grazing the underside of my breast before resting on my hip. He digs his fingers in my skin, pulling me closer, and I moan in response, not sure if this is really happening or if I'm dreaming.

The sound of a phone ringing bursts through the rose-colored haze surrounding us. With a groan, Andreas pulls back, biting my lower lip before letting go.

"To be continued. Don't go anywhere."

Like I'd be able to move even if I wanted to.

"Hey, Danny. What's up?"

"Where are you?" Danny asks.

I'm close enough to Andreas I can hear him clearly.

"Something came up." He looks at me, smiling cheekily.

"Troy is bitching that you left a mess in the kitchen."

"Ah, crap. I totally forgot about the banana cake."

"What do I tell him?"

"Shit." He threads his fingers through his hair, pushing his long bangs back. "Tell him Lorenzo needed me."

"Okay, but you know you'll have to elaborate on your excuse. Does your disappearing act have anything to do with you-know-who?"

"Yeah, it does."

The heated gaze he gives me makes my entire body go haywire. I'm craving his touch, but at the same time, I have to know what's going on here. This little break worked to get some of my sanity back.

"I have to go." Andreas presses the End button and shoves his phone back in his jacket pocket.

"Wait," I tell him when he steps closer to me. "Why did you bring me here, Andy? I thought you were furious with me."

"I was mad for a hot second, but I was the idiot who didn't realize who you were." He tucks a loose strand of hair behind my ear. "Right now, I'm angry at myself for not remembering much of that evening. You didn't deserve for your first time to be a rough tumble in the sheets with a drunk bastard like me."

"You might not remember much, but it wasn't a bad experience."

"Did I hurt you?"

My cheeks become hot. It's silly to get embarrassed when we've already done more than fool around.

"It hurt just a little."

He kisses me again sweet and fast, and then presses his forehead against mine. "I'm sorry."

"I'm the one who needs to be apologizing here. For tricking you, for lying."

"You've been a naughty girl, sweet Jane." He chuckles. "Now what you said makes sense. I acted like a jackass that night. I've been bad for the longest time. My reputation is not a lie."

"What does that mean for us?" I ease off. "If you don't think you can com—"

He presses a finger against my lips. "I wouldn't have started anything with you if I wasn't serious. But I am a broken asshole, Jane. There's a good chance I'll fuck up. I always do."

I search his eyes and read nothing but the truth. He believes wholeheartedly in his statement and that breaks my heart.

I hold his face between my hands. "I won't let you."

"Well, I already did."

"Let's agree that we both messed up. Which means we get a clean slate."

He kisses my nose, and then the corners of my lips. Goose bumps break out on my arms and a shot of desire travels down to my core.

"I'd like that. I want to make it up to you if you'll let me." He kisses me again, long and hard this time.

I reach for his arms, digging my fingers into the fabric of his jacket. At once, the fire he ignited when he kissed me at Troy's returns. I match the tempo of his tongue beat for beat while I step closer to his inferno. The man is incendiary and I'm burning hot for him.

He breaks the kiss suddenly to whisper against my lips, "Is that a yes?"

"It's a hell yeah." I try to capture his lips again, but he stops me.

"Wait. We're not rushing through this. Since I don't remember our first time, this is a do-over. We're taking things slowly."

"How slowly?"

He smiles wickedly. "I'll show you."

His fingers lace with mine and we head to his bedroom. Everything is as I remember, but this time, he knows who I am. I look at the bed, letting those memories assault me. My clit throbs, recalling the feel of his length inside of me.

Andreas kisses my neck while he pulls my hoodie off. I close my eyes, letting out a whimper. He runs his fingertips over my bruise and whispers, "Does it hurt a lot?"

"Not right now."

He bends over and kisses the spot. "Do you have any other places in need of attention?"

"Yeah, right here." I touch the side of my thigh.

"I'm afraid I'll have to inspect that closer."

He drops into a crouch in front of me and tugs my leggings down. I reach for his shoulders, needing the support to remain upright. When he sees the huge purple mess, he freezes.

"What the hell. How did you get this?"

"Someone collided with me on the banked track and we both fell."

He glances up. "I don't like to see you injured like this."

I furrow. "Do you really want to start this relationship by giving me grief over roller derby?"

"I'm not giving you grief. I'm just saying I don't like to see you covered in bruises."

"You'll have to get used to it."

He narrows his eyes. "Only if I get to see you kick ass on the track."

A bubble of laughter goes up my throat. "I still have to go through bootcamp."

"Yes, you do. Right here in my bedroom." He runs his tongue over my bruised leg, erasing my amusement in an instant. All that's left is yearning for this beautiful man.

He curls his fingers around the sides of my panties and looks up. "May I?"

I nod, unable to form words. My throat is dry now. Anything I say will probably sound like a croak.

Keeping eye contact, Andreas rolls down my underwear, exposing my sex. He keeps going until they're off.

"Did I taste you here, Jane?" he asks in a husky voice.

"No."

"Tsk. That needs to be remedied."

His face disappears between my thighs, and when his tongue finds my clit, I cry out, unprepared for the sensation. He laughs, blowing hot air against my core, and then continues his delicious torture.

"Oh my God, Andy. Take me to bed."

"Why? I'm perfectly fine here."

"My legs are about to give out."

"All right."

He grabs me by the hips, applying pressure to the bruise. I bite my tongue to keep the whimper bottled in. I don't want to get him distracted by my injuries again. He doesn't notice because as soon as I'm sitting at the edge of his mattress, he reaches for my breast with one hand, and pushes me down while he opens my legs with his other. Then he resumes eating my pussy as if it were candy.

The room begins to spin. I'm back inside the vortex, only there's no regaining any kind of control anymore. I let go of all restraint and soon, the orgasm hits me, more intense than the first time. I moan, and call his name, shaking from head to toe.

Andreas only stops when I can't take the assault against my sensitive spot any longer and beg for mercy.

I don't move while I catch my breath. The room is no longer spinning, but I am still floating on air.

The mattress dips to my right when Andreas lays by my side, propping his head against his fist.

"How did I do?" he asks.

"Do you want me to give you a score?"

"Not exactly. I want to pretend this is our first time together."

His eyes soften, and if it's possible, I fall in love with him even more. "Technically, it is. On Halloween, you fucked Harley Quinn."

He glowers. "Don't talk like that. I hate that you experienced my asshole self."

I roll on top of him, holding his arms above his head as I straddle him. "Fine. I won't talk about the past anymore, but only if you stop calling yourself names."

"Why? It's the truth."

He can be a jerk, controlling, a veritable pain in the butt. But when he belittles himself, it causes a pang in my chest. I curl my fingers tighter around his wrists, putting more weight on them.

"Promise me."

"Fine, I promise. Can I have my hands back now? I have plans for them."

"Hmm, I don't know. I kind of like you in this submissive position."

He narrows his eyes to slits. "You know you weigh nothing, and I can easily break free."

"I wouldn't be so sure about th—"

In a swift move, he dislodges me, rolling over to cover me like a blanket. "You were saying?"

"Not fair. You caught me by surprise."

"Do you want to see unfair moves?" He rotates his hips, pressing his rock-hard erection against my clit.

I whimper, drawing a smirk from him. *Oh yeah? Two can play at this game.* I lift my knees, hooking my ankles together behind his ass, and then pull him to me.

"How about my moves?" I capture his lower lip between my teeth and tug slightly.

"One hundred percent unfair. I think it's time to be reintroduced to your sweet pussy."

17

ANDREAS

I ROLL off Jane for a second to search for a condom in my nightstand drawer. The box is almost empty, a sign I haven't been myself for a while. I always make sure I've got plenty on hand. Maybe there's hope for me after all. Maybe my father and Crystal are wrong, and I'm not a fuck-up.

I can't think about those two hateful people now. Not when I have the most beautiful girl—inside and out—next to me.

I turn to her. "Where were w—"

My words get stuck in my mouth. Jane has gotten rid of the rest of her clothes, and is now lying naked on her side, watching me with a Cheshire cat smile. My gaze drops to her glorious breasts, causing me acute pain, especially in my crotch. My dick seems to grow larger at the sight.

"You were saying?" she asks.

"My God, you're beautiful."

A blush spreads over her cheeks, but she holds my gaze. "It's your turn now. You're wearing far too many clothes for my liking."

I jump from the bed and get rid of my jeans and shirt faster than I've ever done anything in my life. Jane's eyes drop to my cock, and I swear they widen a fraction.

"You can touch it if you want to."

She lifts her gaze to mine again. "You said the same thing to me on.... Never mind."

We agreed to leave the past behind, but I'm too curious to let that one go. It's fucking sad that I don't remember the details of that night.

"Oh? And what did you do?"

Groaning, she rolls on her back and pulls a pillow to cover her face. "I don't want to talk about it. I shouldn't have even mentioned it."

Damn it. Now I really have to know. I take the pillow away from her. "Come on, sweetheart. Tell me. This is a safe space." I smile.

She snorts. "Safe space? You're having too much fun at my expense."

"I'm not making fun of you. But like you said, I can't let things go. I'm a dog with a bone."

Her gaze narrows. "Fine. But this is the last time we're going to discuss that night."

"Cross my heart and hope to die." I make the sign across my chest.

She sighs, resigned. "I tried giving you a blow job, but I'm pretty sure I sucked at it. You didn't even let me finish."

A burst of laughter escapes my mouth. "That's what you're embarrassed about?"

"Don't laugh!"

"I'm sorry, sweetheart, but it's pretty funny."

"No, it isn't. Shit. Now I'm mortified all over again."

I cover her with my body, pressing my cock against her belly. "I probably didn't want to come in your mouth."

"That's what you said, but I wasn't sure if it was true. I've never sucked a guy before."

Her confession makes me feel crazy good. "Don't worry, babe. I'll teach you, but now, I want to fuck you until you see fireworks."

She opens her legs wider and arches her back. "Hmm, I'm fine with that."

I pepper her neck with open-mouthed kisses, loving the goose bumps that form on her skin. "Tell me, Jane," I whisper in her ear. "Did I make you come the first time?"

"Yeah."

I draw my tongue across her collarbone. "Good. It wasn't a total bust then."

"No, you were amazing and considerate, despite not knowing who I was."

I lean on my elbows to peer at her face. "I'll never forgive myself for that."

She cups my cheek. "You have to, because I already did."

My chest overflows with emotion and I can't breathe for a moment. I thought I knew what I felt for her. I mistakenly confused it with the same feelings I had when I was a naïve teenager. But this is different. It's so much more and I can't quite describe it.

I bring my lips to hers again, kissing Jane deeply and slowly. I want to savor her mouth, be consumed by her taste. Jane's hands find my back, her nails scratching my skin softly. She begins to gyrate her hips underneath me, and immediately, I mimic the movements of what's to come.

My cock is now pressed against her heat. She's so slick between her legs that it won't take much to slide in. I can't let that happen. One pregnancy scare is way too many.

"Hold on, sweetheart. I have to put protection on before I lose my mind."

I reach for the condom, and then sit on the balls of my feet.

I keep my eyes locked with Jane's as I tear the wrapper and fish the condom out.

"Can I put it on?" she asks.

"Yeah," I say in a voice I barely recognize.

Her fingers are nimble and gentle, but her hands on my cock is absolutely torture. My balls tighten. This could very well end up with me pulling a quick draw move on her. I squeeze my butt cheeks and focus on not coming yet.

As soon as the condom is in place, I fumble forward, locking my lips with hers as I sheathe myself inside her tight pussy. I said I was going to take things slow, but my body seems to have other ideas. I'm fighting against three years of lusting after the impossible, three years of wanting to the most beautiful girl I've ever laid my eyes upon.

Jane's hands find my back again, but this time she digs her nails deep. It will leave a mark and I don't care. She can brand me all she wants because I'm as much hers as she is mine.

The bed begins to rattle. The headboard is banging against the wall loudly and in sync with the pumping of my hips. I'm glad this isn't Jane's first time. I'm fucking her so hard, it'll be a miracle if we can walk straight afterward.

Her knees are up, her legs crossed behind me. She's kissing with tongue and teeth. This isn't as a sweet moment as I thought it would be. This is raw need. This is letting go and being consumed by a passion that's been brewing for the longest time.

"Jane, babe, please tell me you're close," I whisper against her mouth.

"Oh my God," she breathes out, capturing my face between her hands.

Her body convulses, her walls tighten around my dick, and I lose it. I'd scream if I wasn't busy kissing the hell out of her. Now my body is shaking too as I empty myself inside of her. I don't stop moving. I piston in and out even faster, trying to prolong the best orgasm of my life.

Eventually, all good things must come to an end. I shudder with one final thrust, and then collapse next to her.

"Fuck," I say out of breath.

When Jane doesn't reply, I roll on my side toward her. Her eyes are closed, but her breathing is as erratic as mine.

"Jane, babe. Are you okay?"

"Give me a second. I'm trying to reassemble my body after it burst into a million pieces across the galaxy."

"Are you saying I gave you an out-of-this-world orgasm?" I ask, amused.

She pries one eye open. "Yes, you turned me into stardust."

Unable to resist her beautiful, sexed-up face, I kiss her. It was meant to be a quick one, but now that I've tasted her, I'm greedy for more. She brings her body flush with mine, as eager to keep going as I am.

"Hold on, babe. I have to get rid of the condom first."

"Oh, sorry."

It takes me only a few seconds to discard the condom in the bathroom bin, but when I return to my room, Jane is already half dressed.

"What do you think you're doing? I thought you wanted round two."

"I heard my phone ring in the living room. I bet it's Troy asking me where I am."

I push my hair back. "Oh shit. I totally forgot about the barbecue."

She pulls her leggings up, and I know I won't be taking them off again today. The magnitude of what we did hits me at once. Troy will kill me when he finds out about us.

Hastily, I put a pair of sweatpants on and follow Jane to the living room. My eyes drop to her sweet ass, and I don't feel an ounce of guilt. I can finally ogle her freely now—at least when we're alone.

"It was Troy. I'd better call him back."

"What are you going to tell him?"

She turns around. "I don't know. Definitely not the truth. I don't want his reaction to spoil things for us yet. I hope he hasn't spotted my car."

"We can't keep our relationship a secret from him forever."

She bites her lower lip, causing a stirring in my pants. *Jesus, settle down, Andreas.*

"I know we can't, and I don't want to. But this is so new, I don't even know yet where we stand."

I walk over, and then pull her closer to me. "I want you, Jane. I've wanted you for a long time. I'm not going to let you slip through my fingers. I'm yours."

"Exclusively?"

"What kind of question is that? Of course, exclusively. Unless you want to date other people."

She twists her face into a scowl. "Now you're being thick on purpose. It has always been you, Andy."

"Good. That means I'm taking you to the debutante ball."

Her eyebrows arch. "It's in six weeks. That means we have to come out to Troy way sooner than that."

"Why?"

"You don't know your best friend? He's going to flip, and it will probably take him ages to get over his overprotective brother issues and accept that you're my boyfriend."

I smile from ear to ear, letting the happiness flow freely through me. "I love that you called me your boyfriend."

"You do?" Her eyes twinkle.

"I do, sweet Jane." I kiss her on the cheek—it's safer—and then step back. "Now call your annoying brother back so we can resume our activities."

18

JANE

I wish I could have spent the entire day with Andy, but if I didn't come home, my mother would probably call Troy and my ruse would be up. Andreas had to drive me back to my car. For the first time since Troy moved to Grandma's house, I was glad finding a parking space on this street during the weekend is a nightmare.

I was hoping Mom wouldn't be around when I got home, but unfortunately, she is, and she has company. Her friend Lorena, the one who arranged my date with Hanson van Buuren, and another woman who I believe is also on the ball committee. They're all around the dining room table, which is now overrun by packages and samples of merchandise.

Mom lifts her gaze in my direction. "Where have you been?"

Crap, can she tell that I've spent the entire afternoon having mind-blowing orgasms?

"At Troy's. He had a barbecue."

"You spent the whole day at your brother's?"

"Yeah. Why?"

"A text letting me know would have been nice."

"Oh, Elaine, leave the poor girl alone," Lorena pipes up. "So, how was your date?"

"I wouldn't know. Your boy Hanson van Buuren canceled last minute. What a gentleman, huh?" I reply sarcastically.

The pitiful look on Lorena's face is comical. "Oh no. I'm sure he must have had a good reason to cancel."

"I wouldn't know. He didn't say."

Mom shakes her head, making a disapproving sound. Of course she's going to blame Hanson's assholery on me.

"It's back to the drawing board then. Who else is still free?"

"Enough already with trying to pawn me off on some random guy. I can find my own escort."

"Jane Marie, we've already discussed this. Your escort must be from a reputable family."

"No, it doesn't. I looked into it," I lie. "There's no rule that says the escort of a debutante has to belong to an elite family."

"It's not a rule, my dear, but it's tradition," the other friend says.

"Screw tradition."

"Jane! That's unacceptable behavior."

"Oh really? Like you having an affair with a married man was?"

I never thought I'd use Mom's affair with Charlie's dad as a weapon, but I'm sick and tired of being her punching bag. She's not perfect by any stretch of the imagination. Why does she want me to be?

"How dare you?" She rises from her chair. "Go to your room and don't come out until you're ready for school tomorrow."

"Gladly." I turn on my heels and stomp away.

Maybe now that I fought back, she'll stop pestering me about the ball. If I'm lucky, she won't make me attend it at all. *Yeah, that's wishful thinking.* She'll do it out of spite. I could refuse to go, but unfortunately, while I'm still living under her roof, I can't declare open war against her. Besides, I can't risk her getting suspicious and searching through my things. If she finds out about roller derby, she might ship me off to a boarding school in the middle of nowhere.

Once in the safety of my room, I pull my cell phone out to text Alicia and ask when she wants to meet to practice. But a message from Andy is waiting for me, which I read first.

HEY, babe. Missing you already.

Missing you too. The dragon was home and she went ballistic when I told her I'd find my own date to the ball.

The dragon? LOL. She needs to suck it up. Besides, I'm a pretty good catch.

Yes, you are. Did you talk to Troy yet?

No. I need to speak to Lorenzo first since he's my alibi.

Are you telling him about us?

Yeah. He's cool. He won't tell anyone.

I'm not worried about that.

Hold on. He's calling me back now. I'll call you later to wish you goodnight.

Okay.

I KEEP my gaze glued to the phone, smiling like an idiot for a minute. I also re-read Andy's texts several times. I still can't believe this is all real. Andreas Rossi is my boyfriend.

My phone pings, announcing an incoming text. It's from Fred. *Ah shit. What am I going to do about him?* I don't click on it yet. I'm afraid he's texting to ask me on a date and I'm not ready to deal with that. I hate disappointing people, especially kind ones like him.

I text Alicia instead, remembering the reason I grabbed my phone in the first place.

. . .

HEY, when do you think you can practice this week?

Hey, girlie. Yikes. It's going to be pretty tough. My schedule is hell. One of my coworkers is sick and management is forcing me to work a double shift.

Oh no. Can they do that?

Technically, no. But they know I need that job. It's cool. I can use the extra cash.

No worries then. I'll see you next Saturday at bootcamp.

You betcha!

I FLOP ON MY BED, suddenly bone-tired. I showered at Andy's, but I should change. My clothes smell like I've been in a sex dungeon. But they also smell of him. I hug one of my pillows, and pretend I'm hugging him instead. There's a delicious ache between my legs that reminds me of the most amazing day I've ever had. I'm pretty sure if I could spend the night at Andy's, he'd fuck me all night long.

I become hot and bothered again, and now, another shower is in order. A yawn catches me by surprise. I look at the time. It's only a little bit past eight. Not late at all. But I'd better get ready for bed. I need to get enough rest. This week promises to be hella busy. Between school, practicing, and sneaking around to see Andy, I don't know when I'll have time to slow down. And that's not taking into account whatever social function Mom will try to shove in my schedule. She insisted I not take any volunteering work this month, which means she plans to keep me occupied.

I take my time in the shower. I'm sore in several places, and the sex marathon didn't help. Not that I mind that at all. The bruise on my arm and thigh is more purple than before. I have to be extra careful to hide them from Mom. That means no trying on clothes in front of her. Thinking about it reminds me that I still have to pick a dress for the ball. I only got the blue one for the stupid date with Hanson.

Silver lining: I'm sure Andy will love that dress. I'm still smiling when I walk out of the bathroom, but it vanishes immediately when I find my mother there, waiting for me. Panicking, I look for me phone. I left it on my bed, but the screen is face down.

"What are you doing here?" I ask.

"This is my house. I can go wherever I please."

"So privacy doesn't mean anything to you anymore?"

"You'd better watch your tone. If you think behaving like that in front of my friends will get you kicked out of the debutante ball, you're mistaken. And since you don't have a date yet for the ball, don't even think of skipping the marina luncheon next Saturday."

The blood drains from my face. The fucking luncheon. I completely forgot about it. *How am I going to get out of that?*

"I said I'll find my own escort," I grit out.

She laughs. "Who? Some loser from your school?"

"Any loser from school would be better than that prick Hanson van Buuren."

"Well, Lorena was overreaching with him."

My phone rings. It must be Andy calling. *Crap.* I ignore it, hoping Mom will too.

She doesn't even glance at the device. She's busy staring me down. "I already put a dress on hold for you at Nordstrom. Go try it on tomorrow after school."

"Really? No personal stylist anymore?"

"It's pointless to get you in an exclusive gown. Off the rack will do just fine."

She walks out, leaving me fuming. I can't wait to get out of this house. If I didn't like my life here in LA, I'd attend a school across the country just to stay away from the woman.

Before I check who called me, I lock my bedroom door. I know Mom has a spare key, but it makes me feel a little better to do so anyway.

The missed call was from Andy. Seeing his name on my screen makes me crazy happy, even if I'm still angry at my overbearing mother. I press the Call button. He answers on the first ring.

"Hey, babe. Where were you?"

"My mother was in the room, giving me a hard time."

"Ah hell. Was it because I kept you hostage the entire day?"

"No. I told her I'd find my own date to the ball and she flipped."

I decide to keep the nasty details to myself. He knows how bad my mother can get. I don't need to elaborate.

"Do you want me to come over and officially request to be your escort?"

I laugh. "How gallant of you. But that won't be necessary. I do, however, have to find a way to miss the bachelorette luncheon next Saturday. I have roller derby bootcamp all weekend."

"Ah man. When am I going to see you?"

"After bootcamp. But can you please focus for a second? How am I going to evade the dragon? She'll be at the luncheon, watching me like a hawk."

"What time is it at?"

"It probably starts at noon."

"And bootcamp starts at eight, right? I suppose you have an hour of lunch break?"

"Yeah, I think so."

"You could show your face at the luncheon, and then head back to bootcamp."

"I'll never be able to pull that off with LA traffic."

"Don't worry about the logistics. I'll get you where you need to be."

It's so sweet that he's determined to help me, but unless he can rent a helicopter, I don't see how his plan will work. Maybe I can fake food poisoning.

"Let's not talk about my problems anymore. What are you doing now?"

"Baking the banana cake I started at Troy's. Well, not that one. I had to start from scratch."

"When did you get into baking?"

"My mother introduced me to it. After she died, I forgot about it for a while, but now it's back in my life."

"Oh, I'm going to get so fat. You know I love treats."

"I don't care if you get fat. You'll still be the most beautiful woman I've ever seen."

"Yeah, yeah. You say that now. Wait until I look like the Pillsbury Doughboy."

"You're silly. What's your favorite cake?"

"Hmm. That's a tough one. Probably chocolate lava cake."

"Okay, I'm making a note of that. Anything else?"

"Wait. Do you want a list?"

"Yeah, I want a list."

"Who is being silly now?"

"Why is it silly to want to spoil my girl with delicious treats?"

Giddiness overtakes me at hearing him call me his girl. I'm so happy, I could burst into song, Disney style.

"I have to stop by the mall after class to try on a dress my mother has on hold for me. Do you want to come?"

"Is this the dress for the luncheon?"

"Yeah."

"I'm definitely coming then."

"Don't be a pest like you were at the other store."

"To be fair, those clothes *were* provocative. Were they for roller derby?"

"Yep. And full disclosure, I still want to go back there. I liked those clothes."

He groans. "God, it's going to drive me insane to see baboons drool over you."

"That's what you get for dating a hot piece of ass," I laugh.

"Shit, babe, don't remind me of your booty. I have a hard-on already only imagining you in those skintight clothes."

"Really? And what are you going to do about it?"

"I guess I'll have to make do with my hand. Keep talking. I'll pretend you're here."

Heat rushes over me. I've never imagined I'd be having phone sex with Andreas, not even in my wildest dreams. But in this case, the reality is so much better than the fantasy.

19

ANDREAS

I'M STILL on cloud nine when I enter the classroom. It's Norman's class—the douche professor who wants to see me fail —and I'm smiling from ear to ear. No surprise, Taiyo is already here, face buried in a book. *Damn, the dude is serious about his academics.*

I drop on the chair next to him as loudly as possible. "Morning."

He jumps on his seat, startled. "Jesus, where did you come from?"

"Don't you know? I'm a wizard. I can apparate."

He stares at me blankly. Not a Harry Potter fan then.

"Anyway, what are you studying so hard there?"

"I have a Finance quiz after this class. I feel wholly unprepared."

"Ugh. I barely passed that class. Can't help you there."

A guy with wild curly hair takes the seat in front of us. He dyed the tips of his hair blond, which immediately makes me think of Justin Timberlake circa the nineties. Yikes.

He turns around and asks, "Hey, what you guys think of Professor Norman?"

I snort. "You don't want to know."

"Yeah, he didn't seem to like you very much. Total jackass move, in my opinion."

I nod, not wanting to agree and risk getting caught dissing the guy by a teacher's pet or the man himself.

"Anyway, my name is Ricky Montana. Big fan."

Taiyo looks at me. "I didn't realize you were famous."

"You don't like sports very much, do you?" I ask.

"No time for that."

"Dude, this guy is a legend," Ricky replies enthusiastically. "It's wild that you're taking the same class as me," he tells me.

"I'm not a legend. Calm down," I joke.

"Sorry. I tend to get overexcited easily. Hey, do you know of any cool parties happening this week?"

"Not really."

"Well, if you hear about any, please, let me know." He scribbles something on a piece of paper and hands it over. "Here are my digits."

"Sure." I tuck Ricky's note inside my book, knowing very well I'll forget about it by the time this class is over.

Professor Asshole walks in, silencing all the chatter in the room. He has a reputation, and no one seems to be willing to get on his bad side. He gets settled behind his desk, and not a minute later, begins his lecture. This time, he doesn't put me on the spot, and I start to hope he's forgotten about his dislike of me.

I get into the zone, not daring to look away from the white board, and taking notes as furiously as Taiyo. Ten minutes before the class is over, he announces he has the schedule for the hands-on portion of this course. We're expected to work at the Rushmore Hotel in different functions to get real life experience.

I log in to the class's portal to see what my first assignment will be. I'll be serving at the hotel's restaurant during my first week. I curse when I see my schedule. I'm supposed to work this Saturday during the lunch shift. *Fuck.* I promised Jane I'd help her sneak out of the luncheon. I can't let her down.

I raise my hand. "Sir, what if the schedule conflicts with prior plans?"

He glowers at me. "Then I suggest you change your prior plans. Like I said before, I'm not going to give any student special treatment. If you can't take this class seriously, I suggest you quit wasting my time."

Asshole.

"Am I allowed to switch with another student?"

He sighs, intensifying his death glare in my direction. "If you can find someone willing to trade with you, then be my guest. However, if they don't show up to cover your shift, you are the one who will get an F."

Ricky raises his hand. "Sir? Does that mean if we get sick and miss a shift, we get an F too?"

"For Christ's sake. Of course not, Mr. Montana. This is America, not China." He glances at Taiyo meaningfully.

What a racist prick. I can't keep my mouth shut.

"Taiyo is from Japan."

"Actually, I'm second genera—never mind," he whispers.

I don't glance at him. I'm too busy in my staring contest with Norman. I'm not going to look away first.

"Oh, okay," Ricky mumbles.

Norman caves first, giving the classroom a glance. It's a small victory, but I know I just made my life ten times more difficult.

"Anyone else have an asinine question to ask? No? Good. Class dismissed."

People can't get out of their chairs fast enough. I refuse to rush out. Ricky turns in his seat.

"I can trade shifts with you," he says in a low voice, probably afraid to be overheard by Norman.

"Oh yeah? What do you have?"

"I've got serving on Friday, dinner shift. Does that work?"

I'm not keen on wasting my Friday evening. I'd much rather spend the time with Jane. But I don't have a lot of options. I doubt anyone else will want to trade with me now that I'm on Norman's shit list. They're probably afraid to attract his wrath too if they help me.

"I'll take that. I'm on Saturday lunch shift. Are you sure you can cover for me? I can't get an F."

"Yeah, man. I got your back. But... I need a favor in return."

I knew there was a catch.

"Spill it already."

"Can you get me a date with a cheerleader?"

From the corner of my eye, I notice Taiyo sitting straighter in his chair. Finally something catches his interest, but I'm too annoyed right now to care.

"Do I look like a pimp to you?" I ask.

Ricky's eyebrows shoot up. "I heard you got Leo Stine a date with Heather Castro."

Shit, I did do that. But Leo is the Pike's president. It wasn't that difficult to convince Heather to go out with him.

"Those were rumors. But I can introduce you to a bunch of chicks the next time there's a Greek Row party."

"For real? Man, that would be awesome."

"Can I come too?" Taiyo asks.

I turn to him. "I thought you didn't go to parties."

"Right, I don't. Never mind."

"You can come if you find the balls to do so." I switch to Ricky. "You have a deal. You'd better not screw me over, Montana."

"Are you crazy? I'd never do that to you." He stands,

hoisting his backpack over his shoulder. "When is the next party?"

"Don't have a clue. I've been out of the loop. I'll text you, but it won't happen this weekend. I have plans."

"Right. No worries." He glances at his phone. "Oh fuck. I'm late for my next class."

"Shit, me too," Taiyo says in a panic.

Both hurry out of room in an ungainly fashion. I shake my head, wondering when the hell I turned into the king of nerds.

"Is the situation with Lorenzo resolved?" Troy asks me.

I forgot I made plans to meet the guys for lunch today. Danny, who was about to take a big chunk out of his burger, pauses to look at us. *Damn, could he seem any more suspicious?* Luckily, Troy and Paris aren't paying attention to him.

"Yeah, I called a repair company. They came over and fixed the glass on our father's trophy case in a jiffy. He'll never know it was broken in the first place."

The lie feels bitter in my mouth. I hate that I have to lie to my best friend like this, but I can't tell him why I bailed yesterday before Jane is ready to deal with Troy's reaction.

"Damn. Your father must really love those trophies to send Lorenzo into panic mode," Paris pipes up.

"You have no idea," I say.

I'd never have come up with an alibi involving my asshole father. That was my brother's plan. The story worked because everyone knows my old man is a self-absorbed jerk.

"Barbecue was fun, but man, when are we going to go on a guys-only trip?" Paris asks. "Now that football season is over, I need a healthy dose of adrenaline."

"Are you sure you're allowed to go on a trip without your girlfriend?" I tease.

"Bite me, Andy. Geneva is not my keeper. I can do things without her."

"Could have fooled me." I shove a piece of fry in my mouth.

"I'm game for a trip. We could go rock climbing at the Arches. I haven't done that in a while," Troy says.

"You want to go all the way to Utah?" Danny frowns. "I don't think I can swing buying a plane ticket."

"We could go somewhere closer," I suggest. "Like Yosemite Park. But when are you thinking? I started my practical portion of Intro to Food Service Management and I have to check my schedule. Some are weekend shifts."

Plus, I don't want to leave town for a whole weekend and miss spending time with Jane. *Jesus, I sound as whipped as Paris and Troy.*

"I don't know. I have to check with Charlie," Troy replies.

"Oh, look who is actually in jail," Paris laughs.

"Shut up, jerkface. I don't have to ask for Charlie's permission, but maybe she already has things planned for us."

"Like LARPing." Danny chuckles.

Paris perks up on his seat. "We have to come see Troy run around in a full troll outfit. How come we haven't done that yet?"

"LARPing is not a performance. You can only come if you participate," he replies.

Paris makes a face of disgust. "No, thank you."

"Don't dismiss it until you try it." Troy throws a fry in Paris's direction.

"Not happening, bro." He shoves the food missile in his mouth and smirks.

I thought hanging out with Troy today would be weird as fuck. The guilt for keeping shit from him is still in the background, but it's easy to ignore that while this banter is going around.

"Did you read the email Coach sent us about that benefit gala?" Danny asks.

"Ugh, don't remind me of that." Paris sighs in an exaggerated manner. "Geneva read the email and now she can't stop talking about ball gowns."

"First of all, why is she reading your emails?" I ask.

"She was sitting next to me when I clicked on it."

"Why are you asking about the gala, Danny?" Troy asks.

"I don't want to rent a tux. Any of you have one to spare?"

"Wait? That's a blacktie event?" I glance at him.

"Galas usually are," Paris pipes up.

"I barely glanced at the email," I confess. "When is it again?"

When my phone vibrates in my pocket, my remorse heightens. I bet it's Jane calling. She said she would let me know when she planned to go to the mall. I reach for it and press the Ignore button. A moment later, my phone pings again with an incoming text. I shouldn't check now that all eyes are on me, but I don't want her thinking I'm blowing her off.

I glance at it quickly, making sure no one sees the screen. She wants to go the mall now. My heartbeat picks up its pace as excitement takes hold of me. I can't wait to see her again and it hasn't even been twenty-four hours since I saw her last.

"Who is that?" Troy asks.

I try to school my face into the perfect mask of innocence, but I'm not sure if I'm pulling it off. Remorse returns with a vengeance.

"No one. I actually have to go." I stand, taking my food tray with me.

"No one, huh?" Troy leans back, smiling knowingly. "I bet that was a booty call."

Shit. I'm so transparent. He wouldn't be smiling like that if he knew I was about to nail his sister.

"Yeah, yeah. You got me. Later, fools."

I walk out of the cafeteria as fast as I can, hating myself for being such a douche. I don't disagree with Jane. Troy is a fucking pain in the ass when it comes to her. But I also know that if the situation were reversed, I wouldn't want a guy like me messing around with my sister either. If I were a better man, I would have never let things get this far. But I'm too weak and Jane is everything I've ever wanted.

20

JANE

I'M GIDDY WITH EXCITEMENT, restless as I pace back and forth in front of Nordstrom. I told Andy I'd meet him here. It's better if we go in together instead of sending the poor guy on a wild goose chase inside the store.

It's risky meeting him in a public space when no one is supposed to know about us, but as long as we don't do any PDA, it will be okay.

I let out a yelp when strong arms wrap around me, and Andreas's lips find my neck. There goes the no PDA idea down the drain.

"Hey, babe. Miss me?" He spins me around so now I'm facing him.

"Andy! People can see us."

"So?" He ends any further protest I might have with a long and sensual kiss that makes me melt on the spot.

I find myself leaning into his body while my own bursts into flames. Oh my God. This man is going to be the end of my sanity. I could kiss him forever, and proof of that is that he's the one who eases off, breaking the moment too soon in my opinion.

"You were saying?" He chuckles against my lips.

"We shouldn't be kissing in public," I whisper without making any motion to move away.

"I know, I know. But I couldn't resist. You're breathtaking today." He steps back and gives me a once-over. "I love school uniforms. Does that make me a perv?"

"It totally does. You're lucky that I'm into the forbidden stuff."

"Is that why you want to keep our relationship a secret?"

His question erases my amusement in an instant. *He doesn't really think that, does he?*

"Of course not."

"Hey, I was joking. I get why. Troy is my best friend. I know him better than anyone."

"Sorry. This situation is giving me a lot of anxiety. I feel like I'm keeping too many secrets and eventually they're going to come crashing down on me."

He caresses my cheek. "I'm sorry, sweetheart. I'm ready to let the world know about us. Just say the word and I'll message Troy right now."

Panic grips me. "No. That's not what I meant. We *will* tell Troy, but I can't afford to have him angry at me. I need an ally in case Mom finds out about roller derby."

"It's okay, babe. I'm not pressuring you to do anything. But it's so fucking hard to be in your presence and keep my hands to myself."

"If it makes you feel any better, I feel the same way."

He scrunches his eyebrows together. "No, it doesn't make me feel better."

I sigh, defeated. "Let's go. I can't wait to see what kind of atrocity Mommy Dearest thinks is suitable for me."

Andy reaches for my hand, but I pull away with regret. *This sucks.*

"Oops. Sorry. Told you it was hard," he says.

"I know."

We walk side by side, leaving a gap between our bodies. For all intents and purposes, we're just friends.

"Who picked that blue dress you were wearing the other day?"

"I did. Mom was against that choice."

"Hmm."

"What?" I glance at him.

"Just wondering why you chose that dress to go on a date with a random guy."

Andy is jealous, something that used to irritate me, but it warms me like a soft blanket now that we're together.

"I wasn't planning to stay. I just wanted Hanson to see I wasn't a charity case. I had roller derby tryouts that afternoon."

Andreas touches the back of my wrist with the tips of his fingers. It's an innocent caress, but it sends a zing of pleasure to my core.

"No one in their right mind would think you're a charity case, Jane. You're perfection."

I don't know if I should laugh or jump in his arms. "I'm perfection?"

"Too corny?" He gives me a crooked smile.

"A little."

My cheeks are warm, and I'm a second away from breaking my own rules and kissing him in the middle of the store. A cheerful sales associate saves me from myself when she welcomes us to Nordstrom.

"This store has so many departments. Do you know where you're going?"

"Yeah. Follow me."

I find the department that has my dress on hold. While I

speak with the sales associate, Andreas hangs back and pretends to be interested in the accessories displayed on the mannequin. He's completely out of his element, but seems to be enjoying himself. Many guys seem to get an allergic reaction when they have to go on a shopping trip with their girlfriends, and here's Andy, the most macho guy I know, taking everything in stride.

While the associate goes to the back to find my dress, I join him in his exploration.

"I bet I'm not going to like what my mother picked. Help me find alternatives?"

"Really? You want my help?"

"Of course. You're the one who has to see the dress on me."

"Okay." He turns to the rack behind him and quickly browses through the options.

I look at the dress on the mannequin. It's cute and I wonder if they have it in my size.

"Hi." The associate returns. "This is the dress your mother put on hold." She shows me an off-white dress that's as boring as they come. It's also too long to be cute.

Andreas steps closer. "What's this? A grandma's nightgown?"

The woman laughs politely. "It's a little on the conservative side. I have other options that are a bit more fun."

"I like fun," he pipes up, and then looks at the dress on the mannequin, the one I had been eyeing before. "What about that one?"

"We just got it in. It's my favorite dress in the collection."

"I'd like to try that on, please," I say.

"Of course."

She finds my size on the rack without having to ask—she can probably judge by looking at me—and asks us to follow her to the fitting room, which is bigger and more private than the ones I'm used to. When Andy slips in with me, she doesn't bat an eyelash.

He takes a seat on the velvet bench, getting comfortable while I stand in the middle of the room in my school uniform, feeling awkward all of a sudden. *Nonsense, Jane. He's seen you in your birthday suit already.*

"I'm ready for my show." He leans back, lacing his fingers behind his neck.

"Ha ha. I didn't ask you to come for your entertainment."

I begin to unbutton my shirt, remembering at the last minute I'm wearing a boring cotton bra. I should have worn sexier underwear today. Andreas doesn't seem to care though. His eyes are hooded, swimming with desire. His heated gaze feels like a sensual stroke against my skin. My breathing turns shallow. My panties soak through. He got me hot and bothered with a single glance.

"Oh? And why did you ask me to come, sweetheart?" He leans forward, resting his elbows on his knees now.

"To help me pick a dress." I lob my shirt in his direction, and he catches it with perfect dexterity.

"I can't help you if you don't try it on. You'd better hurry up, or that sales chick will think we're up to no good in here."

He had to go and remind me that the woman is only a few feet away from us. *Ugh!*

Quickly, I take off my skirt, and then put on the strapless dress. The zipper is in the back, and I can't quite close it all the way up.

Andreas jumps from his seat. "Allow me."

With him close behind me, it's impossible to ignore how much I crave him. My pulse skyrockets.

He zips me up slowly, sending ripples of pleasure down my spine. Then he captures my gaze in the mirror's reflection and tugs the bra straps with his index fingers.

"You don't need this," he whispers seductively.

"No," I croak. "I didn't want to tempt you too much."

He kisses the corner of my neck, making me shiver. "That's an impossible task. I'd burn for you even if you were wearing a shapeless potato sack."

He continues his torture, drawing his tongue up my neck until he captures my earlobe between his teeth. His left arm snakes around my waist, pulling me flush against his muscled body—and obvious erection—while his right hand disappears underneath the skirt of the dress.

"Andy." I melt against his embrace, reaching behind me to keep his head where it is.

He touches the edge of my panties, and there go my legs, turning into jelly. He tugs at the fabric, sliding it to the side so his fingers can play with my sensitive flesh without barriers.

"Oh my God." I close my eyes and arch my back.

"Do you like that, sweetheart?"

"Yes," I hiss.

He makes small circles over my clit, quickly building a delicious tension between my legs. A moan escapes my lips.

"I'm obsessed with the sounds you make," he whispers, blowing hot air against my skin.

And I'm obsessed with you. I don't say that out loud, instead, I whisper, "I love your hands on me."

In response, he inserts two fingers inside of me.

"How about now, babe? Do you love that too?"

"Ye—oh my God. Don't stop," I beg as the first wave of the orgasm hits me.

"Open your eyes, babe. I want you to see how beautiful you look when you come."

I do as he says, and watching Andy finger fuck me as I climax is the hottest thing I've ever seen. The image seems to double my pleasure, and I have to bite my lower lip to keep from moaning out loud again.

Andreas works his magic until my body goes slack against

him and the tremors subside. My heart is pumping like a factory and sweat dots my forehead now.

With a smile, he fixes my underwear back in place, and does something utterly shocking. He licks his fingers.

"Fucking delicious," he says.

"How did the dress work for you?" the sales associate asks outside our door.

My face bursts into flames. I jump out of Andy's embrace, mortified now. What if she heard us? He chuckles at my reaction, earning an exasperated glance from me.

"I love it. It fits like a glove," I reply.

"Great," she says.

Andreas still has a stupid grin on his face after she leaves. I slap his arm. "Quit laughing. This isn't funny."

"Sorry, babe, but it kinda is." He sits on the bench again, and I notice the bulge in his jeans is still there.

"I don't know what you find so amusing when you have to deal with your lack of release."

He drops his eyes to his crotch for a second. "This is nothing. Besides, I know you're going to take care of me soon."

Smirking, I reply, "Maybe."

"You're a mean one."

I stick my tongue out at him. Then I take the dress off and place it back on the hanger while still in my underwear. I know I'm making the situation for him worse, but that's what he gets for laughing at me.

"I'm not mean," I laugh.

"I don't know about that. And if you don't want me to fuck you against the wall in the next second, you'd better put your clothes on. This is cruel punishment."

Crap. Now I want him to follow through on his threat. But if I stay another minute alone with Andy in this room, I won't be able to face the associate outside.

"Okay, okay." I hastily button my shirt and put on my skirt.

I said I wanted to be a bad girl, but one orgasm in a public place is all I can handle today. When we finally walk out of the fitting room, there are more customers browsing through the department. I feel like they all know what Andreas and I were doing. I can't look the sales associate in the eye when I pay for the dress, and I practically drag Andy with me as I stride away.

"Babe, what's the hurry?" he asks with humor.

"I just want to get out of here."

"Are we going to the other store now?"

Ah shit. I forgot about that. But I can't take Andy to that store and try on a bunch of sexy outfits in front of him. He *is* going to want to bang me in the fitting room and I won't be able—or want—to stop him.

"No, I think we should go home."

"Oh? I thought you were coming to my place."

I stop in my tracks when I realize I meant his place when I said the word home. It's probably too soon to be thinking that way. We literally just start dating.

"I didn't want to assume you didn't already have plans," I reply to save face.

"You'd better start getting used to the idea that any plans I have involve you, babe."

The butterflies in my stomach become radioactive. I beam, smiling like the crazy-in-love girl that I am.

"Is that so?"

Still holding hands, he tugs me closer to him. I know we shouldn't be doing this out in the open, but right now, I don't care about being discreet.

"You'd better believe it."

He kisses me softly, a quick peck on the lips. I obviously want more, but Andreas has more restraint than me.

He steps back and says, "Let's get out of here before I drag you back to that fitting room and make good on my promise."

21

ANDREAS

I'VE NEVER HAD a hard-on last this long. I'm usually able to take care of the problem or it goes away naturally—and painfully. But after a thirty-minute drive back to my place, my cock is still as hard as a rock. Maybe if I hadn't kept talking to Jane on the phone during the ride, this wouldn't have happened.

We agreed that I would go up to my apartment first, and she'd wait five minutes and follow me. It's one thing to steal kisses in the middle of a packed shopping mall, but quite another to walk into my apartment building with Jane in my arms. There are too many people coming and going, and everyone knows Troy and me.

I'm grinning like a fool when I open the front door, but a sickly sweet perfume reaches my nose the moment I walk in. Immediately, my muscles tense. I know that fucking smell too well. Crystal is sitting on my chair, holding a glass of whiskey in her hand as if this is her house.

"What the fuck are you doing here? How did you get in?"

She takes a sip of her drink before replying. "My, my. Is that how you greet your stepmother?"

"Answer the fucking question, Crystal."

"I might have borrowed your father's spare key. What's the matter, Andy? Aren't you happy to see me?" She smiles wickedly, knowing very well her presence here is unwelcome.

"Quit with the bullshit. Why are you here?"

She stands up, revealing another skintight outfit. "I thought we should continue our conversation from the other day."

"Are you out of your goddamned mind? We have nothing to talk about."

She sashays in my direction, once again trying to pull her old tricks on me. "I know you don't mean that."

"Oh my God. This was the most inten—" Jane walks in but stops abruptly when she sees Crystal there. "Oh, hi. I didn't know Andy had company."

"She was just leaving," I grit out.

Crystal turns to me, smirking. "Of course. I don't want to ruin your afternoon delight." She chugs the rest of her drink before heading for the door. "We'll catch up another time, sweetie."

I'm fuming. Any happiness I had in me Crystal sucked out with her vile presence.

"That was your stepmother, right? Is everything okay?" Jane asks as soon as the bitch walks out of the door.

I glance at Jane, all innocent and pure, and I hate myself for allowing her to come into my corrupted world. Crystal's presence here reminded me that I'm tainted, unworthy of someone like Jane.

Shit. I need a drink.

Without answering, I make a beeline for the booze cabinet in my kitchen. I need something stronger than beer. The bottle of expensive tequila I keep hidden from Danny needs to make an appearance. I twist the cap off and drink from it, not bothering with a glass.

"Andy?" Jane walks over. "What happened?"

I close my eyes, letting the warmth of the tequila wash away my guilt. "Nothing happened, babe."

She stops in front of me and pulls the tequila bottle from my hand. "Bullshit. Don't lie to me."

"Sorry. I don't mean to push you away. My home life growing up wasn't exactly all sunshine. Crystal's presence here was... triggering."

"Did she let herself in?"

"Yeah. She knows I wouldn't have let her come in otherwise."

Jane steps into my space, wrapping her arms around me. I hug her back, kissing the top of her head. She doesn't comment on my confession, and my affection for her grows. Just the feel of her body against mine is enough to dissipate the darkness swirling in my chest.

"Are you hungry?" I ask. "I can cook you something."

She lifts her gaze to mine. "The only thing I'm hungry for is you."

And just like that, my body is on fire again. I take her face in my hands and crush my lips to hers. My mouth takes possession starvingly, as if I want to drown in her taste, in her essence. The world ceases to exist. It's only Jane and I lost in each other.

I let go of her face to lift her off the floor. My hands find her sweet ass while her legs wrap around my hips. Without breaking the kiss, I stride to my bedroom. I'd take her right there on the kitchen counter, but Danny could come in at any time.

Hands busy squeezing her tight ass, I shut the door with a backward kick. Then we're falling on the bed together, already tugging at each other's clothes, fighting to get them off as fast as possible. I don't know if I should rip her uniform shirt off or kiss the bit of skin already exposed.

Roughly, I push her bra up and suck her nipple into my mouth. I guess it's tasting her with clothes on for now. She arches her back as she threads her fingers through my hair.

"Ouch," she blurts out when I get too eager and bite her a little too hard.

I lift my eyes to hers. "Sorry, babe. You're too delicious."

"I want to taste you too."

God, the idea of her mouth on my body almost makes me climax on the spot. I've never felt such insatiable hunger for anyone before.

"That can be arranged." I lean back and impatiently get rid of my shirt.

Jane's hands find my chest and then my abs. I don't move, letting her explore me with soft fingers and hungry eyes.

"I love your body. It's almost not fair how perfect you are. I could look at you all day."

"I wouldn't mind that at all as long as I can touch you as you do so," I reply.

Her hands travel south. She unbuttons my jeans and pulls the zipper down. "I want your cock in my mouth."

"Babe, I'm hanging by a thread here. This could end fast."

She curls her lips into a grin. "If it does, we'll just start it all over again."

With that sassy smile across her face, she sits up, pushing me down as she does. I'm now lying on my back and Jane is straddling my thighs.

"You know, I wish you were a Scottish lad wearing a kilt. That would make things so much easier." She pulls my pants low enough to grant her easier access to the goods.

"I don't have an ounce of Scottish blood in me, but I can role-play."

"Don't tease me, or I'll be ordering you a kilt as soon as I get home."

I chuckle. "That's okay."

She holds my gaze for a couple of beats before her eyes drop to my crotch. I notice her slight hesitation when she tugs my boxers down and frees my dick.

"Do you want me to tell you what I like?" I ask softly.

She meets my eyes again, and I see as clear as day the vulnerability and insecurity shining in her gaze.

"Am I lame if I say yes?"

I run my fingers over her exposed thighs. "No, on the contrary, sweetheart. Although I'm sure you know exactly what to do to drive me wild."

She rubs her thumb over the sensitive skin, spreading precum over my cock's head. My balls tighten, making me hiss.

"Do you like that?" she asks.

"God, yes."

A little smile appears on her lovely face. She leans forward, bringing her plump lips closer to my shaft. I inhale deeply, bracing for the sensation. I don't want to come too soon. I never had this problem before until Jane came along. This must be pent-up desire thanks to all the long nights I spent fantasizing about her.

Her fingers curl around the base, then she licks my length from bottom to top. My hips buckle, and I dig my fingers into her legs.

"How about this?"

I nod, closing my eyes, fighting to maintain control, but it's pretty fucking hard. I thought she was going to keep taking things slowly, but she surprises me when she swallows my cock all the way to the hilt.

"Fuck!" I blurt out.

Jane is not playing around anymore. I know she wasn't lying when said she never sucked a guy before me, which means she's just talented. With expert hands and tongue, she quickly takes me closer and closer to the edge.

"Oh my God, babe. You're a magician," I whisper.

I give everything I have to keep my shit together, to fight the tidal wave that's fast approaching. But this is a fight I can't win. My release crashes against the shore like a tsunami, obliterating everything in its path. My body seems to disintegrate and become whole again in the span of a second.

I realize I kept my eyes shut in the final moment like an idiot. Maybe it was instinctual to try to maintain some kind of control because looking at Jane as she sucked me into oblivion would be my demise.

When I open my eyes, I catch her wiping off the corner of her mouth. There's not a drop of my release in sight. She took it all.

I reach for her open shirt and tug her forward. "Come here."

She leans closer, and I use the opportunity to roll over her and switch positions. Now she's trapped under me, my reawakened cock lodged between her legs. She laughs, but I cut the sound short by kissing her long and hard.

I'm already ready to go for round two, but I decide to take my time now and make out in bed like teenagers, something I never did, all thanks to Crystal. I can't change the past, but maybe I can have something good for once.

22

JANE

"Wow. I didn't think guys could recover that fast," I say against Andy's chest.

After I gave him the best blow job of his life—his words, not mine—we did nothing but kiss for an hour. I thought he needed that time to recover—not that I minded in the least. But I was so wrong.

"Most don't, but they don't have a Jane in their bed."

I lift my chin to look at him. "Are you saying I have magical powers that can recharge your dick with a mere touch?"

He chuckles. "Yeah, you do."

I rest my face against his chest again. "I wish I could spend the night and put that theory to the test."

The sun has set already. I have to leave soon or my mother will start hunting me down. I completely blew off my plan to get some skating practice. I don't want to be one of those girls who drop everything to spend time with their boyfriends, but considering our illicit affair, finding the time to spend together might be more complicated.

"I wish you could stay here too, babe." He kisses the top of my head.

His phone vibrates on his nightstand, an invasion of our peace. The world has come knocking. I try to sit up, but Andy's arms around me become tighter.

"Stay for just another minute."

"You don't want to see who's calling?"

"Whoever it is can wait."

I relax in his arms, loving the feel of them around me. Exhaustion is slowly creeping into my bones. I've done a lot of physical activity in the past few days. Between roller derby and screwing Andreas's brains out, it's no surprise I'm beat. I'm sore now in a lot of places, some I don't mind one bit. My bruises from roller derby are still tender to the touch, but they're already beginning to yellow out. I'll probably gain new ones next weekend, though. I'm glad it's not bikini season yet.

I should get up, especially when my eyelids grow heavy and my eyes begin to shut. I'm beginning to doze off when loud male voices in the apartment makes me tense on the spot. Danny is home, and he brought company. *Shit.* I hope whoever it is it doesn't have a big mouth.

"Hell. Our solitude is over," Andy murmurs.

We both get out of bed and start to get dressed. All he does is put some sweatpants on that don't hide much. I get now why some girls from school love sweatpants season. You can see everything, especially when guys don't wear underwear like Andy isn't now.

He snaps his fingers in front of my face. "Hey, my eyes are up here."

"If you don't want me to objectify you, don't wear provocative clothes. You're asking for it." I smirk.

"Well played, babe. Well played."

I'd love to shower first before doing the walk of shame, but it's really getting late. Andy leans against his desk with arms crossed and watches me get dressed. He's ogling my body on purpose now, payback for my earlier comment. A tent forms in the front of his pants, and I can't help my laughter.

"Oh my God. Again? Did you take Viagra or something?"

He twists his face into a scowl. "Please. I don't need help in that department. But man, I do love that uniform on you."

I finish fastening the last button, and then I try to smooth the wrinkles on the skirt. It's pointless. I make a quick run to the bathroom to check the state of my hair. *Crap.* It's as bad as I feared. There's no way in hell I'll be able to comb through this tangled mess, so I just make a quick bun, securing it with a strand of my own hair since I don't have a hairband, and if I find one in Andy's bathroom, I'm going to go blind with jealousy. I'd better not open that Pandora's box.

"Okay, I'm ready to go," I say as I walk out of the bathroom.

Andy has his cell phone in hand. He turns to me, his face completely ashen.

"We have a problem. Troy is here."

"What?" My voice rises to a pitch.

Then I berate myself. What if Troy heard me?

"Danny was the one who called to warn me. Then he texted."

"Why is my brother here?" I shout-whisper, panicked.

"We were hanging out before I went to meet you at the mall. I have no fucking no clue why Danny came home with Troy and Paris. I'm so sorry, babe. I'll go out and try to get rid of them as quickly as possible."

I can tell that Andy feels guilty as hell over the situation, but this is not his fault. I'm the one who's afraid to tell Troy I'm in love with his best friend.

"No, this happened for a reason. It's ridiculous to keep our relationship a secret from him when Danny and Charlie know. Lying about it is only going to mess things up more."

"Wait. Charlie knows about us? You told her?"

"She doesn't know that we're together. She knows we hooked up at the Halloween party."

He passes a hand over his face. "Man, now I get why she looked so guilty when I asked her about it."

"Yeah, I put her in a super-tight spot with my brother and it's not fair. I'm doing the same to you. The longer we keep this a secret, the more betrayed Troy will feel."

"I'm ready to face the music if you are." He offers me his hand.

We lace our fingers together, but before we step out of his bedroom, Andy leans in and kisses me on the lips. "It will be fine."

Yeah, right. We both know that's a lie. My heart is thundering inside of my chest as we step into the living room. Troy is on the couch, playing a video game with Paris, and doesn't see us right way. Danny, on the other hand, is in the kitchen and balks at the sight of us.

"Shit," he says.

Troy begins to turn around. "What is it?"

He freezes the moment his eyes land on Andreas and me holding hands, my uniform looking like a cat chewed it and spat it out, and Andy wearing nothing but sweatpants.

"What is this?" Troy stands, body coiled tight with fury.

"Bro, calm down," Andy says.

"Calm down?" He walks around the couch, eyes bulging out of his skull. "Jane was your afternoon hookup?"

"I'm not his hookup," I retort angrily, but Troy doesn't even spare me a glance. His murderous gaze is on Andreas.

"I can't believe this. You could have any girl on campus, but you had to go after my sister, didn't you? Nothing is off-limits to you."

"I don't want any girl. I want Jane," he replies calmly.

"Yeah, for how long? A day, a week?"

I step in between them. "Back off, Troy. You don't have a say about who I date and don't. If I want to date Andy, I will."

"Date Andy?" he scoffs. "Don't be naive, Jane. Andreas doesn't date. He's a player, he always has been."

"People can change," Andy replies. "I care about your sister. I've cared about her since the day I met her."

Troy's eyes widen. *Fuck. That's not good.*

"Are you telling me you've had a thing for my sister for three years?" he shouts. "Three fucking years? She was fifteen, you perv."

He advances, hands curled into fists. If I weren't standing in between them, he would have punched Andreas by now. Danny and Paris, who had been trying to stay out of the situation, must have noticed that Troy is about to blow. Paris pulls Troy back while Danny stands next to Andy, worried.

"Let go of me!" Troy pulls his arm free from Paris's grasp.

"Calm down, bro," he says. "You're not thinking straight."

"Andy didn't do anything, you jackass!" I yell. "He stayed away from me this whole time. I was the one who started this."

Troy snorts. "Are you saying you seduced the biggest manwhore on campus?"

"Yes. That's what I'm saying." I throw my hands up in the air. "Get a grip, Troy. I'm no longer a kid. I'm eighteen. I'm capable of making my own decisions."

He looks at me with contempt. "So, you want to hook up with him until he gets tired of you and breaks your heart? Is that the plan?"

My eyes burn. I'm about to cry, but not out of sadness. I'm so fucking angry I could punch Troy in the throat. I knew he would get ugly, but I didn't imagine it would be like this.

Andreas walks around me. "I'm not going to break your sister's heart. I wouldn't have let things get this far, wouldn't have risked our friendship, if all I wanted was to bang her."

Troy laughs without humor. "Oh, you're worried about our

friendship now? That's rich. You should have thought about that before you screwed my sister behind my back."

I wince, mortified that we're airing dirty laundry in front of Danny and Paris. The tears finally spill, making me even angrier that I let them fall in the first place.

"You're such a jerk!" Propelled by fury, I pull my arm back and punch Troy in his gut, something I haven't done since we were kids.

Back then, all I accomplished was to tickle him. Now, he doubles over, and grunts, "Jane, what the hell!"

Andy throws his arm around my shoulders and pulls me closer. "That's my girl."

Pride surges within me. Not because Andy validated what I did, but because Troy is finally seeing me, instead of arguing with Andreas as if I wasn't in the room or like my opinion doesn't matter. I don't know why he's like that with me. I know he doesn't treat his girlfriend with that backward attitude. She wouldn't date him if he did.

"She's not your girl." Troy straightens to his full height.

"Yes, I am. Get used to it."

ANDREAS

Seeing Jane stand up for herself and put Troy in his place is hot as hell. For three years, I had this image of a shy and sweet girl. I had no idea there was a lioness inside of her, ready to fight for what she wanted. And the fact that she's fighting for me, someone who doesn't deserve that fierce loyalty, is humbling.

"Are you seriously going to date *him*?"

The venom in Troy's voice cuts like a knife. I knew he wouldn't be happy about this situation, but the way he's staring at me with such loathing rips me apart.

"Yes, and you either support my decision, or you stay out of my life," Jane replies.

His face falls. "I'm just trying to protect you. I don't want you to get hurt."

I open my mouth to rebuff his words, but he looks at me and cuts me off. "Don't even try to deny it. You know you're going to break her heart, even if you don't mean to."

The words to defend myself won't come. Troy knows me better than anyone. He might not know all the sordid details of my past, but he can see I'm rotten inside. I've told him time and time again I'd never settle with anyone. Why would he believe me now?

But he's upsetting Jane with his behavior. Despite her bravery, she's shaking next to me. And no one is going to make her feel that way, especially not in front of me.

"You'd better leave before you say something that can't be unsaid," I grit out.

"I'm not going anywhere without Jane."

My spine goes taut as I prepare to forcibly remove him from my apartment. But Jane surprises me once again.

"Fine. I'll go with you, only because I don't want Andy to kick your ass for being such an idiot."

He snorts. "Like he could."

I narrow my eyes to slits. "Don't push your luck, pal. I can whoop your ass with one arm tied behind my back."

"Okay. No one is going to whoop anyone's ass today," Paris pipes up. "Unless it's in video games."

I glance at Jane. "You don't need to go if you don't want to. Don't let Troy bully you into anything."

"I'm not bullying her!" he yells.

"Just wait outside, Troy," Danny chimes in. "You're not helping anyone with that attitude."

"Fine! But if Jane doesn't come out in five minutes, I'm coming back in."

"Bite me, Troy," she retorts. "You're not my keeper."

He spares me another murderous glower before he strides out of the apartment and shuts the door with a loud bang.

With him finally gone, I turn to Danny. "Why the hell did you bring him here?"

"Hey, I called to warn you."

"Five minutes before you got here. Fantastic timing."

"It was my fault. I wanted to play your new game," Paris chimes in.

"Guys, please don't beat yourself up for this. I'm the one to blame. It's my mess." Jane looks at me. "I'm sorry, Andy. I'll talk to Troy. He'll come around."

"Don't worry about me, babe." I caress her cheek. "Call me when you get home, okay?"

"Okay."

I plant a soft kiss on her lips, dying for more, but refraining from devouring her mouth in front of my friends.

My heart feels like lead as I watch her leave. She's putting on a brave face, but she must be torn inside over her fight with her brother. I wish I could do something to ease her pain, but I've caused enough damage as it is.

23

JANE

TROY IS LEANING against the wall opposite Andreas's apartment
with his arms crossed and an expression capable of leveling an
army. I match his furious glare and then walk away from him
without a word.

"Jane, wait."

"What for? So you can yell at me some more? Humiliate me
in public?"

"That's not my intention. But you have to understand where
I'm coming from. I just found out that my best friend is
sleeping with my sister behind my back. That's fucked up,
Jane."

"Yeah? And whose fault is that? If you weren't so pigheaded
when it comes to me, maybe we would have told you we were
together from the start."

"That's a lame excuse. He should have manned up and
told me."

I stop and whirl around, stepping into his personal space to
poke him in the chest. "He wanted to tell you from the start.

The only reason he didn't was because I asked him to wait. So if you need someone to aim your misplaced anger at, I'm your target."

I resume my escape, getting angrier by the second. Troy follows me, but at least he refrains from saying another word until we reach my car.

Before I can get in, he touches my arm. "I'm never going to blame you for what happened. You're only eighteen. Even if you think you started all this, he should have put a stop to it."

"You're so full of shit, it's not even funny. Do you know how Andy and I got together the first time? He didn't know it was me. That's right. I tricked him into sleeping with me."

Troy's eyebrows shoot to the heavens. "Why would you do that?"

"Because I've been in love with Andy for three years, but I knew he would never cross that line with me. I'm not denying it was a terrible thing to do. Andy was furious when he found out. He felt horrible he didn't recognize me."

"And that doesn't tell you to run for the hills? Come on, Jane. I thought you were smarter than that."

"Don't patronize me!" I snap.

"I'm not. I'm just trying to open your eyes. I get being so infatuated with someone that you ignore the red flags."

"I don't need your help. I know about the risks. But Andy is worth all of them."

Troy clenches his jaw hard, narrowing his eyes. "I hope he feels the same way about you."

There's a myriad of things I want to tell him, the top one on the list being a big "fuck you," but I don't voice any of them. Troy walks away, and I lose my chance to have the last word. My pulse is pounding in my ears when I slide behind the steering wheel. My eyesight is blurry thanks to all the unshed tears, and my chest is heavy. I don't know what makes me sadder—the fact this is the biggest fight I've ever had with

Troy or that he spoke out loud all my fears in relation to Andreas.

Mom's ringtone breaks the silence inside the car. I let out a string of curses. It's already past eight. She must have just gotten home, and now she's wondering where I am. I'm too wretched to deal with her, so I let the call go to voicemail, and then put the radio on as loud as I can. I have at least half an hour to come up with an excuse for why I'm out.

About five minutes into the drive, I see the sign for an In-N-Out restaurant. My stomach grumbles, reminding me I haven't eaten anything in hours. That's my alibi right there. Delicious junk food. Mom doesn't need to know I haven't been home since the trip to the mall.

I order all my favorite items from their menu, including their six-hundred-calorie strawberry shake. After the day I've had, I've earned it. I start drinking it as soon as I get a chance, but the treat is not making me feel any better. I hate that I fought with Troy. He's a pain in the ass, but I love him.

I've never felt more alone than I do now. I don't have any close girlfriends who I can trust with my problems. The only person who could actually give me some advice is Grandma, but even so, I'm afraid to tell her about Andreas. What if she agrees with Troy that I'm risking too much, that I will get my heart broken? I can't handle another person I trust and love telling me I'm making a mistake.

I should be on cloud nine. I'm dating the boy of my dreams, but I've never been more depressed. And when I walk through the front door, knowing I'm about to be on the receiving end of criticism and reproach, my stomach bottoms out.

Mom is sitting at the dining room table busy working. A glass of Chardonnay is next to her laptop, but no sign of food. She subscribes to the idea that wine is an excellent meal replacement. If I were a better person, I would have bought her at least a burger. She's eternally on a diet, but she eats junk food like everyone else.

She lifts her face from the computer. "Where have you been?"

"I went to grab dinner." I lift the In-N-Out bag.

"Junk food on a Monday, Jane? Really?"

"Alcohol on a Monday, Mom? Really?" I mock.

She watches me through slits. "Don't start with me. Did you pick up your dress?"

"Yep," I reply.

She doesn't need to know I didn't pick the dress she selected. It's better if she finds out at the luncheon Saturday. My stomach ties into knots. I still don't know how I'm going to manage bootcamp and that event.

"I've made a list of all the candidates that are still available. They aren't at the same level as Hanson van Buuren, but beggars can't be choosers."

I grind my teeth, fighting hard to not fall for her trap. I know she's goading me to talk back so she can either ground me or say more hurtful things.

"Sounds good, Mom. Just shoot me an email." I veer for my bedroom.

"Where do you think you're going with that greasy bag? You know you're not allowed to eat in your bedroom."

I count to ten in my head. I'm not going to engage. With a fake smile on my lips, I say, "Right. I forgot. I'll eat my dinner in the kitchen."

She keeps watching me with her resting bitch face. I'm sure she's raving mad that she doesn't have a solid excuse to grill me further. I'm almost out of earshot when she adds, "Oh, your father called. He wants to have dinner together to discuss your application to Stanford."

"I'm not going to Stanford," I blurt out, and just like that, I give her the opening she needs.

"If you botch your application to Stanford on purpose, we aren't paying for any other school. So I suggest you reconsider your attitude."

I give her the mother of all death glares while saying in my head, *Fuck you, Mom.*

24

ANDREAS

GOING against Danny and Paris's advice, I decide to pay Troy a visit after class the very next day after our fight. They said I should give him more time to cool off, but I can't stand to see Jane suffering. I have to patch things up with him because I'm not giving her up.

I call Charlie to make sure he's home. It rings for a long time and I fear it will go to voicemail. She finally answers it, but judging by the tone in her voice, I might have called at a bad time.

"Hey, I want to check if your boyfriend is home."

"He is, but if you're planning to swing by, I'd suggest you don't."

"Why is that?"

She sighs. "I told him I knew you had hooked up with Jane at the Halloween party. Now he's mad at me too."

"Ah hell. I'm sorry. Troy can be such a stubborn jerk sometimes. I'm coming over anyway. I'll see you in a few."

Maybe Charlie is right and going right now while Troy is

already pissed is not such a great idea, but I can't leave things alone. I can be as pigheaded as he is.

I snag a prime spot in front of his house, but I stay in my car for a minute, running over in my head what I'm going to tell him. Saying that I care about Jane is not going to be enough for him. But I won't lie and tell him that I love her, because I don't even know if that's true. To be honest, I don't know what the hell I feel for her. That's how fucked up I am. I crave her body like nothing else, and she makes me crazy happy. But is that love?

"Shit! I'm a bastard."

"You got that right," Troy says, looming only a few feet away from my car.

I was so immersed in my thoughts that I didn't even hear him walk out of the house. I get out of the car. It's time to do what I came here for.

"I'm glad we're in agreement about something then," I reply.

"What do you want, Andreas?"

"I want a chance to explain things."

"Nothing you can say will change the fact you pursued my sister after you told me countless times that you'd never commit to anyone. Do you want me to be happy that Jane is now another notch in your bedpost?"

"That's not what she is to me. I ca—"

"Care about her, yeah, I heard you the first time. And the second. Even Charlie tried to feed me that bullshit. But I've seen you in action too many times. I have watched you leave a parade of girls brokenhearted after you fucked and ditched them. Do you think I want Jane to be one of them?"

"That won't happen. I'm giving you my word."

"You can't promise me that."

"Why not? Because I have a reputation? Maybe I slept

around because I didn't know what I was missing until I found Jane."

Troy presses a closed fist against his forehead. "As angry as I am right now, I do want to believe you, man, but I just can't." He glances at me, his eyes shining with conflict. "Jane might have finally found the confidence to speak her mind, but that doesn't mean she isn't vulnerable. Don't you fucking know how hard she has it now at the hands of my narcissistic mother?"

"I do know. And that's why I'm here, risking getting punched in the face. She's miserable about your fight. Don't let your anger with me drive you away from her."

"If you're that worried, there's a simple solution. Walk away now before it's too late."

"It's already too late!" I lose my patience. "I can't walk away from Jane. She's all I think about."

"Are saying you love her?"

Damn it. He had to ask me the only question I'm not able to answer truthfully.

He laughs without humor. "Never mind. Your face says it all. Don't worry about Jane. I'm not going to shut her out of my life because you're now in hers. Someone will have to be around to pick up the pieces when you obliterate her heart."

He walks away, leaving me feeling worse than I did before I came here. I didn't expect him to forgive me. I don't think he ever will, even if end up marrying Jane and we have a bunch of kids. Warmth spreads through my chest at the thought of one day starting a family with her. Right now, it seems like a dream and I don't dare let my thoughts go there.

I knew patching things up with Troy would be impossible. My main goal was to make sure he wouldn't stop talking to Jane on my account.

I text her once I'm in the car. I probably should give her some space, but I wasn't lying to Troy. I can't stop thinking about her.

. . .

HEY, what are you doing today, babe?

SHE DOESN'T TEXT me right away, and I begin to worry, which is fucking stupid. She might be busy. *Hell.* I went from Casanova to clingy boyfriend in the span of days. I'd better find a distraction fast before I head to her house uninvited. Wouldn't it be the cherry on the top of the cake if I got Jane in trouble with her mother too?

You already agreed to help her escape the luncheon, dumbass. What do you think is going to happen?

I did agree and I can't back down now. Her mother will be furious, but at least Jane will get what she wants, which is to play roller derby instead of being paraded around like she's a fucking prize horse.

Anger surges within me, making me tighten my hold on the steering wheel. Her mother is almost as bad as my father. Mine punished me with his fists, hers does so with words and actions. Maybe that's why I'm so drawn to Jane. We both have fucked-up parents.

My phone chimes, announcing a new text message, and my heart skips a beat. I glance at the screen, smiling from ear to ear when I see it's her reply. At a traffic light, I read the whole message.

I HAVE a ton of homework to do, and I have to get my skates on later.

I'M DISAPPOINTED THAT, most likely, I won't have a chance to see her today. The feelings I keep having are a surprise to me.

Another text pops up.

. . .

I'M GOING to Hermosa Beach to practice. Do you want to come?

AND JUST LIKE THAT, my spirits are lifted. I feel giddy like a kid on Christmas Eve. I say "Yes" before thinking things through. I never learned how to skate properly. *Shit.*

DO YOU HAVE ROLLER SKATES? I should have asked that first, huh?
   No, but I'll figure it out. I'll pick you up. Just tell me when.

I HALF EXPECT her to say it's better if I don't or her mother might create issues, but when she texts back with an "Ok," a stupid grin appears on my face. Now I have to find some skates.

JANE

I can't focus on my homework to save my life. And once Andreas's text comes through, impossible. But I can't let my grades slide off. I need to maintain my GPA, or forget getting accepted at Rushmore. They might not be as prestigious as Stanford, but they have a tough selection process as well.

   I'm still reeling from Mom's latest threat. I bet it was her idea to withdraw financial support if I refuse Stanford. One more reason to graduate top of my class. I might have to apply for a scholarship if that's the case. The only issue is that I'm not a star in any sport, and since my parents are wealthy, it will be tough getting financial assistance any other way.

   I wish Troy were speaking to me. He'd have a word of

advice. But knowing him, he'll stew on his anger for a while.

I force my mind back to the book in front of me. I have to memorize all these historical facts by the end of the day. I have a quiz tomorrow, and I want to head to Hermosa Beach to practice later. I'm jonesing to go skating.

But my phone with Andy's message keeps taunting me. I glance at the screen every thirty seconds. *God, forget it.*

He asked what I'm doing today. I guess he wants to hang out. So tempting. With the way we left things off last night, I'd like nothing more than to see him in person to make sure he hasn't changed his mind about me. Any other guy would say the hell with it if they had to deal with a brother like mine.

With regret, I tell him that I have homework to do, and I'm going to practice after. He doesn't reply immediately, so I shoot another message, asking if he wants to come.

The "Yes" comes swiftly, and like a fool in love, I let out a shriek. I didn't stop to think if he has skates or not. I've never seen him rollerblading before. He says he doesn't own a pair, but he'll figure it out. The worry in my chest eases a little. If he wasn't sure about us anymore, he wouldn't go through the trouble.

When he tells me that he's going to pick me up, a sliver of worry pierces my chest. The last thing I need is Mom finding out about Andreas and forbidding me to see him. She would do it out of spite—or jealousy. Then I remember she won't be home until much later. She texted earlier to let me know she has a dinner with a client.

That thought and the prospect of seeing Andy today is all the motivation I need to get done with schoolwork as fast as I can.

25

ANDREAS

IT TOOK me a while to find someone who had a pair of skates I could borrow. Buying was also an option, but I didn't feel like going all the way to the mall. In the end, I got a pair of rollerblades from a dude on the hockey team. In hindsight, in the amount of time it took me to find these damn things, I could have gone to the mall and back in less time.

I'll be late to pick up Jane, and I feel horrible, knowing she probably wants to get as much practice as possible. I tell her she can go ahead of me and I'll meet her there. She doesn't sound upset over the phone, but I could be completely wrong. My lack of experience having a girlfriend is coming back to bite me in the ass, big time.

After suffering the brutal LA traffic during rush hour, I finally arrive in Hermosa Beach, but I can't find a parking space near the pier to save my life. I end up parking closer to Redondo Beach, which is the next neighborhood south of Hermosa. I call Jane as soon as I'm out of the car, but it rings and rings until it goes to voicemail. *Hell. What now?*

I text her instead, and walk toward the beach, carrying my borrowed rollerblades. I won't put them on until it's absolutely necessary. The sun is about to set, and the boardwalk is busy. Too many people to witness my poor skating skills. I look at my phone again, and nada.

"Come on, baby. Where are you?" I mutter to myself.

I hope she didn't forget her phone in the car. It seems I won't have a choice but put the skates on and look for her on wheels. I hope I don't break something in the process.

JANE

When Andreas said he would be late and told me he'd meet me here, I was disappointed. I was looking forward to the ride with him. I even dressed like a cute eighties roller skater girl especially for him. But now that I'm at the beach, I'm glad he gave me the option to practice longer.

The boardwalk is as busy as I expected it to be. The weather is lovely and the sunset promises to be phenomenal. I put my roller skates on, and then I make sure my phone is off vibration mode. I don't want to miss when Andy calls. I brought a mini crossbody bag that fits the device, my wallet, and my car keys. It's small enough that it won't get in the way.

I skate from my car to the boardwalk, and it feels like I'm in a video game where the objective is trying to reach the beach without running over any of the pedestrians. This is good practice for me. I'm sure there will be obstacles on the banked track this Saturday.

I finally reach the boardwalk without killing anyone, and then skate toward Manhattan Beach. Andy said he was probably running thirty minutes late, so that should give me enough time to get there and back. Then I'll wait for him near the pier.

My legs are still a bit sore from the tryouts. It was good that I wasn't able to practice yesterday—in more ways than one. Remembering what kept me busy brings a blush to my cheeks and a wonderful feeling in my belly. I couldn't have imagined, not even in my wildest dreams, how wonderful it would be to be with Andy.

My brother thinks it's crazy to be so in love with someone I don't really know well. But the heart wants what the heart wants. Besides, he only knows one side of Andreas. Even when he was drunk out of his mind, he was kind and gentle. A true asshole wouldn't have cared if I was comfortable or not.

I reach the edge of Manhattan Beach in ten minutes. I could keep going farther, but I decide to head back in case Andy manages to get here earlier. Sweat is pouring down my back and covering my face. I'm no longer as cute as I wanted to be, but there's nothing I can do about it. I'm blazing past a busy restaurant with an outside area when I hear someone call my name. I look over my shoulder and find Fred waving at me. Sylvana and Katja are sitting at the table with him.

I whirl around and head back to them. Fred jumps over the restaurant's pony wall, grinning from ear to ear.

"Jane, we have to stop meeting like this," he says.

"I know, right? What are the odds?" I glance past his shoulder and wave at the girls. "Hi."

"Are your ears burning, Jane? We were just talking about you," Katja pipes up.

"Really?" My smile wilts a bit.

I hope it wasn't Fred talking about me. With everything that happened recently, I forgot all about him and the date I postponed. A raincheck is not a refusal, and judging by the way he's looking at me, he believes he has a chance.

"Yeah, Fred was spewing poetic shit about you," Sylvana laughs.

My face becomes as hot as lava while my chest tightens. *Crap.* I really wish she hadn't said that.

"I was not!" Fred retorts. "Don't listen to my cousin, Jane. She's crazy. I was just saying how awesome you were during tryouts."

"Thanks. I'm still pinching myself that I made it through."

"You did really well," Katja says. "I'm glad to see you're training. Bootcamp is intense."

"I have a question about the schedule. Do we have a lunch break or something?"

"Yeah, of course. You'll get an hour, but I advise you to eat something light. Puking on the track is never fun."

An hour. I still don't know if I'll be able to make an appearance at the luncheon and then get back in time. Andreas said he could make it happen. I have to trust him because with the way things are between Mom and me, if I miss the luncheon, I don't know what she'll do to me.

"Right," I reply.

"What's with the furrow?" Fred asks.

I shake my head, forcing a smile on my face. "Nothing."

"You look like you need a break. Do you want to join us?"

"Uhh...."

"Yeah, Jane. Join us." Sylvana smirks.

"Jane!" I hear Andreas yell my name from somewhere nearby.

I turn toward the boardwalk, squinting to try to find him in the crowd. Suddenly, he appears, coming fast on rollerblades. He doesn't slow down, even when people walk in his path.

"What is he doing?" Fred asks.

"Oh my God. I don't think he knows how to brake," I reply.

And I'm right. Andy manages to miss a couple in his way, but only because he swerved to the right at the last second. He's going to crash into us if I don't help him. I skate in his direction, but instead of meeting him straight on, I loop my arm around his waist, using his momentum to spin us. It would have worked if he didn't freak out and flail around. I can't maintain my balance and compensate for his lack of it at the same time. We're going to fall and it's going to hurt.

My back meet someone's chest and hands reach my arms, stopping my descent.

"Gotcha," Fred says near my ear.

I'm still holding Andreas in my arms, so this must look like the most awkward scene ever. But since we stopped moving, he finally finds his balance and eases off me.

"Are you okay?" I ask.

"Mortified, but yeah." He looks over my shoulder at Fred. "You can let go of her now, pal."

There's no mistaking the hint of threat in his tone. Fred steps back, but he leaves a hand on my lower back. *Crap on toast.* I'd increase the distance myself if Andy wasn't blocking my way.

"Maybe you should be the one to give her some space after you almost killed her with your poor skating skills."

"I didn't—"

"You're both smothering me. Back off, please," I say.

Andreas glances at me, surprised, but then gives me some room. Fred also drops his hand and stands next to me.

"I'm sorry I almost made you fall, babe."

"*Babe?*" Fred's tone rises to a pitch. "Are you two dating?"

I turn to him. "Yeah."

"Since when?"

I feel Andy's stare burn a hole through my face. *Oh boy, that's going to be a bitch to explain.* I hope he doesn't have another fit of jealousy in front of everyone.

"Why do you care?" he asks.

Fred doesn't try to hide his disappointment. He ignores Andy and glances at me. "You could have told me."

"I'm sorry."

He cuts a quick look in Andy's direction, and then back at me. "I'd better go before your boyfriend punches me in the face."

Damn it. I feel awful now. Fred heads back to the restaurant with his shoulders slumped forward. I was a total ass for not being straight with him from the beginning.

"What was that all about?" Andy asks.

His posture is tense, but it's the hardness in his gaze that worries me. Now he's upset with me too.

"It's not what it looks like."

"Whenever someone says that, it is *exactly* what it looks like. Were you going out with him before we got together?"

"What? No! Can we go somewhere else and talk, please?"

He turns toward the beach, skating away without answering. I follow him until he sits on the pony wall separating the beach from the boardwalk. He removes his rollerblades, still not saying a word or meeting my gaze.

"Are you mad at me?" I ask in a small voice.

He lifts his face to mine. His green eyes are softer now. *Thank God.*

"I'm not angry at you. I'm just trying to come to grips that my girlfriend is a knockout, and it's my own damn fault for taking too long to stake my claim."

Sweet baby aliens. I've just melted on the spot. I move into his personal space, then I run my fingers through his hair. "There's no need to be jealous. It's always been you, Andy."

His eyes focus on my lips, and in the blink of an eye, I'm blazing from inside out.

"Did you get enough practice already?" he asks.

"Yeah, why?"

"I want to do something, but unfortunately, what I have in mind is NSFP."

"What's that?"

He curls his lips into a crooked smile, and then he whispers in a husky tone, "Not safe for public, meaning it involves my cock buried deep inside your pussy."

26

JANE

ANDREAS WALKS me to my car. Since I left my shoes in the vehicle, I have to skate slow so I can match his leisurely pace.

"You didn't answer your phone," he says.

"I didn't hear it. I'm sorry. But you found me anyway." I squeeze his hand.

"Don't remind me of that scene."

"Why didn't you tell me you didn't know how to skate?"

"I know how to skate," he grumbles.

Through laughter, I say, "Fine. Why didn't you tell me you didn't know how to skate well?"

He reaches over and pinches my waist. "Ouch!" I drop his hand and move away from his naughty fingers.

"I wanted to see you today. If that meant making a fool out of myself, so be it."

"That's the sweetest thing someone has ever done for me. Who said romance is dead?"

"Some schmuck who never had anyone loveable in their life."

When we reach the sidewalk, I ask, "Where are you parked?"

"All the way at Redondo Beach."

"Wow, really? Well, my car is right there." I point to my right. "I can drive you to yours."

"Hmm, sure, but later."

"Later? Where are we going?" I unlock the doors, waiting for an answer.

Andy doesn't say a word. He gets into the car, leaving me hanging. I quickly follow suit, dying to know where he wants to go first. While I remove my skates, the suspense gets to me. "Are you going to tell me or is it a secret?"

"It's not a secret."

"So where?" I press.

"Not far."

"You're acting very mysterious." I toss my skates to the backseat and then turn the engine on. "But if I'm driving there, I need a location."

"Just drive, babe. I'll give you directions on the way."

I watch him through slits. "You'd better not be taking me to fleabag motel."

He throws his hands up in the air. "Ah hell. There goes my plan."

"You were seriously going to take me to one?"

He looks at me, trying to maintain a serious expression, but the twitch of his upper lip gives him away. "Nah, I'm just yanking your chain."

I smack his chest. "You're awful."

He grabs my hand, keeping it trapped under his, and tugs me to him. His lips find mine, possessive and hungry, like always. I soon forget that what we were talking about a minute ago, and get lost in the feel of his stubbled chin against my face, in the taste of his tongue as it dances with mine.

A familiar throbbing between my legs makes me wish we

were anywhere but inside my car. Even a fleabag motel would do. I want to straddle him and take care of the ache so badly, I could cry. But there are too many people walking around.

I pull away before my brain short-circuits and I do something foolish. "What was that for?"

"I realized I didn't say hello to you before."

"Hmm, I like the way you greet me."

"And let me add that I fucking love what you're wearing." He runs his fingers over my exposed legs.

"I'm glad you approve. This is all for you."

He smiles broadly, revealing the dimples I adore. "Good. Now, what was the deal with Fred? Why did he sound so butthurt to find out about us?"

Way to kill the mood, Andy.

"Uh...." I look forward, putting distance between us. "I was trying to get over you and might have encouraged him a little."

"Only a little? You didn't go out on a date with him, did you?"

I glance at him, trying to guess how jealous he is right now. I can't tell.

"No. He wanted to go somewhere to celebrate me surviving the tryouts and making the team."

"Wait? You told him about that?"

Ah hell. He's probably not going to like this. But I can't lie to him. "Fred was there."

"I see." Andy faces forward, clenching his jaw hard.

I touch his arm. "Hey, the only reason he knew about it in the first place is because his cousin's girlfriend is a player on the team."

"Hmm."

"Are you mad?"

"Nope." He crosses his arms over his chest. "Not mad at all."

"You could have fooled me."

He watches me sideways. "Fine. I'm jealous as hell, okay? But I'm trying my hardest to get over it."

"There's no need to be jealous, but I get it. I'd be jealous too if the situation were reversed. Let's not talk about Fred anymore, okay? Where do you want to go?"

He's still pouting when he answers, "I wanted to take you to a boutique hotel a block away, but maybe that's not much better than a motel. It's okay if you just want to go home."

Heavens above. Guys can be such babies sometimes.

"I was joking about the motel. I don't care where I am as long as you're with me."

I can tell he's trying not to smile, but the grin wins. "Okay, babe. Then drive."

No sooner do I pull out of my parking spot than Andreas's hand finds my pussy. He presses his fingers against my clit through the fabric of my shorts, making me gasp.

"Andy, you're distracting me."

"You can't multitask, babe?"

With regret, I bat his hand away. "Not when one of the tasks has the power to send me into oblivion."

He chuckles. "Okay, okay. I'll try to keep my hands to myself. Turn right at the next traffic light."

The boutique hotel appears as soon as I turn on the next street. It's so close to where I was parked that we could have walked. There's a tiny parking lot in front of the building, full save for one spot.

"We got lucky," he says.

"No, you got lucky. Imagine if there was no free space. You would have made me lose my parking spot for nothing."

"You sound way too grumpy for someone who's about to have some awesome sex." He gets out before I can offer a retort.

I grab my bag and follow him. He didn't go far. He's waiting just in front of my car with his hands shoved in his pockets. The pose makes his jeans hang lower on his hips, showing a peek of tanned skin. It's impossible to stay annoyed when the man looks like Adonis. He offers me his hand once I'm near, sending a zing of pleasure everywhere in my body.

I hate to admit it, but he's right. Grumpiness has no place with him next to me. I ignore how strange this situation is, getting a hotel room just for sex. I feel all grown-up and a little dirty too.

Andy got us a suite with a separate living area from the bedroom. There's also a huge balcony with an ocean view.

"This is incredible, but we're not spending the night. Why waste the money?"

"Because I can."

He grabs me by the waist and spins me around. Then he leans in and rubs his lips over mine, teasing me with the promise of another mind-blowing kiss. He doesn't follow through though. Instead, he presses his forehead against mine and takes a deep breath. His fingers run up and down my arms, leaving a trail of goose bumps in their wake.

"I thought you said something about awesome sex," I murmur.

"In good time. Let me just breathe you in."

"Is this going to be our thing? Fancy hotel rooms?"

He pulls back, frowning. "No, I just knew I couldn't make the drive back to my apartment in my condition."

"Your condition?"

He takes my hand and guides it to his crotch.

"Ah, this condition." I smile.

"Be straight with me, Jane. Does it bother you that I brought you here? I don't want you to feel uncomfortable."

"It doesn't bother me. I just wish I had my own place to make things easier for us."

"You're always welcome in my apartment. And your mom works, right? I can come over when she isn't around."

"I think I'd rather go to your place. My mother's schedule is unpredictable."

"That's fine." He tucks a lose strand of hair behind my ear. "I went to see Troy today, by the way."

His confession takes me by surprise. I step back so I can look at his face properly. "What happened?"

"He's still mad as hell at me. I don't expect him to forgive me any time soon. But I wanted to make sure he didn't make you pay for my sins. I don't want to be the reason you don't speak with your brother."

"You're not the reason. Troy's stubbornness is."

"Even so, I had to explain to him I'm not simply fooling around with you. I'm serious about us, Jane. I haven't been this happy in a long time and I'm not going to give you up."

My heart takes off, skipping gleefully toward the sunset. If I wasn't already in love with Andreas, I'd fall in love now. I throw my arms around his neck and crush my mouth to his. He matches my enthusiasm, encircling my waist with his arms and pulling me closer to his body. Together we create an inferno. His heat fuels my own, and suddenly, I no longer know where I end and he begins. Clothes get snatched off urgently, and then we're tumbling down on the white leather couch.

Andreas abandons my mouth to place open kisses on my neck and then he moves south, sucking my nipple into his mouth while he plays with my other breast with his hand. I arch my back, begging for more.

"Andy, shouldn't we head to the bedroom?"

"What for, babe? I got you right where I want."

He lets go of my nipple to continue kissing my stomach until he's in between my legs. He lifts one of them over his shoulder, exposing me even more to him. When his warm tongue finds my clit, I cry out. He licks my bundle of nerves with gusto while he continues to play with my breast.

I'm quickly losing control. I'm floating on air. I want to hold on to sanity for as long as I can, but Andreas is too good at sex. He inserts two fingers inside of me, torturing me in every possible way.

"Oh my God," I moan just a second before he makes me come.

His fingers fuck me harder; his tongue works my clit faster while my body shakes from head to toe. I don't realize I was screaming until I stop and find my throat hoarse. My eyes are closed when Andreas finally shows me mercy. I'm boneless.

I hear a condom wrapper rip, and a moment later, Andy's body is covering mine, and his length slides into me. *Holy fucking shit.* I didn't think I was ready for round two. But I guess I am.

27

ANDREAS

Eventually we made it to the bedroom. It would have been a waste to not take advantage of the king-sized mattress. I'm now resting my head against Jane's stomach and she's running her fingers through my hair. I could seriously fall asleep like this. It's heaven.

"How was your day today?" I ask.

"School was a bore. I'm so ready to graduate."

"Only a few more months and then you'll be a Rushmore Rebel."

"That's what I want. But my parents want me to go to Stanford, no matter what."

I lift my head to look at her. "They can't force you to go to a school you don't want to."

"As long as they control the financial strings, they can. My mother told me the other day that if I botch my Stanford application on purpose, they won't pay for my tuition anywhere else."

"That's seriously fucked up, babe."

"I know. But even if I did try to sabotage my chances, I'd still be a shoo-in with my father being a famous alumnus and all."

"I don't want you to move to San Fran," I say. "But I'd respect that if it were your choice."

"It's not my choice and I won't go. I love my life here in LA. Now I have you and roller derby. If that means attending community college and working my way through, so be it. Lots of kids in America do it. I can too."

"Of course you can, babe. Have you talked to Troy about it?"

"The last time we spoke, he wasn't completely against Stanford."

"Maybe he was trying to keep you away from me. I think, deep down, he suspected I had a thing for you."

"Why do you say that?"

"He never wanted me to tag along when he had plans with you."

"You say you had a thing for me, but tell me the truth. When exactly did that start? It can't possibly have begun after I stole that kiss from you."

I frown. "Why not? You were a damn good kisser for a first-timer."

She yanks a fistful of my hair. "Hey. How do you know it was my first kiss?"

"Are you saying it wasn't?"

Her cheeks turn a beautiful pink color. "No, Mr. Know-It-All. For your information, my first kiss happened when I was in seventh grade. His name was Enrique Garcia, and he wore braces."

"Fine, I accept that I wasn't your first everything. But I'm sure my kiss was the first one that made you go weak in your knees."

"Aren't you cocky?"

I roll on my belly, resting my chin in between her lovely tits. "Are you saying that it isn't true?"

She narrows her eyes. "Fine. It's true."

I chuckle. "There's no need to feel embarrassed about it."

"Who says I'm embarrassed?"

I poke her cheek. "Your lovely red face."

She bats my hand away, and then leans on her elbows, dislodging me from my comfortable position. "All right. Enough of making fun of me."

"I'm not making fun of you."

I'm about to blurt out that she's the first girl who ever made me feel alive, but the truth gets stuck in my throat. Her phone interrupts the moment.

"Crap. That's Troy's ringtone."

I roll off her and reach for the device on the nightstand. "Here, you should answer it."

She bites her lower lip, staring at the phone without making any motion to take it from me. "I'm not sure I'm ready to talk to him."

"Babe, he's probably calling to apologize for being an ass. Give him the chance. And he if doesn't, then I'll head back to his house and kick his ass for making you suffer."

Her beautiful eyes turn as round as saucers. "Please don't. I don't want you two fighting because of me again. I feel bad enough as it is."

"Please, Jane. Answer the phone."

She finally takes the device from my hand and clicks the Accept button, putting it on speaker.

"Hi, Troy."

"Hey, Jane. Are you busy?"

"No. But with I'm Andy."

"I figured as much. Anyway, I want to apologize for the way I reacted Sunday. To be honest, I'm still reeling from it."

I roll my eyes, making the same gesture Jane does. Troy can be so dramatic sometimes.

"You make it sound like I'm dating the devil."

"Not the devil, but close enough."

I twist my face into a scowl. As apologies go, this is one of the worst.

"I thought you were calling to say you're sorry. All you've done so far is criticize Andy."

"Right. Well, I *am* sorry for the way I treated you. But I'm not sorry for the things I told hi—ouch! Charlie, come on."

I laugh, guessing that Charlie must have pinched him or something. If she's comfortable doing that, then it means they've made up. No surprise there. Troy is crazy about her.

Just like you're crazy about Jane.

The random thought takes me by surprise. Up until now, I couldn't make sense of my feelings. Sadly, my only experience with love is too fucked up. Danny said what I had with Crystal wasn't real. She manipulated me. He's right, but that doesn't mean she didn't leave scars deep enough to confuse the hell out of me.

I shouldn't be listening to this conversation, so I slide out of bed and return to the living room. Jane must have taken the call off speaker because I can still hear her talking although Troy's voice vanishes. It's better this way. He's clearly too angry, and all the things coming out of his mouth were beginning to get to me.

I put my boxers back on and head to the balcony. Fresh air will do me good. It's much colder now that the sun has set. A T-shirt would make me more comfortable, but the cool air against my skin isn't too awful.

The boardwalk is much quieter now, and I can hear the waves crashing against the shore. I take a deep breath, enjoying the peaceful moment. A few seconds later, Jane hugs me from behind, resting her cheek against my back. I feel a pang in my chest like a broken piece clicked back into place. I can't breathe for a moment, caught between being scared and elated.

I cover her arms with mine and ask, "All good?"

"Yeah. After you left the room, Troy was much more reasonable. I think he was saying all those hurtful things because he knew you were listening."

"I figured as much. Did you tell him about Stanford?"

"Not yet. We made plans to visit Grandma this Friday. I'll tell them both at the same time."

"Are you also telling Ophelia about us?"

Jane releases me from her hold and steps to my side. "Yeah. I don't want to hide from anyone that you're my boyfriend."

I throw my arm over her shoulders, pulling her closer. "Only your parents," I chuckle.

"Not even them." She turns in my arms, looking up. "I'm telling Mom at the luncheon that you'll be my escort to the ball because that's what boyfriends do."

My face splits into a grin. "That's right. And I'm going to prove to you that I'm the fucking best boyfriend in the world."

"Better than Troy?" She arches an eyebrow.

"Hell yeah. No offense, but your brother's got nothing on me."

"All right. But now that you've raised the bar, you'd better deliver."

I kiss her long and hard, loving how she immediately melts into me. When I pull away, her face is ethereal.

"Oh, I'll deliver, sweetheart. You'd better believe it."

28

JANE

I've been avoiding Mom since we clashed over Stanford. But I couldn't keep that up forever. This morning she reminded me that we were meeting my father for dinner tonight, which totally blew the plans I'd made with Andreas and left me in a bad mood all morning.

I didn't text him right away because I knew I had to vent, and messaging wouldn't do. As soon as I come home from school, I call him, knowing he should be home already.

"Hey, babe. How's your day so far?" he asks.

I flop on my bed and stare at the ceiling. "Pretty crappy. I have to cancel our plans. I'm having dinner with the parentals tonight."

"Oh, no worries. Is Troy going to be there?"

"I don't think so. This is a dinner to talk about my future at Stanford. Gag me."

"I've been thinking about that. Maybe it's better if you just pretend to follow along with their plan until you have a solid counterattack strategy."

"Yeah. It's good advice. The problem is, now that I've found my voice, it's hard to keep quiet. Meek Jane is gone."

He chuckles, infusing my body with warmth.

"You were never meek."

"I beg to differ."

"A meek girl wouldn't have attacked me in the laundry room."

"Oh my God. You're never going to drop that, are you?"

"No. I'll be telling that story to our grandkids."

I stop breathing for a second. *Is he only joking or is he serious about that statement?* Andy has told me I make him happy and he's not giving me up, but he's never mentioned a distant future like that. He knows I'm in love with him, and yet, he has never said it back.

"Hello? Jane? Are you still there?"

"Yeah, I'm here."

"Anyway, just think about what I said."

I want to ask which part, but I know he's referring to dinner with my folks. "You're right. The smart thing to do is to bite my tongue. Dinner is going to be brutal though."

"Why don't you ask Troy to tag along?"

"I thought about it, but he's been protecting me from Mom my entire life. Maybe that's why he feels entitled to an opinion about us. I need to do this on my own."

"And you will, babe. I wish I could come over right now, but I have to write a paper."

"It's okay. I also have schoolwork to do."

"Call me when you get home from dinner, okay?"

"I will. Love you," I say automatically and immediately freeze.

Fuck me. I can't believe I blurted that out. Maybe it was his talk of grandkids that made me daft for a moment. The line goes silent, but I can hear his breathing. *Oh my God.* If he says thank you, I'm going to die.

"I know," he finally replies. "Talk later."

He ends the call, leaving me reeling. My heart feels tight, and my stomach is now twisted in knots. The urge to cry comes swiftly like a tidal wave. He didn't say it back, and it hurts so damn much. I know I'm being melodramatic. We have been dating for less than a week. The fact I've been in love with him for three years doesn't change that.

But what if he thinks I'm a pathetic, needy girl?

"I'm such a moron." I hit my mattress with a closed fist.

My phone vibrates, sending me into a flutter. But it's not Andreas texting me back. It's a message from Hanson van fucking Buuren. *What the hell does he want?*

I should delete it after the douche move he pulled, but I'm too curious for that.

Hi, Jane. I'm sorry it took so long to get back to you. I feel awful for canceling our lunch the other day, but I want to let you know I'll be at the luncheon this Saturday. I hope we have a chance to talk then. Looking forward to meeting you in person.

Oh joy. I'm sure Lorena has something to do with Hanson's resurrection. Mom might have given up pairing me with a top candidate, but her friend clearly didn't.

ANDREAS

"I'm a fucking idiot." I stare at my phone, fighting the impulse to throw it against the wall.

"What did you do?" Danny asks.

He has an uncanny ability to show up at the exact time I'm doing or saying something stupid.

"Jane said she loved me, and I replied with 'I know.'"

"So you pulled a Han Solo on her. That's not too bad."

"No, it's bad. I hesitated. Besides, I've never said those words to her before. The Han Solo line only works after the fact in real life. I haven't risked my life for Jane time and time again like Han did in the movies."

Danny's eyebrows arches. "Wow. And I thought I was the romantic sap in this household."

"Just because I know my pop culture doesn't make me a romantic. Han wore his feelings on his sleeve, unlike me."

"You haven't been dating long. I'm sure she didn't expect you to say it."

I push my long bangs back. "I'm not sure, man. She's sensitive. The last thing I want is to hurt her."

"You're feeling awfully guilty about this. Is it possible that you're already on the same page as she is, but you're just too afraid to admit it?"

I throw him a glower. "Stop psychoanalyzing me, Dr. Phil."

He lifts both hands up. "Hey, I'm just trying to help. I'm going to hit the gym. Wanna come?"

"I can't. I have to finish a paper for Professor Douchebag's class."

My phone pings with an incoming message. My heart skips a beat, thinking it's from Jane, but when I glance at it, it's from a random chick, wanting a hookup. This one included a picture of her rack. *Jesus.* What if Jane saw it by accident? I can't give her any reason to believe I'm still a player.

The problem is so many girls have my phone number. Most of the time, I don't know who they are or how they got my digits in the first place. That detail never bothered me before. Now it's a fucking problem. This is the fifth text I've received since I started dating Jane. And like the others, I delete the message and block the number.

"Why are you glaring at your phone now?"

"Just another random message from a stranger."

"Ah, booty call. Maybe you should make an announcement on the school paper that you're officially retired as the campus Casanova. I'm sure Charlie can hook you up."

Danny's eyes are swimming with glee as he drinks his pre-workout shake.

"You're such a comedian, Danny. I thought you were leaving."

He sets the glass down on the counter. "Don't be a hater. I'm just trying to help."

"Sure."

I get comfortable on the couch and fire up my laptop. This damn paper won't write itself. Danny doesn't say another word, and five minutes later, he walks out the door. I should be able to get into the zone now that the house is quiet, but my mind keeps going back to my phone conversation with Jane. I didn't want to tell Danny, but the reason I was cursing to myself is that I almost said the L-word back but choked in the end.

The only time I've said those words before was to Crystal, and now, I'm terrified to open myself up for more heartbreak. Crystal was a fucking bitch who only used me to get to the top prize, my father. Even knowing I was played when I was too naïve to know better doesn't make the memory of that pain less acute.

I'm hardwired now to walk away from any chance of getting hurt again. Admitting that I've fallen for Jane could be the hardest thing I have to do.

29

JANE

WHEN WE ARRIVE at the restaurant, my father—punctual man that he is—is already there waiting for us.

"You're late," he says as soon as we take our seats.

"I had an important call with a client," Mom replies without looking in his direction.

They've been divorced for ages, and still, they can barely tolerate each other's presence. I can't remember the last time they exchanged more than a few words at social events. The fact they've agreed to this dinner means it will be an uphill battle to convince them I don't belong in Stanford.

He glowers at my mother for another second before switching his attention to me. "How have you been, Jane? It seems like I haven't seen you in months."

"That's because you haven't. The last time was last year at your employees' barbecue party."

"Ah, that's right."

"Your father is too busy for family, Jane. You should know that by now," Mom retorts.

I let out a heavy sigh. *Here we go.* I wonder how long they'll keep tossing barbs at each before they remember the reason for this dinner from hell. I look around until I catch the waiter's attention. He walks over to our table and takes our drink orders. His interruption serves to reset my parents. They stop bickering for a moment to pay attention to the menu. I'm not hungry, but if I don't order anything, it's just going to cause me more grief with them.

"So, how's school?" Dad asks, resuming his phony interest in me.

"School is fine. Same old, same old."

"I hope this silly debutante ball business is not distracting you from your studies." He gives Mom a meaningful glare.

"This 'silly debutante ball' will help Jane's chances of getting into your precious Stanford. Her extracurricular activities were lacking."

"That's bullshit." I set the menu down, fuming.

My parents look at me as if I had suddenly sprouted a second head. I promised Andy I wouldn't antagonize them, but I can't keep my mouth shut and let Mom walk all over me.

"Jane, what in the world?" Dad says.

"See what I have to deal with? Jane has suddenly developed a rebellious side. Back talking, staying out late, and God knows what else she's doing."

"I've finally found my backbone, and I'm not going to apologize for that. I've been busting my ass, picking up any volunteer work I can, and you know it."

"You're not doing any volunteering work now."

"Because you told me not to!" I snap.

People are now staring, which is probably what's bothering Mom the most. Like she's one to talk after the spectacle she pulled last year in front of Charlie's family.

"She didn't want me to sign up so I'd have free time for debutante events," I continue in a lower tone.

Dad continues to stare at me calmly without saying a word. Mom, on the other hand, looks like she's about to blow a fuse. The waiter returns then with our drinks, and no sooner does he set her martini on the table than she chugs half of it. Dad glances at her in disgust before thanking the man.

"I'd be more than okay if you didn't participate in such a ridiculous affair, Jane," he finally tells me.

I want to shout, demanding why didn't he say something before, but then I remember he's not that type of parent. The only thing he cares about is making sure I attend his alma mater.

"You'd have to be involved in her upbringing to have decision power."

"Mom already put a lot of work into it. I think it will be fun," I say.

She looks at me, surprised, and I don't blame her. She knows I'm not keen in the least. However, now that Andy is coming with me, the prospect of a dull gala is not daunting anymore. I can't wait to show him off to all those snobby bitches I know talk trash about me behind my back.

"I'm glad that some sense has finally returned to you." She takes another large sip of her drink.

"Anyway, I didn't ask for this dinner to discuss frivolous social affairs." Dad folds his napkin on his lap, keeping his shrewd eyes on me. "Your mother told me you don't want to attend Stanford, and I want to know why."

"I don't have anything against it. I just don't think it's the right school for me."

"I don't see why you would think that. You loved the campus when I took you on a tour."

"I was eight. I didn't care about the school's campus. I enjoyed spending time with you."

He seems taken aback by my honest remark. Maybe he's

just too focused on his career and is truly unaware of his short-comings as a father.

"Besides, how come you've never pressured Troy to attend Stanford?" I continue, taking advantage of a weakness in his demeanor.

"Because John Rushmore has a better sports program, and that's where your brother excels. Your talents would be wasted there."

"Rushmore is a good school."

"Stanford is better. Jane, I'm sorry, but I'm not going to back down on this. You're going to Stanford. You *will* thank me later."

Tears gather in my eyes and I hate myself for showing weakness. "No, I won't. I happen to like my life in LA."

"Oh, please. San Francisco is only a few hours away. You're being dramatic, as usual," Mom pipes up.

She flags the waiter again since she's already finished with her drink.

It's clear that there isn't a way to win this argument. Nothing I say will convince my father to let go of his Stanford dream. I have to swallow this bitter pill for now and, like Andy suggested, come back with a strategy in place.

I check out during the rest of the dinner, only replying with short answers whenever I'm asked a question. I lose count of the number of martinis Mom drinks, and when the dinner is finally over, she's positively drunk. I have to drive us back home.

She stumbles out of the car when I park in the garage. It's a miracle she doesn't fall on her stiletto heels. I guess she's had a lot of practice. She disappears into her room and I know she will be dead to the world until late morning tomorrow. It's a blessing and a curse. I'm free of her annoying presence tonight, but I'll have to deal with her bitchy hangover mood tomorrow.

I get ready to call it a night, feeling immeasurably drained from the whole affair. I pick up my phone and pull up Andy's contact info. I promised to call him, but I'm not sure I want to after I blurted out that stupid love declaration. I set my phone on my nightstand, deciding it's better to just go to sleep and hope he forgot what I said.

Twenty minutes later, he calls. If I don't pick up, he's going to think there's something wrong.

"Hey," I say.

"Hi, babe. Did you just get home?"

"Yeah," I lie.

"You sound upset. How bad was it?"

I didn't think I sounded upset. I don't know how he could tell. But hearing the worry in his tone does something to me. Sadness and a sense of impotence overwhelms me. My eyes burn as the tears form once again.

"Jane?"

I let out shuddering breath, which I'm sure he heard.

"It was exactly like I thought it would be," I say through the choking in my throat. "My mother got stinking drunk and nasty, whereas all my father cared about was my future at Stanford. He's determined to send me there. He thinks he's doing what's best for me."

The hot tears finally roll down my cheeks. I'm glad Andreas is not here to see me bawl my eyes out, but I can't keep talking and hide the crying. I feel so weak and pathetic; I don't want him to know.

"Jane, bab—"

"I'm actually super tired. Can we talk tomorrow?"

There's a poignant pause before he replies, "Yeah. Sleep tight, babe."

I end the call without replying, burying my face in my pillow. I know I'll feel better tomorrow, but tonight, I'm going to let misery win.

ANDREAS

Something is wrong. Jane was crying, I'm sure of that, and trying to hide it from me. There's no way in hell I'm going to wait until tomorrow to check on her. I jump off the couch, grab my keys from the entryway table, and head out. I'm glad Danny is not home to try to stop me. It's not that late yet, and Jane said her mom got drunk, which means she's probably passed out already.

I drive as fast as I can, propelled by a gripping sense of dread. I wish Jane lived closer to campus, but the twenty-minute drive is nothing compared to the six hours from here to San Francisco. I told Jane we would find a way for her to stay here, but there's a small part of me that fears that might not be possible. I still have another year of school to go, which means not seeing her every day until I graduate.

The thought fills me with anguish, spurring me to press the gas pedal harder. I'm lucky I don't get a speeding ticket. When I park outside of Jane's house, all the lights are off. I could jump the gate, but there's a security camera mounted on top. Plus, there's the issue that I don't have the house keys and I can't pick a lock. Besides, I don't want to surprise Jane. I just want to make sure she's okay with my own eyes.

I call her, hoping she hasn't fallen asleep yet. It rings and rings, until finally, her croaky voice comes through.

"Hey."

"Babe, I'm outside, can you open the gate for me?"

"What? You're here?" Her voice gets more agitated, and then I hear the sound of sheets being tossed aside.

"Yeah. I couldn't sleep without checking on you."

"Okay, I'm coming."

The call goes silent. She must not want to be overhead on the phone. A moment later, the gate opens, and I slip through. Jane is waiting by the front door wearing loose flannel pajamas.

There's barely any light save for the crescent moon. It's enough to see the streak marks of tears on her cheeks though.

"You didn't need to come. I'm fine."

"Well, I'm here now. Are you going to let me in?"

"Yeah, but you have to be super quiet. The dragon sleeps for now."

She closes the door softly after me, and we tiptoe to her bedroom. We're lucky that it's at the opposite side of the house from her mother's suite.

As soon as Jane closes her door, I pull her into a bear hug, hiding my face in the crook of her neck. She hugs me back, and we don't move for a minute or so. I'm in not in a hurry to let her go.

"You didn't need to come, Andy. As you can see, I've survived."

I pull back to look at her face. "You don't need to lie to me, sweetheart. It's okay not to be all right."

She drops her eyes to my chest. "I don't want to be the girl with all the emotional baggage. First my brother goes berserk, and now my insane parents are dead set on making my life a living hell."

"You don't think I have enough baggage to fill a jet plane?" I pinch her chin between my index finger and thumb and lift her face back to mine.

"You seem to be handling it better than me."

"Babe, I wish that were true. I think I just learned to hide it better."

"You know you can tell me anything, right?"

"Yeah," I say, even knowing it's unlikely I'll ever confess my dirty secret to her. "You know that applies to you too. So tell me. You're feeling down only because of your parents, or did I contribute to it as well?"

Her eyes widen a fraction. "What do you mean?"

"You were hurt that I didn't say I love you back."

She steps back, putting an unwanted distance between us. "No, I wasn't. I didn't expect you to say it."

"I want you to know that I want to say it, but... I can't."

"Why?" she asks in a small voice, breaking me.

I'm such a fucking mess. I'm hurting the girl of my dreams and I can't help it. "Because I'm broken, babe. It's not you. It's me. I'll never be able to say those words out loud. It's beyond what I can give."

She wipes away the tear that rolls down her cheek. "Why is that? What happened to you, Andy?"

I swallow the huge lump in my throat. "I can't tell you that either."

"You don't trust me?"

I bridge the distance between us and capture her face between my hands. "I do, babe. I do. I'm just not ready yet. I need time."

It's a cop-out. I'll never be ready.

"I can give you time. This is not a race."

I kiss her lips softly. "You're too good to me, sweet Jane."

She steps away from me again, leaving me adrift. But when I look into her eyes, I don't see sadness anymore. I see passion and love. She undoes the buttons on her shirt slowly, not stopping until the swell of her breasts peek through the open fabric.

"You said you can't say you love me. But can you make love to me, Andy? Even if it's only tonight?"

I inhale sharply. My pulse accelerates, and other parts of my body react accordingly at the sight. Not only my cock, but also my stomach that now seems to house a thousand butterflies.

I step into her space again and rest my hands on her hips. "I can make love to you tonight, and every other night. I'm damaged goods, but I'm yours, babe. For as long as you want."

30

JANE

My alarm blares, ending a pretty good dream prematurely. With my eyes still closed, I reach for my phone on my nightstand, trying to shut it off. A male grumble makes me open them in a flash. *Oh my God.* In my semi-asleep state, I forgot that Andreas spent the night. He tosses his arm over my stomach, trapping me against his solid chest as he spoons me.

"Andy, you have to go," I whisper.

"Five more minutes, babe."

"I have to get ready for school. And don't you have class too?"

"What time is it?"

"Quarter to seven."

He pulls my hair off my shoulder and kisses my neck. "Plenty of time for a morning quickie."

I want to say no, but his hand finds its way between my legs, effectively shutting off the cautious side of my brain.

"You really know how to make your case."

"Is that a yes?" he whispers in my ear.

I moan in response, and he bites my earlobe before releasing me to search for his jeans on the floor.

Wanting to get a better view of his ripped backside, I lean on my elbows. Andy straightens when he finds the condom he was looking for and then turns to me with lopsided grin on his face.

"The last one. I need to keep you stocked."

"Why? Are you planning more midnight visits?"

"First of all, I didn't come at midnight. And secondly, why not?" He rips the wrapper and quickly rolls the condom down his length.

My eyes remain focused on his erection when Andreas returns to bed.

"My eyes are up here, babe," he smirks.

"Is that s—"

A knock on the door cuts off my sassy reply. My heart jumps to my throat at the same time that Andreas jumps off the bed, grabbing a pillow to cover his crotch area.

"Jane, are you up?" Troy asks outside the door.

He glances at me, panicked. If Troy finds him naked in my room, God only knows what's going to happen.

"Barely. What are you doing here?" I ask.

"I thought we could have breakfast together."

"Is Mom up yet?"

"I walked by her room. Heard her snoring pretty loudly."

"I have to shower. I'll be out in a minute."

"You do that, but tell Andy to come out first."

"Shit," he curses under his breath.

"I saw your car parked outside, moron," Troy replies.

Andreas gives me a look that's equal measures guilt and exasperation. It would have been comical if I knew what's going to happen once he walks out of my room alone. Maybe I should forget the shower.

He removes the condom and gets dressed in a flash. My

lady parts are crying now that the morning quickie got canceled. Stupid Troy. Why did he have to show up unannounced like that? It's almost like he knew Andy would be here. I wonder if it's a big brother radar thing.

I get going as well, putting my underwear back on before finding my school uniform.

"You're not showering first?" Andreas asks.

"I don't want to leave you alone with Troy."

He walks over with a smile. "Babe, I can face Troy by myself. I don't need you to be my lady in shining armor."

"I don't need to shower," I pout.

He leans closer and takes a whiff of my neck. "You smell like you've been thoroughly fucked all night. I think that will set your brother off more than me having a conversation with him alone."

"Okay, fine. But please, try to not to argue. We don't want to wake the dragon."

"I hear ya. Don't worry, babe. I'll behave."

He leans down and kisses me softly on the lips. I'd enjoy it more if my stomach didn't feel like it was filled with pinballs.

ANDREAS

I can't believe Jane bought into my reasoning. If she smells like sex, so do I. However, I'm sure it would bother Troy more to smell my scent all over her then the other way around.

I find him in the kitchen making way too much noise for my liking as he prepares breakfast.

"What are you trying to accomplish here, buddy? Wake your mom up so she can bust Jane too?"

He stops in his tracks and glances at me, sporting a glower.

"No. I'd never unleash my mother on Jane on purpose. I can't believe you'd think that."

"You sure are making a ruckus." I pull up a chair and rest my elbows on the counter.

"I got a text from my father last night. I know Mom got trashed. She won't be waking up before noon."

"You need to help Jane out with this Stanford deal," I say, even though Jane told me she'd tell Troy and their grandmother later today.

He crosses his arms over his chest. "Why? Would you be upset if she moved to San Fran?"

"Of course I would." I pull my hair back, yanking it at the strands. "I can't bear the thought of her going to live almost four hundred miles away from me."

Troy doesn't say a word, but his eyes.... They feel like a drill trying to make a hole in my brain.

"I don't know what else I can say to you to prove I'm not messing around with Jane," I continue.

"I guess only time will tell. But if you're that worried about not getting her in trouble, you shouldn't be sneaking in and spending the night."

"I was worried about her. She sounded off when I called her after dinner."

Troy's hard stare softens. "I wish she'd told me she was having dinner with our folks last night. I'd have come."

"She wants to fight her own battles."

Jane walks into the kitchen, looking like a ray of sunshine as usual. Her hair is damp, and her cheeks are still flushed from the hot shower. She's not wearing any makeup, but she doesn't need it. I feel a stirring in my pants, and immediately curse my body for betraying me.

"Are you talking about dinner last night?" She looks from me to Troy.

"He wanted to know why I risked being caught by your

mother. I was explaining I had a valid reason."

"Dad won't change his mind about Stanford. He's a stubborn son of bitch," Troy tells her.

"Like father, like son," I mutter under my breath.

He throws me a warning glare. "Watch it, pal."

"Please don't start," she says. "I really wish you wouldn't be at odds because of me."

"I'm not the one being difficult here," I reply.

"I'm trying, Jane. But seeing you two together is going to take time getting used to."

"Well, that's better than nothing. Are you going to help me get Dad off my case about Stanford?"

"I don't know what I can do to help. Like I said, he's committed to sending you there."

"Shit. I don't know what to do." She pulls her hair back, frustrated.

I wish I could do something to help, but if Mr. Alexander won't listen to his own son, he won't listen to me either.

"Would it be so terrible to move to San Fran?" Troy asks, earning the mother of all glares from me.

I just told him how I'd feel if she moved. *What a jerk.*

"Really, Troy? You're that petty?" Jane retorts.

"I'm not being petty. And before you say it, I'm not playing devil's advocate because I want to separate you two. I just don't want you to make this decision because of a guy."

"This has nothing to do with Andy, and you know it," she grits out. "Besides, he's not the only thing that I'd be giving up if I moved."

"I'd visit you."

"She's not talking about you, jackass," I butt in, annoyed as hell. "And you're not going to be around anyway. Aren't you going to Europe with Charlie?"

He narrows his eyes at me, probably dying to say something, but in the end, he simply turns to Jane and asks, "What are you talking about then?"

"What in the world is all this yapping in my house?" Jane's mother whines as she walks into the kitchen.

My spine becomes tense in an instant. Jane and I lock gazes, and I read fear in her eyes. *Fuck.* I'm about to make her home life a thousand times more difficult.

"Troy, what are you doing here?" his mother asks.

She hasn't acknowledged my presence yet, and I suspect it's because she's still drunk. I can smell the alcohol she drank last night from where I sit.

"Having breakfast with my sister. Why? Do you have a problem with that?"

"I fucking do have a problem when I have a migraine and you're talking so loudly." She whirls around and finally sees me. "And why are you here?"

"He came with me," Troy answers. "But don't worry, we're leaving. Come on, Jane. Let's have breakfast out."

"Let me get my bag." She runs back to her room, and away from a very uncomfortable situation.

Staggering to the fridge, their mother mutters, "I can't wait for Jane to start college and get out of my hair."

My hands curl into fists as I scowl at the back of her head. Troy shakes his head, a sign for me to keep my mouth shut. It's with effort that I stay silent. Jane deserves so much more than the awful parents she has. At least I had a mother who love me unconditionally.

Jane also deserves a man who can offer that same kind of love, not someone who is too fucked up to even say the words out loud.

My conscience is my fucking worst enemy. *Jesus.*

She returns with backpack hanging from her shoulder, and an expression that says let's get out of here. I get up and follow her and Troy to the front door. I don't bother saying goodbye to their mother. She's too hateful to warrant proper manners.

Outside the house, Jane seems unsure of what to do.

"Well, I guess I'd better head home. You kids have fun," I say.

"Will I see you tonight?" she asks me.

"Sorry, I can't tonight. I forgot to tell you. I have to work at the Rushmore Hotel as part of the practical portion of my Intro to Food Service Management class. But don't worry, I haven't forgotten about my promise." I move to kiss her on the lips, but Troy is watching us like a hawk, so I kiss her on the forehead instead.

There's no need to poke the beast with a short stick.

31

ANDREAS

BEFORE I DRIVE to the hotel for my shift, I make a pit stop at one my father's dealerships. There's something I need to arrange. I figured out a way to get Jane to the luncheon and back to the tryouts in time.

I hate my father's guts, and I wouldn't use his resources under normal circumstances. But for Jane, I'll make a deal with the devil if necessary. For this to work, I need to talk with the right person. Being the heir of my father's empire doesn't mean I can do whatever I want. The asshole has loyal employees who would immediately call him to inform him of my visit.

But I have my own contacts, people who would gladly help on the down-low in exchange for the right amount of cash. The entire transaction doesn't take more than ten minutes.

I'm in good spirits when I leave the place, but as I approach my final destination, apprehension takes hold of me. I've never served in my life. In hindsight, I should have practiced carrying a tray at least. One of the syllabi had the basic rules, but nothing beats the real deal.

The instructions said to use the employees' entrance at the back, and wear black slacks, a white button-down shirt, and tie. I took a selfie before I left the house and sent to Jane, asking what she thought of my new look. She replied with a thirsty emoticon and told me to save the tie.

She is the fucking best.

I'm grinning like a fool when I finally join tonight's crew. But sadly, Professor Douche is also present, killing my good humor in an instant. He gives me a loathing glance before introducing us to Paul Leggett, the restaurant's manager, who will be our instructor tonight. The restaurant opens in an hour, which means Paul only has time to explain things once.

A petite brunette wearing glasses bigger than her face moves closer to me and whispers, "Do you think this is going to be like Ramsay's *Hell's Kitchen*?"

"I hope not. I might punch someone in the face."

She chuckles, earning a glare from Paul and Norman. She doesn't say another word throughout the rest of the lecture.

Paul assigns our sections and then all we have to do is wait for the crowd to come. I'm in my designated section, ready to engage, when suddenly Norman appears next to me.

"I'm surprised that you actually found someone to trade places with you. Must be that star power."

"Must be," I reply through clenched teeth, fighting the urge to ask what his problem with me is.

But I can't start an argument with the man here of all places. He'll take great pleasure in flunking me. He departs soon after, and all I can do is stare daggers at this back.

"What did you do to piss off Professor Norman like that?" glasses girl asks.

"Nothing. I think he hates jocks."

"I'm Amelia, by the way." She offers me her hand for a handshake.

This is probably the first time a girl in school introduced

herself to me in such a businesslike manner. Her expression is neutral too; I see no signs of flirtation.

"Andy," I say.

"Nice to officially meet you, Andy." Her gaze travels past me. "Oh, the first customers are coming in. Shit, I have butterflies in my stomach."

"It will be fine."

"I hope so."

Soon, a party of three sits at a table in my section. I'm a little nervous when I greet then and take their orders. As the time goes by, I get more comfortable with the job, and the first hour passes by in a flash.

I'm feeling pretty good about myself, but the feeling goes up in smoke when I catch sight of my father and his fucking wife being escorted to a table in my section. This can't be a coincidence. The question is, how did he know I'd be working here tonight?

I need to take a couple of calming breaths before I veer for their table. I have every intention to treat him like he's just a regular customer, but my tongue has a mind of its own.

"What are you doing here? This is not your regular spot."

"I had to see for myself this despicable display," he replies with disdain, looking me up and down.

"How did you know I'd be here?"

"Norman is an old buddy of mine." He smiles wickedly.

Mystery solved. Now I know why Norman had it out for me since the beginning.

"Did you pay him to make my life a living hell in his class?"

He ignores my question and picks up the menu. "I have to say, the service is appalling. Do I have to call the manager to get my order taken?"

"I'd like to start with a cocktail. What do you suggest, Andy?" Crystal asks in overly saccharine tone.

"How about a Redheaded Slut?" I blurt out without thinking.

Dad whips his face up, glaring, but Crystal simply laughs.

"Nah, I think I'll have a Cosmo. I'm feeling *Sex and the City* tonight."

The way she watches me as if I'm a piece of meat twists my stomach. And to think I used to crave her heated glances once upon a time. The recollection makes me feel dirty, unworthy of my sweet Jane.

My father opens his mouth to order, but I cut him off. "Yeah, I know what you'll have, Dad. I haven't forgotten."

How could I when the smell of his expensive whiskey was always on his breath whenever he pounded me with his fists?

I put their drink orders in the computer, fighting the sudden nausea that has gripped me. Amelia joins me, and makes a comment about something, but I don't know what. My mind is reeling, stuck in the past.

She touches my arm. "Andy, is everything okay? You look ill."

"I'm fine. I just want this evening to be over already." I stare at my father's table, and the loathing and sickness grows.

She follows my line of vision. "Do you know them?"

"Unfortunately, yes."

"Do you want me to cover their table for you?"

"No, but thanks."

Accepting Amelia's offer would be cowardice. No, I'll serve Daddy Dearest and his Stepford wife with a smile on my face even if it kills me.

The evening that was going by in a blur suddenly begins to move at a snail's pace. Every time I have to attend to their table, my skin crawls. When the asshole finally asks for the check, I can't help the sigh of relief that whooshes out of me.

He signs the bill without looking or speaking to me. I

expect him to not give me any tip, so when I see the amount he wrote down, I can't hide the surprise.

"I think you've made a mistake here. There's one zero too many."

"No mistake." He stands. "Consider this my parting gift. I've warned you I'd cut you off if you insisted on dragging the Rossi name through the mud. Surviving on tips will be your life now."

"What the hell are you saying?"

"I'm done with you, Andreas. You can finish the semester since it's already paid for, but if you want to remain a student at Rushmore, I'd suggest you find a way to pay your tuition fees from now on. Oh, and I'll be collecting rent too."

I remain rooted to the floor, fighting to get air into my lungs. I can't believe he's actually following through with his threat.

"Don't look so sad, darling," Crystal purrs. "I can try to convince your father to give you a second chance, for old time's sake."

She takes advantage of my paralysis and kisses me on the cheek before sashaying away.

Her unwanted touch works like an electric shock. I can move again, and I use my recovered ability to run to the restroom to empty the contains of my stomach.

I'm not even that upset about the loss of financial security or the fact I'll have to drop out. I'm distraught because now I have nothing to offer Jane. Absolutely nothing.

32

JANE

ANDREAS SAID he'd call me after his shift. I ended up falling asleep early last night, but this morning there wasn't a missed call or single text. His radio silence worries me, so I call him right away.

"Hey babe," he answers on the second ring.

I exhale in relief. "Hi. You didn't call last night."

Great. Way to sound needy, Jane.

"I know. I'm sorry. It was late, and I was pretty tired."

"Oh. How was it?"

"It was... okay, I guess. I didn't drop spaghetti on anyone."

His attempt at a joke falls flat in my ear. He sounds miserable. *What is he not telling me?*

"Are you ready for tryouts?" he asks.

"Yeah, I'm just about to get ready. I have to sneak out before my mother wakes up."

"I can't wait to see you in that dress you picked. It's giving me happy memories."

Even though I know he's distracting me from whatever is

bothering him, I can't help the smile that spreads across my lips.

"I know there will be hell to pay afterwards, but I can't wait to see the look on my mother's face when I tell her you'll be my escort to the ball."

"You know, we don't need to tell her today. Maybe I'll just wait outside and let you do the rounds."

Disappointment floods through me. "You've changed your mind about being my date?"

"No, babe. Not at all. I'm just thinking logistics. We don't have a lot of time before I have to take you back."

"Right. I still don't know how you're going to work that magic."

"Don't worry. I'll make it happen. Do you trust me?"

"Yeah, I trust you."

I wish you would trust me too.

"Lunch break is from noon to one," I continue.

"I'll be there at a quarter to twelve. Now go get ready. I don't want you to be late."

"Okay. I'll see you later."

I keep staring at my phone for at least a minute after I ended the call. Even though Andreas said all the right things, I still sensed something off about him. If there's one thing I wish he would do, it's to let me in. I actually crave that more than hearing him say he loves me.

I MANAGED to slip out of the house without Mom being any the wiser. My dress for the luncheon is safe in the backseat of my car, and I'm already wearing makeup. It's probably going to be ruined by lunchtime, but it's easier to retouch than apply everything from scratch.

As much as I hate that Mom is forcing me to attend this

stupid luncheon at the marina, I want to make an impression. I want Hanson van Buuren to know what he missed out on. I'm no longer upset that Andy doesn't want to come in with me. I don't need to have a gorgeous man on my arm to prove to everyone I'm worth it.

My head is still filled with thoughts of him, my mother, and the debutante ball when I step foot in the gymnasium. The sound of skates on the banked track and the excited chatter of the other new recruits push all my personal problems to a corner in my mind. A rush of excitement goes through me. This is where I belong.

I head to the locker room and find Alicia sitting on a bench, lacing up her skates.

"Ready for this?" I ask, setting my duffle bag next to her.

"Jane. How are you, girlie?" she replies with a smile.

"I'm good. Excited."

"Same. It's too bad we didn't have a chance to meet this week to practice. Work was brutal."

"It's okay. We have the weekend to catch up. Did you manage to get any skating in at all?"

"Here and there."

She waits for me to put my skates on and together, we head to the track. The same guy who was judging us during tryouts is in the center of the track with a clipboard in his hand. Katja is standing next to Scary Samantha, the mean brunette who ended up helping me get picked for the Second Time Around Divas.

"Good morning," I greet them cheerfully.

Scary Samantha sneers in my direction. "Great. Kindergarten has arrived."

She skates off before I have a chance to reply.

"She's upset that Jane broke her record, huh?" Alicia pipes up.

"Right. She never forgets shit. You'd better keep an eye out for her. She's one of the most savage players in the league," Katja tells us.

"I'm not afraid of her," I say.

"Good." She smirks. "So, who was that hottie at the beach the other day?"

"Oh, that's Andy. My boyfriend."

"I didn't know you had a boyfriend," Alicia chimes in. "I thought you had a thing for Fred."

"Oh no. Fred is just a friend. And I just started going out with Andy."

"I think you broke poor Fred's heart," Katja says. "I've never seen him so quiet as I did after that encounter."

Guilt enters my chest and squeezes my heart tight.

"I didn't mean to hurt his feelings."

"The face of an angel, the attitude of the devil." Alicia laughs. "I knew I liked you for a reason, girlie."

"I'm not the devil," I reply, faking indignation.

I like that for once, I was not described as meek or shy. I'm a fucking badass rebel.

"I do hope you have a devilish streak in you. There's no room in roller derby for nice girls." Katja smirks.

"Nice girls can be bad." I follow her to where the rest of the girls have gathered.

It seems we're about to start training.

"I like that," Alicia says. "We should make T-shirts with that quote. So, do you already have a game name?"

I had been thinking about several options, but it wasn't until Scary Samantha sneered at me that I settled on the winner.

"Yeah, Blaze Jane."

"Blaze Jane," Alicia repeats. "I love it."

33

JANE

MY LUNGS ARE ABOUT to burst when the whistle finally echoes in the gym. Our trainer, Roger, is in fact, a torturer. Sweat covers my skin, and I know there's no chance that my makeup survived the intense workout. I need a shower. I glance at the giant clock on the wall. It's a quarter to noon, which means Andy should be already waiting for me outside.

Alicia skates to me slowly with her hands on her hips. Her breathing is coming out in bursts like mine.

"Fuck. That was intense. My legs are liquified. I don't think I'll survive the afternoon."

"Do you think we can start break before noon?"

She glances at the group being tortured now by Roger. "I don't think we'll be going back on the track until after lunch. Do you want to go somewhere to grab a bite to eat?"

"I can't. I have to be somewhere."

"Oh?" She raises an eyebrow.

"My mother is forcing me to attend a luncheon at the marina. I have to make an appearance."

"Why?"

"Because she doesn't know about roller derby. If I don't show up, she'll probably wonder where I am."

"Not to sound negative, but how are you going to make it to the marina and back before our break is over?"

"I don't know. Andy said he could make it happen."

"Oh, is Andy Superman then?" She laughs.

"Maybe he is. Anyway. Can you cover for me? I have to shower first."

"Yeah. You're good. If anyone asks me where you are, I'll tell them you have the shits."

I wrinkle my nose. "Gee. Thanks."

I look around, making sure no one is paying attention to me. Not that this is a jail or anything. I'm allowed to use the restroom. In the locker room, I practically yank my clothes off and jump into the shower. My hair, unfortunately, I can't wash. Showing up with damp hair will surely be seen by mother as an affront. But I had the foresight to pack dry shampoo. It should do the trick. I'll have to do my makeup in the car.

Five minutes later, I'm running to the gym's front door, hoping no one will see me sneaking out in my fancy dress. But it's my luck that Scary Samantha is standing there, talking on the phone.

She gives me a once over and smirks. "Where's the ball, Cinderella?"

"Shut up," I say as I run past her.

My reply will probably come back to bite me in the ass, but I can't worry about that now. Outside, I search for Andreas's Bronco in the parking lot. My heart sinks when I can't find it. *Shit. Is he late?* In my hurry to get ready, I didn't even check my phone. I dig for it in my bag, but the sound of a motorcycle's engine approaching catches my attention. The rider stops right in front of me and then removes his helmet.

"Andy! Oh my God. Whose bike is that?"

"I borrowed it for the day." He pulls an extra helmet from his backpack, and a leather jacket. "Here, put them on."

I hesitate and the smile on his face wilts. "What's the matter?"

"I've never ridden a motorcycle before."

"You can add that to our list of firsts."

His dimples make an appearance, turning me into goo. I put the jacket on first, and then helmet—there goes my idea of putting on my makeup on the way to the marina—and hop behind him. The smell of leather and Andy's cologne reaches my nose, infusing me with heat. I wrap my arms around his waist, getting as close to him as I can.

"Are you comfortable?" he asks over his shoulder.

"As comfortable as I can be."

"All right. Hold on tight, babe."

He revs the engine, making me acutely aware of its power. Then he takes off and my entire body tenses. I curl my fingers around his jacket, pressing my helmet against his back.

"Relax, babe."

"I'm trying."

"I'm not even going fast yet."

"I know."

Stop being pathetic, Jane.

In another minute, we enter the freeway, and my heart lodges in my throat. I'd scream if I could, but I'm too busy closing my eyes and pressing my face against Andreas's back. It can't be comfortable for him with my helmet jamming into him like that, but he didn't complain when he had the chance.

Okay, I'm not pathetic. This is awful, and I'm going to die.

I keep my eyes shut during the entire trip, but I'm keenly aware that Andreas is zigzagging through traffic. The ride that would normally take thirty minutes, we make in ten. When he finally slows down and I open my eyes, my heart is beating so fast, I'm afraid it's going to burst through my chest. I lean back and remove the helmet, but I make no move to dismount.

"Are you okay back there?" he asks.

"I need a minute."

I glance around and take in my bearings. We're in the parking lot of the fancy marina restaurant, which is almost full, save for the few motorcycle spots. I guess there aren't a lot of guests riding bikes today. The luncheon started a half an hour ago, so we're the last ones to arrive. My legs are still shaking, but the whole point of this hellish ride was to save time. I'm not going to waste it now by sitting outside.

I jump off and try to smooth the wrinkles from my dress's skirt. Andreas hops off and then removes his jacket. Underneath, he's wearing a jacket, shirt, and tie.

"I thought you wanted to wait outside," I say.

"I'm sorry I said that. I was having a rough morning, and I thought that by suggesting that I was being helpful. I was an idiot. If you still want me to be your date today, I'm here."

"I do, but for different reasons now. Before, I wanted to show you off. Now, I just want you by my side because you're my boyfriend, and that's where you should be."

He pulls me to him and kisses me deeply. I'm glad that I'm not wearing makeup because this is a lipstick-smearing kiss. When he pulls back, I'm a little breathless.

"Okay, then," he replies with a lazy smile.

I step back from his embrace and take off the leather jacket. "How do I look?"

"Hot as sin."

I frown, looking down. "My dress is a disaster."

"Who cares if your skirt has a few wrinkles?"

"I do, and not because I'm afraid what my mother is going to say. I really dislike wrinkled clothes."

"Really?" His eyebrows shoot up.

"Yeah."

He chuckles. "Okay. Well, there's nothing we can do about it now." He offers me his arm. "Shall we? I'm kind of hungry."

ANDREAS

Hungry for you, I want to add, but getting Jane hot and bothered now is not going to do me any favors. I'm already sporting a semi all thanks to that kiss. I swear I must have reverted to a horny teen because my dick is out of control whenever I'm in her presence.

I know she wishes she looked more polished, but she's stunning no matter what.

The restaurant's maître d' greets us and lets us know where to go. The affair seems to be pretty casual. There are high tables spread around an open room, a buffet with food, and an open bar. The presence of that surprises me.

"Aren't all the debutantes under twenty-one?" I whisper to Jane's ear.

"Yeah, but not all escort candidates are. Plus, the organizing committee depends on alcohol to survive."

I chuckle. "What's the plan?"

"Find my mother, eat something, and bail."

"Jane Marie Alexander," a woman shrieks behind us.

"Ah, I believe she found us," I say.

We turn around, coming face-to-face with a veritable dragon. The woman is spiting fire from her nostrils.

"Where have been? I woke up to find you gone. You don't answer your phone, and you show up late and wearing..." She gives her a glance over, twisting her face in disgust. "That."

"Sorry, Mother. I had things to do in the morning. But I'm here, aren't I? Now, what's for lunch? I'm starving."

She makes a motion to grab Jane's arm, but my protective

instinct takes over. I block her without stopping to think about it.

"I wouldn't touch her if I were you. Besides, everyone is looking."

If looks could kill, I'd be dead on the spot. She takes a step back, yanking her fancy suit down as if it's she trying to smooth invisible lines.

"I'd like to know what you're doing with my daughter."

"Andy is here because I asked him to be. He's going to be my escort to the ball."

She snorts. "*Him?*"

I try not to wince when she stares at me with profound disdain. *Who the fuck does she think she is to judge me?* But I keep my mouth shut because I don't want to embarrass Jane in front of all these people.

"Why not? He's Troy's best friend, and his father is a legend and filthy rich. Isn't that all you care about? Money and connections?"

Shit. I wish Jane wouldn't have mentioned my asshole father. At least that wasn't the first qualification she mentioned. I know she doesn't care about status, but how would she feel if she knew my father disowned me?

"Sorry to interrupt, but are you Andreas Rossi? Son of Giancarlo Rossi?" a preppy-looking dude with pushed back straw-colored hair and a fucking chin dimple asks me.

"Yes, that's me."

"I'm Hanson van Buuren. Huge fan of your old man." He extends his hand, and I stare at it without taking it.

After an awkward moment, he drops the offending appendage, and continues. "You must be Jane. I'm so pleased to finally meet you."

"I bet you're regretting canceling that date now, huh?" I ask, not hiding the aggression in my tone.

He looks at me, surprised. "Of course. I wouldn't have done it if I hadn't had an emergency."

"Sure, pal. Or maybe you didn't know how smoking hot she was."

Jane tugs on my arm. "Let's get something to eat, Andy."

"We're not done yet, young lady. I demand an explanation for all this," her mother tells her.

"With all due respect, Mom, I've done what you asked me to. I'm here, and hey, I have a date to the ball who isn't a teenager covered in pimples."

Her mother opens and shuts her mouth without making a sound. The fish-out-of-water look is great on her. Pride fills my chest. Jane keeps surprising me every day.

We hit the buffet, but in reality, I'm not hungry at all. Jane doesn't seem to have much of an appetite either. To be fair, the food looks too pretentious to be enjoyable.

I take the plate of uneaten appetizers from her hand, setting it down on the high table. "Let's get out of here. Like you said, you've done your part."

"I still have to eat something. I won't survive the rest of bootcamp running on fumes."

"Don't worry, babe. I got you covered."

With her hand firmly in mine, I rush out of the restaurant. I'm sure our attitude will be the talk during the rest of the event, which will mortify her mother to no end.

Jane and I put our leather jackets and helmets on, and then I take her to a place that can make any day better, an In-N-Out restaurant. When Jane hops off the bike and takes her helmet off, I see her grin.

"The gym building is just around the corner. We have fifteen minutes. I hope you're okay with my choice."

"Are you kidding me?" She jumps into my arms and kisses me soundly.

I could taste her mouth forever, but she does need to be somewhere.

"As much as I enjoy your lips on mine, I do need to get you fed, babe."

"I know. Thank you so much for taking the time to help me today. If there's anything I can do to repay you, just say the word." She watches me from under her eyelashes.

Jesus fucking Christ. There she goes again, making me wish we were somewhere private with one single glance. *God, I'm crazy about this girl.*

Stepping away before I attack her mouth again, I reply, "I can think of something."

34

ANDREAS

AFTER I DROP Jane off at the gymnasium, I return to the dealership to get my car. I drive the motorcycle to the service lot and leave the key with the service area receptionist, per my agreement with Juan, the guy who I paid to loan me the bike.

I left my car in the clients' area, however, when I walk to the spot I parked, I find another vehicle in its place.

"What the hell."

Did I park at a different spot and forgot? I run around the lot, covering the area in less than a minute. My Bronco is most definitely not here. There's no way some asshole came in and stole my car out of the lot in broad daylight. There's got to be an explanation for this. I head inside and look for the dealership's manager. I've met him once, and he's a total jerk.

He's in his office on the phone. I don't fucking care.

"What the hell have you done with my car?"

He gives me an impatient glance and tells whoever is on the line that he'll call them back. Then he leans back on his chair, crossing his hands over his protruding belly. "You mean what I've done with your father's car?"

"Don't play games with me. Where is my car?" I grit out.

"Back where it belongs. In Mr. Rossi's garage. I had it towed there per his instructions."

Son of a bitch.

I can't believe he did that. How the hell did he know my Bronco was parked here in the first place? Juan must have sold me out. *Asshole.*

"Now if you'll excuse me, I have work to do." The manager reaches for his phone, dismissing me.

My hands curl into fists, and my body is shaking in anger, but there's nothing I can do. The car was never in my name. At the time, I didn't care. But now I see it was another way for my father to control me.

I stride out of the manager's office, shoving his Nespresso machine to the floor.

"You punk! You're going to pay for that," he yells.

"Send the bill to my father."

I keep walking until I'm off the dealership's property. I wouldn't put it past the manager to call the cops on me. Once I'm out, I call Danny. It rings until the call goes to voicemail. *Damn it.* I can either call Paris or Troy. Paris is most likely with his obnoxious girlfriend. *Pass.* I guess Troy it is.

I'm surprised when he actually answers the phone.

"What do you want?"

"I need a favor."

"Is that so? Why don't you call Danny?"

"I tried. Dude, this a fucking emergency, okay? I wouldn't have bothered you otherwise."

"Does your emergency have anything do with Jane and the stunt you pulled at the luncheon?"

"You know about that?"

"Yeah, I know. I just spent the last twenty minutes listening to my mother yell in my ear that I let you corrupt Jane."

I pinch the bridge of my nose. "This has nothing to do with Jane. She's back at...." *Hell, he doesn't know that she's at roller derby bootcamp.*

"She's back where? Home?"

"Yeah," I lie.

Shit. This is fucked up. I can't keep lying to Troy and expect him to forgive me.

"What's the emergency then?"

"My father cut me off. He took my Bronco away and now I'm stranded in front of one of his dealerships."

"Damn. Is that because you switched majors?"

"Yup. Can you give me a ride home or what? I could call an Uber, but I'm afraid my credit cards probably aren't working right now."

"Yeah, man. I'll be there as soon as I can."

"Thanks again for picking me up," I say to Troy.

"As much as I don't like you right now, I'd never leave you stranded like that."

I look out the window, thinking about what I'm going to do with my life now. I can't even take Jane out on a proper date without having to ask to borrow one of my friend's cars. I can't afford to take her anywhere either. No more impromptu afternoons at fancy hotels.

Some might call me a hypocrite for spending my father's money without a care when I hate him so much, but I've earned every dime of the money I spent. I paid in blood.

"I can't believe your father cut you off. You need to speak to Coach Clarkson about that. The team needs you."

"I will, although I don't know what he can do besides try to convince my father to reconsider."

"You could apply for a sports scholarship."

"I'd never qualify. They'd look at my father's bank account and laugh."

"You know athletic scholarships aren't need-based. You can't just give up and quit school."

"I'm not going to give up. I just don't know yet what I'm going to do."

"I'll talk to Grandma and ask if you and Danny can move in with me."

Troy knows I charge Danny almost nothing for rent, which means we'll both be homeless soon.

"What about Charlie?"

"She supports the idea one hundred percent."

"You already told her? You just found out."

"Bro, as soon as you told me your father cut you off, I knew that meant you'd have to give up your place."

I let out a heavy sigh. "You're a good friend, Troy. I'm sorry I fucked up things royally between us."

He clenches his jaw. "I know you're sorry. I can also see now that you'd never go after Jane if you didn't care about her. What you did today was awesome. Thank you for that."

"So you're cool with me dating her now?"

"Let's say I'm resigned to the idea. But you hurt one single strand of her hair and I'm coming for you."

"I don't plan to ever hurt her, but if I do, you have my permission to pound my ass to the ground."

He snorts. "Like I need your permission."

When I glance at him, he's smirking.

"How did your visit with Ophelia go? Does she have a solution to keep Jane in LA?"

"Jane didn't tell you?"

"No, there hasn't been time. She had to rush to...." Damn, there I went, almost blurting out Jane's secret.

"To roller derby bootcamp."

"Wait, she told you already?"

"Yeah, yesterday."

"So you knew I was lying and you didn't call me out?"

He turns to me. "I was testing you. Don't get me wrong, I'm not happy that you lied to me, but the fact you did shows me you really have Jane's back."

I shake my head. "Boy, you have a twisted way of seeing things."

"I don't know why she felt like she had to keep that a secret from me."

"Hmm, maybe because it's a savage sport and you think she's made out of porcelain?"

"I don't think she's breakable."

I laugh. "Yes, you do."

"Fine. I guess I *am* overprotective. I'm working on it. But anyway, Grandma said that if Jane is truly set on attending Rushmore, she'd pay for her tuition."

"That's great news. I wonder why Jane didn't tell me."

"I'm sure she was stressing about bootcamp and the luncheon, and she wanted to tell you in person."

No, she didn't tell me because I didn't call her last night like I said I would, and today, she probably forgot. I keep my thoughts to myself though.

"What are your plans for the rest of the day?" Troy asks.

"For starters, I have to look for a job."

"What are you thinking?"

"I have no clue. I could do serving."

"You could probably make some serious money depending on where you work."

"Yeah."

"Doesn't Paris's girlfriend's family own a chain of upscale restaurants?"

"I don't know. I usually check out when he talks about her. She hates my guts, though. I doubt she'd help."

"She doesn't hate your guts."

"Dude, she does. She said that to my face. I'm a bad influence on Paris, apparently." I laugh, even though this situation is far from humorous.

It's better than crying, right?

"It doesn't hurt to ask. Paris is a good guy. He'll help."

"Sure." I look out the window again, hating my situation.

"You don't sound convinced. What's the matter?"

"I don't like this. I'm a fucking charity case now."

"You're not a charity case. You're in a tight spot, that's all. There's no shame in asking for help, Andy."

Maybe for someone like Troy, there's no shame. But I've been told time and time again I'm a failure. At a certain point, you start to believe it.

35

JANE

I DON'T REALLY WANT to face my mother after an entire day of practice, but if I don't come home, it will only make things worse. I'm physically and mentally exhausted. I can't say that altercation at the luncheon didn't affect me, even if it felt fucking amazing to stand my ground against her.

No surprise, my mother is waiting for me in the living room, nursing a glass of white wine. Her expression tells me I'm about to receive a major tongue-lashing.

"Where have you been?"

"I was out with friends."

"Bullshit. I know you were hanging out with Troy's buddy."

"Troy's buddy has a name. And I wasn't hanging out with Andy. I don't care if you believe me or not. I'm done trying to please you. I'll never measure up anyway."

"That's right. You never will. I should be used to your mediocrity by now."

My blood is pumping in my veins. I'm about to blow a fuse, and I don't care.

"You know what? Fuck you, Mom. I'm sorry that your life didn't turn out the way you wanted, but I'm done being your punching bag." I whirl around and stride to my room.

"Jane Marie, come back here this instant!" she yells.

I'm beyond listening to her threats. I go straight to my closet and I take my duffle bag out. She finds me shoving random clothes in it.

"What do you think you're doing?"

"Isn't it obvious?"

"Oh, where do you think you're going to live?"

"I don't care. Under a bridge is better than here."

"You can't leave. I won't allow it."

I laugh like a crazy woman. "I'm eighteen. You can't force me to stay. Besides, I'm sure Dad will be more than happy if I go to live with him."

Now she's the one laughing in derision. "I wouldn't be so sure. You might hate me, but at least I take an interest in your life. He wouldn't care if you were dead or alive."

I wince because she's right about that, but I won't allow her to weaken my resolve. "That might be true, but he will take me in to spite you."

I don't even know what I packed, but I zip the duffle bag shut and walk around her. She grabs my arm, digging her long nails in.

"You walk out that door, you're not coming back."

I yank my arm free from her grasp. "Fine by me. I don't plan on ever returning."

Hot tears are streaming down my cheeks by the time I step outside. I'm glad my roller derby gear is in the trunk of my car and everything else I didn't pack I can either replace or ask Troy to come get for me when the monster is not home.

I drive off, needing to put as much distance between me and my mother's house as I can. But when the anger subsides, I feel hollow and alone. I can't see shit in front of me thanks to my blurry vision. I turn into the first parking lot that I come across because driving in my condition is dangerous.

The silence in my car is broken by the sound of my phone ringing. With shaking hands, I fish the phone out of my bag. My heart does a backflip when I see Andy's name flashing on my screen.

"Hi," I say in a trembling voice.

"Babe, what's the matter?"

"I had a huge fight with my mother and I... I left home."

"Where are you now?"

I look outside my window and notice for the first time where I am.

"I'm in front of a McDonald's five minutes from my mother's house."

"Do you want me to call Troy to get you?"

His question takes me by surprise. "Why would you do that?"

"I don't have my car right now or I would be already on my way."

I should ask what happened to his Bronco, but I don't have it in me for small talk. "It's okay. I just needed a minute to calm down. I can drive."

He curses softly under his breath. "I don't like this, babe. Let me call Troy."

"No. I'm fine."

"Why are you so stubborn? I'm beginning to think it's a family trait."

"Would it be okay if I came over and spent the night? I was planning to bunk with my dad, but I can't handle another parent right now."

"Of course it's okay, sweetheart. Do you want to keep talking as you drive here?"

"Better not. I'll see you soon."

"All right. Please drive safely."

"I will."

ANDREAS

I'm on pins and needles, burning a hole in my living room floor as I pace left and right.

"Relax, Andy. Jane will be fine," Danny says from the couch.

He got home five minutes ago. If he had been home earlier, I'd have borrowed his car and left to get Jane myself. For her to make the decision to move out means the fight with her mother must have been ugly.

"You didn't hear her on the phone. She was broken, man." I pull my hair back. "I hate that I wasn't there to protect her from that viper."

"I know you do. That shows how much she means to you."

I turn to him. "She's my entire world."

He levels me with an intense stare. "Have you told her that yet?"

His question feels like a punch to my chest. I can't answer him, so I do the cowardly thing: I look away. A knock on the door prevents him from pestering me further. I stride toward it, and open it without bothering to look through the peephole. Jane is standing there, carrying a duffle bag too big for her. Her beautiful green eyes are red and tear streaks mar her cheeks.

I pull her to me, engulfing her into a bear hug as I drag her inside my apartment. She hides her face against my chest, curling her fingers into my T-shirt.

"It's going to be okay, babe."

She eases off and glances up. "I know it will be. I feel a million times better already just being here with you."

"Do you want anything to eat? I can make you a sandwich."

"No, I'm not hungry."

"A drink then?"

"Maybe some water."

"Okay, coming right up."

I take the duffle bag from her and set it down next to the couch. Danny already made himself scarce, giving us privacy. I couldn't have asked for a better roommate, even when he's acting like a pain in my ass about my inability to voice my feelings.

"Where's Danny?" Jane asks.

"In his room."

She pulls up a barstool and sits at the counter, resting her head in her hands. "I've made a mess of things."

"I doubt it. Whatever you told your mother, she had it coming."

"Maybe. But shouldn't I be feeling relieved then? How come I now have this immeasurable guilt swirling in my chest?"

I set the glass of water on the counter and then I turn her around to face me. "Because you're too good. She doesn't deserve your guilt, sweetheart. Trust me. I know what it's like to be raised by a narcissistic parent."

Jane stares into my eyes intensely, as if she's trying to peer into my soul. She'd only find a black smear there.

"Did your father hurt you, Andy?" she asks softly, probably afraid I'm going to take flight at any moment.

My automatic reaction is to tense and step away. She holds me by my forearms, keeping me in place. "You can tell me anything. I love you and nothing will change that."

I look away, unable to withstand her gaze. My heart is bleeding in agony. I want to surrender to her, lay myself bare at her feet, but my primal survival instinct won't let me. I can't handle the pain of being betrayed again.

"It doesn't matter, babe."

"It *does* matter. Keeping things bottled inside is never good."

I glance at her again. "Why are you asking me if my father hurt me? Did your moth—"

"No. She never laid a hand on me. But not only fists cause pain. She's an expert at verbal torture."

I cup her cheek, needing to offer comfort as much as I need the contact.

"Yes, he used to hit me," I confess. "After my mother died, he became uglier than he already was."

"Did he hit Lorenzo too?"

The possibility that he might be doing to Lorenzo what he did to me robs me off air. The times I spoke to my brother after his races, he was the same cheerful kid as always, but what if he's gotten good at hiding like I did? I shake my head, more to convince myself than anything else.

"No. He never laid a hand on him. Thank God."

"I'm so sorry, Andy."

I close my eyes, hating the pity I see shining in hers. "Don't."

"Don't what?"

"Don't feel sorry for me."

"Andy, look at me."

I do as she commands because there's nothing I wouldn't do for her. *Besides tell her you love her,* my perverse mind reminds me.

She holds my face between her hands. "I don't pity you. I pity your father for being so consumed by darkness that he failed to see what an amazing son he has."

"I'm not that great, babe. Trust me."

"Shut up. I don't want to hear you demean yourself like that. You're great. No, you're amazing. A loyal friend, smart, funny, a beast in bed," she smiles, and that sight fills me with happiness.

I chuckle. "A beast, huh?"

"Yes. My world is better because you're in it. Never forget that."

"For what it's worth, my world is better because of you too."

Her face splits into the most radiant smile, and it's my undoing. I shorten the distance between us and slam my lips to hers. I should be gentle, but I can't restrain myself. If I can't find the courage to tell her how I feel, then I have to show her.

She jumps into my arms, hooking her legs behind me. My hands find her lovely ass, and with our mouths still fused together, I make a beeline for my bedroom. We could tumble down on my bed, but as much as I'm ready to fuck her into oblivion, I want to worship her body first. I set her back on her feet, and reluctantly pull away.

"Where are you going?" she asks, keeping her hooded eyes glued to my lips.

"Maintaining my vow to make love to you always."

"What if I want, no, what if I *need* to be fucked hard?"

Jesus, how can I remain in control when naughty things keep coming out of her angelic mouth?

"Is that what you need, babe? My cock plunged deep in your tight pussy?"

"Yes," she hisses.

I take my T-shirt off. "What else do you need?"

"I need you to pound into me until my body leaves a permanent imprint on your mattress."

Shit. I'm so hard, it's painful. Quickly, I remove my jeans and boxers. But freedom doesn't alleviate the ache. Only doing exactly what Jane wants will give me any kind of relief.

"Take off your clothes."

She follows my request in the same order that I did, first the T-shirt, and then her jeans. She's standing in front of me now wearing no-fuss black underwear with pink roller blades printed on them.

I smile. "I love those."

"I figured I should wear something thematic today."

Unable to keep my distance any longer, I step into her space, kissing her again so hard that she can't tell whose air she's breathing. She runs her fingers down my abs, leaving a trail of goose bumps. I smirk against her lips, knowing exactly where she's going. When she wraps her hand around my shaft and gives it a little tug, I bite her lower lip softly.

"Do you want to do something new, babe?" I whisper against her lips.

"Another first?"

"Yeah."

"Is it a sixty-nine?"

I chuckle, nodding my head. "How did you guess?"

"Hmm, maybe I'm a psychic."

"Oh, yeah? Can you guess what my next move is, then?"

"That's easy. I don't need special powers. You're going to toss me on the bed and eat my pussy."

"Damn straight I am."

"Not if I toss you first." She yanks me by the arm and lobs me toward the bed. I could have put up resistance, but I'm having too much fun.

I bounce on the mattress, laughing like I haven't in a long time. Jane joins me, taking advantage of my lowered guard to straddle me. She's still wearing her underwear though, and that's way too much of a barrier in my book.

My cock is nudged nicely between her folds, and when she gyrates her hips, the friction makes us both moan loudly. She doesn't stop, driving me wild with need. If she keeps at it, I'm going to come. I flip us over, caging her in now with my arms on each side of her head.

"Are you trying to make me want to skip foreplay and fuck you right this second?"

"No, I want to do the new thing first."

I invade her mouth with my tongue again, while hooking my fingers on each side of her underwear.

"Okay, then we need to get rid of a certain piece of clothing."

Peppering kisses on her chin and continuing my trip south, I roll her panties down her legs. I run a lazy tongue around her belly button, loving how Jane arches her back and whimpers like a kitten. But now her pink secrets are exposed to me, and I can't resist the temptation of having a quick taste. I sweep my tongue over her clit, once, twice. *Shit, I can't stop.*

Jane threads her fingers through my hair and pulls hard.

"Ouch!" I complain.

"This is not a sixty-nine."

"Okay, okay." I flip on my back. "Come on, it's easier if you hover over me."

She moves slowly, and a little awkwardly. Her cheeks are bright pink, and I want to tell her there's no need for embarrassment, but then her pussy once again comes within reach of my tongue, and what can I say, I'm easily distracted.

I grab her by the hips and bring her closer to me. Jane cries out when I resume my merciless assault. Like me, she's at the edge of pure ecstasy. I groan when she takes my entire length into her mouth while holding the base with her hand.

Fuck me. I'm not going to last. But hell if I'm going to let that happen before I take care of her. I suck her clit into my mouth, and that does the trick. Her body convulses, and her ministrations turn a little clumsy with the distraction, but I was already on the verge. I dig my fingers deeper into her hips and suck her clit harder as I climax. I'd keep eating her up if she'd let me, but she moves away from me and collapses sideways on the mattress.

For a moment, neither of us move. We're both trying to catch our breath. I run my fingers up and down her thigh—the only thing I'm capable of doing. I never thought I'd say this, but I'm boneless. Jane has taken me to a state of pure bliss and I never want to leave it.

36

JANE

IT'S ALMOST MIDNIGHT, but neither Andy nor I are ready for bed. We're in the kitchen eating ice cream. I feel a bit better, but I'm still worried about the future. What if Dad takes my mother's side? There's no way in hell I'm going back to live with her. I might just have to move in with Troy.

"Penny for your thoughts," Andy pipes up.

"I'm just thinking about practical things."

"Like what?" He licks his spoon slowly, distracting me for a moment. "Jane?"

I blink out of my lustful daze. "Whether my father will let me live with him or not."

"Isn't his house far from your school?"

I shrug. "I don't mind the commute. It beats living with my mother for sure."

"I might have to move out too."

"Why?"

He takes a deep breath, avoiding my gaze. "My father cut

me off. It's the reason I couldn't come pick you up. He took my Bronco, and said I have to pay for tuition next year."

"Why would he do that?"

"Because he's an asshole." He shoves his bowl of ice cream to the side. "I recently switched my major from business to hospitality against his wishes."

"Are you serious? Because of that he decided to cut you off?"

"Hey, who's winning the awful parents award now?" He smiles, but it's a sad one.

I reach over, covering his hand with mine. "It's going to be okay. I'll help you."

"I need to find a job ASAP. I'm sure my credit cards have been canceled by now."

"I have money in my savings. It's yours."

"Jane, I couldn't possibly take money from you."

I sit straighter in my chair. "Why? Because of a macho thing?"

He slides his hand from under mine, and then pushes his long bangs back. "It's not a macho thing. It's a... *pride* thing."

"Andy...."

He stands and walks away from the kitchen counter. His back is to me now, but there's a new tension there that tells me how much this subject bothers him.

"I've spent my entire life trying to please my father. It's fucking stupid, I know." He rests his hands on his hips, and glances at the floor. "The guy used to beat me to a pulp whenever he had a few drinks. But besides the physical aggression, he also loved to bring me down with words. Nothing I did was ever good enough. No matter how many games the Rushmore Rebels won, or how great my performance was, he'd find a way to criticize me."

I walk over and hug him from behind. "I know how it feels. You hear so much that you're not good enough that you start to believe it."

He turns in my arms, revealing his tear-filled eyes. "You're good enough, babe. Don't let that hag get into your head."

"Fine. As long as you don't let your asshole father get into yours."

Andreas's gaze darkens. "I'm trying not to, but it's so damn hard. Do you understand now where I'm coming from? I need to prove to myself I'm not the failure my father believes I am."

My heart is breaking for him. I don't know what to do or say that will make him see the truth. He's not perfect—no one is—but he's perfect to me.

"You're not a failure, but I understand wanting to do it all alone. You don't have to, though. You have me, and your friends."

His lips curl into a crooked grin. "Troy gave me the same spiel."

"Wait? When did you talk to my brother?"

"He helped me out today. We talked. If there's a silver lining in all this it's that we're on the way to patching things up."

A sigh of relief whooshes out of me. The whole feud between Andy and Troy was stressing me out.

"That's great, babe," I say.

"Babe?" He raises an eyebrow. "I think that's the first time you've called me that."

"You don't like it? I can always call you Beast."

He throws his head back and laughs, a sound so infectious that it affects me too.

"What's all the racket?" Danny comes into the kitchen, rubbing his eyes.

He's only wearing pajama pants, and holy moly, the freshman can give Andreas a run for his money.

Andy pinches my arm. "Hey, stop ogling my roommate."

My face becomes hot. "I wasn't ogling."

Danny doesn't seem to register the exchange between us. He opens the fridge and takes a jug of filtered water from it.

"How was your first day at bootcamp, Jane?" he asks.

"Oh, it was intense, but so much fun."

"I can wait to see you in action," Andreas tells me.

"Well, I have another three weeks to go. Grandma already said she wants to come to my first game too."

"With her two boyfriends?" Danny smirks.

"Yeah, of course."

Danny turns his attention to Andreas. "What are you doing tomorrow, bro?"

"I thought I'd hit all the restaurants in the area, see if they're hiring."

"Have you thought about trying a bakery instead? That would you give you a ton of experience that you won't get anywhere else."

"Oh, that's a great idea," I say. "Actually, I might be able to help."

"How so?"

"Grandma. She knows the founder of Sugar Loaf Cupcakes."

"The biggest bakery chain in LA?" Andreas's eyes bug out.

I nod, grinning. "Yep. Do you want me to ask her? I'm sure she can score you an interview."

"An interview would be amazing, but I think I should be the one asking her."

Of course he would say that, but at least he didn't flat out say no to the idea. That doesn't mean I can't give Grandma a heads-up though.

"It'll probably count toward school credit too," Danny pipes up. "It can be an internship."

"As long as it's paid, it can be anything."

I clap my hands together. "This is great. Who wants to celebrate with more ice cream?"

"I can't say no to ice cream," Danny replies.

Andy eyes the one-gallon container greedily. "I don't know if there's enough for three."

Danny opens the lid and widens his eyes. "It's half full. How much were you planning on eating?"

Andreas turns to me, watching me with a smoldering gaze. "All of it."

My face bursts into flames. He's not only talking about dessert. I don't know what part the ice cream plays in his dirty mind, but I can't wait to find out.

37

ANDREAS

WHILE JANE IS AT BOOTCAMP, I spend the day working on school assignments, sending out resumes, and when the restaurants nearby open for lunch, I visit them.

It was a bad call to look for a job while the restaurants are dealing with the Sunday crowd. No one has time for me. I'm told to try during the week when it's less busy. Either way, I'm not very hopeful anything will come out of it.

I stop by the bank to withdraw the money I have left in my account. There's not much in there, but it will cover my living expenses for a few weeks if I'm frugal. No more eating out for sure until I find another source of income. I'm surprised my father didn't zero out my account. It's a joint one. Maybe he forgot. There's no way in hell he'd make things easy for me.

On the way home, I stop by the grocery store. We're getting low on food. I've never shopped before with a budget in mind, and it blows my mind how expensive everything is when you're low on funds. I buy generic shit, and the only splurge I make is buying Jane's favorite brand of ice cream. A smile crosses my lips when last night's memories come to the forefront of my mind. We did finish that half-gallon of ice cream in the exact manner I wanted. Licking every drop of it off Jane's body.

I become aroused in an instant. Thank fuck there's a grocery cart in front of me to hide the bulge in my jeans.

I'm whistling happily while the cashier rings up my stuff. My amusement wanes a fraction when I see the bill. Over two hundred dollars, and I only bought the basics. *Jesus*. The money I got might not last me as long as I expected.

My phone vibrates in my pocket when I'm on my way to Jane's car. Since she'd be in the gymnasium the whole day, it made sense for me to drive her there so I could run errands.

I don't look first before I answer the call. Bad mistake.

"Hi, Andy," Crystal's sugary voice greets me.

Every cell in my body rebels against the sound, and the small hairs on the back of my neck stand on end. She shouldn't be able to reach me. I blocked her number a long time ago.

"What do you want?" I ask.

"Is this the way you greet the only one who can help you out of this mess?"

"I don't know what you're talking about. Being cut off from that dick you call a husband is the best thing that could ever happen to me."

"Oh, Andy. There's no need to play tough around me. You've been a spoiled brat your entire life. No one raised with a silver spoon does well when they lose everything."

"You clearly don't know me at all."

"Oh, we both know that's a lie."

"Fuck off, Crystal. And stop calling me."

I end the call before she can get another word in. I'm ready to block this new number too, but the bitch used Lorenzo's phone to call me. Rage courses through me. If she got her hands on Lorenzo's phone, then she must have read all the messages exchanged between us. I told him about Jane and other personal stuff. I feel violated, which brings back awful memories of growing up with her as my stepmom.

I'm in a funky mood when I come home, a fact that Danny immediately picks up on. "Dude, what happened?"

"Nothing." I dump the grocery bags on the kitchen counter.

The TV is on, displaying a war video game. Paris and Troy have taken over my couch, and barely acknowledge my presence.

"Since when has my place turned into gamers' central?" I ask no one in particular.

"Charlie has a school deadline and kicked me out of the house. She said I distract her too much," Troy replies.

"Geneva is out of town visiting family," Paris adds.

"Basically, their girlfriends let them off their leashes," Danny jokes.

"At least we have girlfriends," Paris retorts.

"Been there, done that. I don't need to enter another serious relationship any time soon. I'm enjoying my freedom," he replies while peering inside one of the bags. "Did you get soap for the dishwasher?"

"That's not in the budget."

"Okay. Did you get detergent then?"

"Ah fuck. I forgot."

"I guess we can use shampoo for the time being."

"Hell no. Do you know how much shampoo costs?"

"I don't know about yours, but I get mine at the Dollar General." He shrugs.

Damn it. Why didn't I think of going there? I bet I could have found half of what I bought for much cheaper.

"So, your dad cut you off for good?" Paris asks.

"He sure did. It's better this way though. He can't control me anymore."

"I can ask Geneva to try to find you a job in one of her family's restaurants."

I grimace, ready to say thanks, but no thanks. One look at Danny's frown and meaningful stare reminds me I can't be picky.

"Thanks, man. I appreciate it."

Paris nods. "No problem."

Troy puts the game on pause. "Listen, I spoke to Grandma. She's okay with you and Danny moving in. Her only condition is that you don't throw rave parties when Charlie and I are in Europe."

"When did I ever throw a rave party?" I ask, offended.

"Sorry, man. You have a reputation."

Shit. That's not good. "Do you think it would be all right if I went to visit her?"

He frowns. "Why do you want to do that?"

"She might be able to help me find a job. Plus, I need someone in your family to not think I'm an irresponsible jerk."

Troy grimaces, and guilt shines in his eyes. "I don't think that about you... *anymore.*"

I should feel offended by his remark, but what's the point? I was reckless and stupid before.

"Fair enough. So, what do you think?"

"I think that'd be okay. You can probably go today. Do you want me to call her?"

"Yeah. Sure."

I SHOULDN'T FEEL nervous about visiting Ophelia Holland. This is not my first time meeting the lady, but I'm jittery when I walk through Golden Oaks' entrance. A youngish receptionist is behind the desk and greets me with an overly cheerful tone.

"Welcome to Golden Oaks. How can I help you?"

"Hi, I'm here to visit Ophelia Holland. I'm Andreas Rossi. She's expecting me."

The receptionist's eyes become wider, and her smile has now the hint of a secret. "Oh, you must be Jane's boyfriend."

I watch her through slitted eyes. "Yes. I don't mean to sound rude, but how do you know?"

An embarrassed flush spreads over her cheeks. "I'm so sorry. I shouldn't have said anything. Ophelia is waiting in the gardens. Just follow the signs and you won't miss it."

"Awesome. Thanks."

After the receptionist's comment, I'm now more nervous than before. I wouldn't put it past the sassy lady to be plotting a trap of some kind. God, what if she's going to tell me I'm not good enough for her granddaughter? She didn't want me living with Troy when she let him stay in her house. I never thought much about it, but now I wonder if there were serious reasons behind her rule against me.

I have no problem finding her today. She has a preference for Easter egg coloring in her hair, and the turquoise blue is hard to miss. She's wearing huge sunglasses and colorful clothes that are either too high fashion for me to appreciate or they're just plain awful. She's sitting at a table with her two boyfriends, Jack Morris and Louis Romano. I'm surprised to see them there. I thought I'd get a private meeting with her.

"Good afternoon, Mrs. Holland, Mr. Morris, Mr. Romano," I say.

She smiles broadly. "Stop with the formality. You can call me Ophelia, like always."

"All right."

I glance at her boyfriends, who, unlike her, are not all smiles. On the contrary, they're glowering at me. *Fuck. What did I do to them?*

"It's so nice of you to visit. Have a seat." She points at the chair opposite them.

It's only when I'm seated that I notice the peculiarity of the seating arrangement. It's a round table, and the trio is facing me as if they're a judging panel. Hell, I bet they are.

"So, Andreas Rossi," Jack starts. "We heard you're now Jane's boyfriend."

"Yes, sir." I squirm uncomfortably in my chair.

Ophelia brings her cocktail to her lips, partially hiding a smirk.

"We're not going to beat around the bush here," Louis chimes in. "What are your intentions with her?"

I blink several times. "Excuse me?"

"We know about your reputation. The manwhore of campus, they say," Jack pipes up.

"That's in the past," I grit out, fighting not to lose my cool.

"So you say," Louis snorts.

I glance at Ophelia, trying to judge if she shares her boyfriends' opinion of me. I can't make sense of her expression. She seems amused. *What the hell!*

"If you came here to ask for her hand, you'd better have prepared a list of reasons for why that should be granted," Jack says.

"What? She's only eighteen!"

Are they for real? I turn to Ophelia, who's trying to hide her amusement, but failing miserably at it.

I narrow my eyes. "You guys are yanking my chain, aren't you?"

The boyfriends look at one another and then burst out laughing.

Son of a bitch. They totally had me for a moment.

"I was wondering when you would figure it out. When Jack and Louis suggested we prank you, I was sure you'd catch on right away," Ophelia replies.

"I hope you're not cross with us," Louis adds, wiping off tears off laughter from the corners of his eyes.

Jackass.

"I'm not mad. You had surprise on your side," I say. "Besides, it was my fear that you would judge me by my bad rep."

"I'm much more inclined to judge you based on your recent actions. What you did for Jane was unbelievable. It showed me you truly care about her," Ophelia says.

Even behind the sunglasses, I can sense her intense stare.

"I do. Very much so."

She nods in approval. "Now, Troy was tightlipped about the reason for your visit."

"Yeah, I asked him to not say anything so you wouldn't have the chance to think it over too much and dismiss me right away."

She raises an eyebrow. "And who is sneaky now?"

I chuckle. "I need all the advantages I can get. He told you that my father has cut me off because I switched majors, right?"

She nods. "Yeah, we know."

"Your father is grade-A asshole," Louis pipes up, sporting a frown now.

"He truly is. But in all honesty, it's better this way. Now I have nothing tethering me to him save for my brother."

"Did Troy tell you I've lifted the ban on male roommates? You and Danny are more than welcome to stay at my house."

"Yes, he did tell me that and I appreciate it. But I'm here to ask you for another favor."

"Anything that I can help."

"I was hoping you could put in a good word for me with the owner of Sugar Loaf Cupcakes."

"Ah, yes, you like to bake, I hear."

"It's my calling. I know that now without a shred of doubt."

Ophelia doesn't speak for several beats, pinning me to the

chair with her stare. I don't dare to breathe while she ponders my request.

She takes a sip of her cocktail, and finally replies, "Consider it done."

38

ANDREAS

I COME STRAIGHT to the gymnasium to pick up Jane after my visit to Golden Oaks. Ophelia told me she'd contact me as soon as she spoke to Howard Honeywell, the owner of Sugar Loaf Cupcakes.

There was some traffic, and by the time I arrive, Jane is already waiting for me in front of the building. She's chatting with a short brunette who by Jane's description must be Alicia.

They glance in my direction when I bring the car to a stop in front of them. Alicia's attention switches to the interior of the car. She's squinting, probably trying to see what I look like. I put the car in park and get out.

"Hey babe. How was practice?"

Jane walks over and kisses me softly on the lips. I'd pull her closer to me and devour her mouth properly if we didn't have an audience. Not everyone is a fan of PDA.

"Practice was good." She turns to her friend. "This Alicia, roller derby legend."

Keeping my arm firmly looped around Jane's waist, I offer my right hand to the girl. "Hi Alicia, nice to meet you."

"Nice to finally meet you too, Andy. And I'm not a legend. Not yet, anyway."

"I like that way of thinking," I reply sincerely.

Jane needs positive role models in her life after all the toxicity her mother gave her throughout the years.

"Anyway. I'd better get my ass home before my big sister freaks out," she continues.

"Okay," Jane replies. "And let's try to meet this week."

"For sure, girlie. See ya."

No sooner than Alicia gives her back to us, I turn Jane around and greet her properly. My mouth covers hers hungrily. My tongue opens the seam of her lips with impatience while my fingers dig into her hips, pulling her closer. Jane clutches my arms, melting into me. She fits perfectly into my embrace, into my world. I never want to let her go. If this is ain't love, I don't know what is. Why can't I tell her that?

She pulls away, and breathlessly asks, "How was the meeting with Grandma?"

"It was good." I lean forward, my eyes dropping to her lips.

Jane presses two fingers against my lips, preventing me from claiming her mouth again. "We should go. You're making it almost impossible to behave in public."

I chuckle, stepping back. "I thought you were a rebel."

"I *am* a rebel, but I'd rather save my bender of rules side for the bedroom."

Jesus fucking Christ. How can she know exactly what to say to drive me crazy?

"Woman, you're playing with fire. Let's go before I break into that gymnasium building and have my way with you pressed against the wall."

A wicked smile unfurls on her lips. "I like that idea."

My body automatically moves closer to her. She flattens her

palms against my chest, halting me. "In your apartment," she continues.

I reply through a groan, "Fine. Get your sweet ass in the car."

"Yo, Danny. Are you home?" I ask as soon as I open the front door.

Jane is supposed to be moving in with her Dad, but he's out of town, which means she can stay with me for a while longer.

Silence greets us, but to be sure my roomie is really not home, I check his room.

"Are we alone?" Jane asks from behind me.

I pivot around, smiling already from ear to ear. "Yeah. I remember something about a wall."

Jane widens her eyes when I pull my T-shirt off and move closer to her.

"Your bedroom has walls."

"The one behind you is just fine."

We're in the hallway, and it would take nothing but a couple of steps to disappear inside my room, but I like the idea of fucking Jane out here where we could get caught at any moment. I cage her in, resting my hands against the wall on either side of her head. Her ragged breathing fans across my jaw, making it hard to maintain my distance and think straight.

Without breaking eye contact, she runs her fingers across my abs, and then she licks her lower lip. "What are you waiting for then?"

"In good time, babe." I lean closer and rub my lips against hers. A distraction while my hands disappear underneath her skirt. She's wearing the simple cotton panties she prefers.

"I love that you're wearing a skirt, but these are in the way."

"Is that so?" She reaches for my jeans, slowly undoes my button, and pulls the zipper down.

Her nimble fingers so close to my cock snap the little bit of restraint I have left. I pull her panties down with the patience of a starving man and crush my mouth to hers. As motivated as me, she pulls my dick free from the confines of my boxers, drawing a feral groan from deep in my throat.

There's no turning back now. I lift her off the ground and she opens herself to me, hooking her legs behind my ass. Her pussy is so wet and ready that one little nudge is enough to drive my cock home. I hesitate though, and curse in my head for forgetting a crucial detail.

"We need protection," I murmur against her lips.

"I'm on the pill." She digs her heels against my ass, pulling me closer

I lose the battle against caution and thrust forward, sheathing myself in her. I don't move for a second, getting used to the feeling. I haven't had sex without a condom in a very long time, and I forgot how fucking amazing it feels.

"Andy?" Jane captures my face between her hands and makes me look at her. "Are you okay?"

"I'm more than okay, babe."

I slam my mouth against hers, kissing her with teeth, branding her with my tongue while I piston in and out of her heat. With each thrust, my grunts become louder. Jane digs her nails in my back, leaving her own mark on me. Our exposed skin becomes slick, and my sweaty hands have a harder time maintaining Jane at the right height. But I keep going, chasing the promised land.

"Oh my God, Andy. I'm going to co—" I cut her off with my mouth because I need to be fused with her in every way possible.

She tightens around me, and her moans of ecstasy are muffled by my tongue. Her body shakes as she clings harder to me. I'm about to lose my mind too. I thrust harder, and when my release finally comes, it's an explosion of bliss. I don't stop moving until I milk every single drop of pleasure.

After a minute, I become still save for my chest, which is keeping my heart from bursting out. My breathing is ragged, just like Jane's.

I press my forehead against hers and whisper, "Jesus. That was...."

"Amazing," she completes.

A chuckle escapes my lips. "Yeah."

"Ah hell." Danny's disgruntled voice reaches us from the beginning of the hallway. "Are you guys kidding me?"

Shit. Roomie is home. I angle my body forward to hide Jane, and glance in his direction. I catch him heading back to the living room.

"Oh my God. I want to die," Jane whispers in my ear.

"Relax, sweetheart. I don't think he saw anything."

"I saw enough," he yells from the couch.

A bubble of laughter goes up my throat and I can't stop. Jane disentangles herself from me, and before running to my room, she hits my arm. "This is not funny."

"Sorry, babe. I don't know what's taken over me."

I have the giggles, and I can honestly say that's never happened to me before. Jane has already disappeared into my bathroom by the time I close the door. I don't follow her, choosing to let her recover from the embarrassing moment alone. I clean myself with my discarded T-shirt and then I go check on Danny to find out how much he's seen.

He's playing a video game while sporting a serious frown.

"Hey." I jump on the couch.

"You're an ass," he says without looking at me.

"Why?"

"You have a room. Why did you have to screw your girl-friend in the hallway, man?"

"Living recklessly, I guess." I shrug. "What's the big deal?"

"The big deal is that I see Jane as the sister I never had, and now I have that racy image in my mind. It's doing my head in. I feel like I need to wash my brain with Purell."

"Nobody forced you to watch."

"I didn't watch, asshole! But the quick glimpse was enough."

I roll my eyes. "You're so dramatic."

My phone rings from somewhere nearby. I don't remember where I left it before Jane consumed my thoughts. I get up and search, finding it on the kitchen counter.

"Great," I mumble.

"Who is it?"

"It's Ricky Montana, the guy who traded shifts with me on Friday." I press the Answer button, knowing he won't stop annoying me until I fulfill the end of my bargain. "Hello?"

"Hey, Andy. My man. What's up?"

"Not much."

"Do you have any plans for tonight?"

"Yeah, chilling with my girl. Why?"

"Rumor has it that the infamous Glitter Club party is happening tonight at Pike's headquarters. Dude, you have to get me in."

I pinch the bridge of my nose. The Glitter Club party is a seventies-inspired event that's always announced last minute and is super exclusive; mainly jocks and Greeks are invited. I probably got an email about it.

"How did you get wind of it?"

"A guy in my dorm did the sound system hookup. Are you seriously not going to this?"

"No, wasn't planning on it. And we have Professor Asshole's class first thing tomorrow morning."

"I know, I know. Dude, you don't need to stay long. Just get me through the door and introduce me to some hotties, and I'll consider us square."

I can tell Ricky won't leave me alone until I help him out. Might as well get this shit over with. There's no chance I'm going to a party without Jane though.

"Fine. I'll meet you in front of library in two hours and we'll walk from there."

"Cool, man. I'll see you there."

I drop my phone back on the counter and then push my long bangs back.

"What was that all about?" Danny asks.

"Fulfilling an oath. Get dressed. If I have to suffer a Glitter Club party, so do you."

"What the hell is that?" He looks over his shoulder.

"Ah, right. You're still a noob. I'll tell you all about it on the way to Troy's."

"Wait. Why do we need to head to Troy's first?"

"Because we need supplies and the only girl I know who has a Halloween costume store in her house is Charlie."

"What about Charlie?" Jane asks as she walks over, freshly showered and wearing clothes that show zero skin. *Overcompensation, maybe?*

"We're going to a dress-up party."

"On a Sunday?" Her eyebrows arch.

"Hey, we're rebels, remember?"

Her cheeks turn bright pink. She glances briefly at Danny. "I'm not so sure about that anymore."

"Don't worry, he saw nothing."

"True. I didn't see a thing," he pipes up.

Still sporting a frown, she looks in my eyes. "What kind of dress-up party?"

"The glitter kind." I smile, loving how her eyes slowly widen in surprise.

"Okay. You should have started with that. I can't wait to see what that entails."

39

JANE

I'M STILL in awe at how quickly our Sunday evening turned into a Club 54 outing. Charlie had everything we needed to glamorize any outfit. The glitter usage went unchecked and now Andy, Troy, Danny, and Paris look like they all came out of a unicorn's ass.

I have on the same eighties outfit I wore to the beach minus the roller skates. My long hair is in pigtails and I'm wearing more makeup than a drag queen.

On the way out of the house, I hear Troy ask Andy, "Are you going to let Jane go out like that?"

I turn around with my hands on my hips, ready to tell Troy to fuck off, but Andy beats me to the punch.

"I see nothing wrong with her outfit. Besides, if any punk even thinks about harassing Jane"—he raises his fists—"he's going to meet Chuck and Norris."

He catches me staring and rewards me with a panty-melting smile. As excited as I am to finally be going to a college party with Andy, I'd trade that for a quiet evening with him in a heartbeat. But he does have to return a favor.

"Did you tell Geneva you were going to a party?" Danny asks Paris.

He rubs the back of his neck, looking sheepish. "Er, not exactly. I said I was hanging out with you guys."

Troy shakes his head and Andy coughs, "Whipped."

"You're both in the same boat as me, so shut up," Paris retorts, walking ahead of us.

"Why do you guys keeping pestering him about his girl-friend?" I ask.

"You'll understand when you meet her." Andreas throws his arm over my shoulders and leans closer to my ear. "You're not cold, babe?"

"I'm fine. But if you want to keep me super toasty, don't let go."

"Sweetheart, I'll be glued to your side like chewing gum on the bottom of a shoe."

"What if I have to pee?" I ask through a laugh.

"I'll come with you."

"Ew. No, you won't."

"Ugh. Can you please cut it out?" Troy opens the door to his car. "Watching you two play the lovebirds game is nauseating."

"That's nothing compared to what I had to witness," Danny says under his breath.

Andy and I cut him a warning glance. He pulls his upper lip in, grimacing. Then he mouths "Sorry."

Troy looks pointedly at us. "Fuck, I definitely don't want to know that."

Charlie giggles, following my brother inside his car. I veer for mine, but Andreas already claimed the driver's seat on the way here, so I take shotgun. Danny is riding with us, and Paris with Troy and Charlie.

"Tell me more about this guy Ricky Montana," I say.

"What's to tell? I barely know him."

"He's not in any of my classes, but he's notorious in the freshman circle," Danny chimes in.

I turn on my seat to glance at him. "How so?"

He shakes his head and laughs. "He's obsessed with meeting girls and keeps talking about his homies from back home."

"Pretty much the real-life version of 'Pretty Fly for a White Guy' then," Andreas laughs.

Danny shrugs. "I guess. It should be interesting going to a party with him."

Ten minutes later, Andy finds a parking spot near Rushmore's main library building. The wind has picked up, and the air is a little chilly. I shiver inside my short jacket, and now my tush is freezing.

"Are you okay, babe?" Andy pulls me to his side, and I feel better immediately. The man is like a human furnace.

"Yes. I'll be fine once we go inside."

"Yo, Andy, my man." A guy ahead of us waves in our direction.

"That's Ricky," Andreas tells me.

He's tall and wiry, reminding me immediately of Shaggy from *Scooby-Doo* even though his hair is curly, not straight. He's not alone. A shorter dark-haired guy is with him.

"I'll be damned. Taiyo?" Andreas asks, amused.

"Hey, Andy. I hope you don't mind that I tagged along."

"Not at all. I'm glad that you found the time to live a little." He turns to me. "This Jane, my girlfriend."

I should be used to Andy calling me his girlfriend by now, but I still get butterflies in my stomach when I hear it.

"Hi, nice to meet you."

"Wait, you're Troy's sister, right?" Ricky chimes in.

"Yep, so?" Troy answers as he walks over, holding hands with Charlie.

Paris is right behind him.

Ricky looks at them and his eyes bug out. "Holy crap. Troy Alexander and Paris Mackenzie. I didn't know you were coming too."

Danny shoves his hands in his pocket. "What's his deal? I'm on the football team too."

"I'm sure you'll have a legion of fans next year," I tell him.

He smiles. "Thanks. I was kidding though. I don't care about having a legion of fans. I just want to play football."

"All right. Let's get going." Andreas steers me toward the beginning of Greek Row, taking the lead.

It doesn't take long to hear the sound of loud music coming from one of the biggest houses in the street. Andy told me this is a semisecret party, but much like Poppy's party in the forest in the *Trolls* movie, anyone in the vicinity can hear the music or see the purple and blue lights coming from the building.

The front lawn is peppered with people wearing skimpy and outrageous outfits. Two huge guys in Greek togas and golden glitter spray all over their exposed skin greet us at the front door.

Andy fits bumps the one closest to him. "Nice outfit, Keevan. Who are you supposed to be? Apollo?"

The guy's lips curl into a grin. "That's right." He glances at Ricky and Taiyo behind us and lifts his chin. "Who are those two?"

"Friends. They're cool."

"All right, then."

And just like that Ricky and Taiyo gain access to their dream party.

Inside, it's crowded and dark. The lights keep changing from purple to blue, but they don't provide much illumination. Music is coming from a small stage set up in the living room where a live band is playing catchy seventies tunes to a crowd of enthusiastic dancers. The disco ball reflects against their glittering costumes and colorful wigs. At one point, I spot a unicorn floatie being passed around until it reaches the stage. As parties go, this is pretty wild.

Andreas still has his arm wrapped around my waist, but it becomes more and more difficult to walk like that. I free myself from his hold and link our hands instead.

"It's easier this way," I shout through the loud music.

"Okay. Stay right behind me."

He carves a path through the throng of people, using his elbows when necessary. No one seems to mind. They're either already too drunk to care, or they idolize Andy too much to complain. We finally reach a spot where there's more breathing room. It's a games space. There are two large leather couches, a pool table, foosball, and a dartboard on the wall.

Once my eyesight adjusts to the difference in lighting—no purple glow here—I notice that this seems to be the make-out room. There are mostly couples here, or people in serious flirtation mode.

Andreas turns to Ricky and Taiyo. "All right. This is it, boys. I'm going to introduce you to some girls, but then it's up to you."

Charlie steps next to me. "Give Andy some room and see what happens."

Curious about her statement and amused tone, I do as she says. Andreas glances at me with eyebrows furrowed and a question in his eyes.

"Go on, help your friends out," I tell him.

Not even a minute goes by before the first flock of pretty girls moves closer to the boys. A stab of jealousy pierces my chest when one overenthusiastic redheaded gets up close and personal with Andy and runs her hand over his arm.

"Is that what you meant?" I cross my arms over my chest, not in the slightest bit happy about the sight.

"Yep. That happens all the time with Troy. It's like I'm invisible to them."

"Pretty sad, isn't it? The boys are like chum in shark-infested water," another girl says next to me.

I turn to find a gorgeous brunette standing there. She looks familiar.

"Vanessa, oh my God. I was wondering if I would see you here," Charlie says.

"You almost didn't. These types of parties are not my jam anymore. Ever since my sister started dating Leo Stine, I avoid Greek events like the plague." She glances at me. "You're Troy's little sister, right?"

"Yeah. Jane. Have we met before?"

"I've seen you on TV during the boys' games. I'm Vanessa Castro. I'm on the soccer team." Her attention switches to the guys, and a moment later, she frowns. "Isn't that Paris Mackenzie?"

"Yeah. Do you know him?" Charlies asks.

"No, I know his girlfriend. She was my neighbor growing up. I fucking hate her. Stupid snobby little bitch."

With wide eyes, I glance at Charlie and we share a similar expression. Maybe the guys were right about Paris's girlfriend after all.

"I'm sorry. I shouldn't have said anything. I'm just surprised she's not attached to his hip."

"It's okay. No one seems to like the girl," Charlie pipes up. "They came to a barbeque at our place, but I can't say I got to know her. She was pretty antisocial."

The guys are still surrounded by the bimbo sharks. Even though Andy has stepped away from the redhead, she's still too close to him for my liking.

"You know what? I've had enough of watching those girls fawn over my boyfriend," I say.

"Yeah, me too," Charlie chimes in.

Vanessa laughs. "And I'm so glad I'm a free agent. No boyfriend for me, especially the pretty ones."

Someone's slimy hand covers my butt, sending a chill down my spine. I jump forward with a yelp, looking over my shoulder.

"Relax, girlie." A drunk jackass smiles leerily at me, stepping into my personal space.

"Back off, asshole." Vanessa shoves him back hard. The idiot staggers back but somehow remains upright.

"I wasn't talking to you, bi—"

A blur appears in front of him, and his face gets knocked back by a punch. He does fall down this time. Andreas looms over him with closed fists by his sides, and then turns to me, eyes gleaming with fury.

"Did he touch you?"

I swallow the huge lump in my throat. If I tell him the truth, he'll go ballistic.

"Oh yeah, he grabbed her ass," a guy standing not too far from us replies before I can.

Thanks, pal.

Andy grabs the drunk from the floor by his T-shirt with one hand, and his right arm is pulled back, ready to deliver another blow.

"You touched my girlfriend, motherfucker?" he yells in his face.

"I-I didn't know she was your girlfriend," he stammers.

"No excuse. You shouldn't be touching anyone without consent."

The jab comes quickly, followed by another. Danny and Troy jump to get Andreas off the fallen drunk before he can get another punch in and drag him far away from the guy.

"That's enough, man," Troy says to Andy.

He's breathing hard, almost as if he's coming down from a

frenzy. I hug my middle, not knowing what to do make this situation better.

After a moment, Andreas shakes himself free. "I'm fine."

Troy and Danny step aside and I move closer. "Are you okay?"

Andy pulls me into his arms and kisses the top of my head. "I'm the one who should be asking you."

"I'm fine."

"Damn," Ricky says as he steps closer to the douche on the floor. "Do you know who this is?"

"Don't fucking care," Andreas grits out.

"That's Professor Norman's nephew," Taiyo chimes in. "Shit, man. If he didn't like you before, now he's really going to hate you."

40

ANDREAS

I SHOULDN'T HAVE LET my anger take control like that, but the moment I saw that asshole get near Jane, my vision turned crimson. Leaving her alone for a minute was a mistake. Guys at those frat parties can't see a pretty girl alone without thinking she's there for their entertainment.

The ride back to my apartment was quiet. Jane looked out the window the entire time. Even Danny, who usually tries to defuse tension, was tightlipped in the backseat.

Troy asked Jane to stay over his place, but she denied him. I should take that as a sign that she's not mad at me, but the doubt has entered my chest and it's now festering. I'm not even concerned about the fact that the jerk I knocked out is Professor Norman's nephew. I guess the apple doesn't fall far from the tree.

Maybe I went too far and spooked her. I am a hothead; I've never hidden that. With me it's punch first, ask questions later. It might earn me an F in Norman's class, which is a small price to pay to protect Jane. What I hope I didn't achieve is making her afraid of me.

No sooner are we alone in my room with the door closed than I pull her to me and look into her eyes.

"Are you okay, babe?"

"I'm fine. Why do you keep asking me that?"

"Because you haven't said a word since we left the party."

"I'm just sad that it ended on such a sour note. I was having fun up until that moment."

"I'm sorry you had to see me like that."

Her delicate eyebrows furrow. "That guy deserved what he got. I'm not sorry you punched him. I'd have done the same thing after I recovered from the initial shock."

"I'm still raving mad he laid his hands on you. I would have kept punching him if Troy and Danny hadn't stopped me. That's who I am, Jane. Impulsive, reckless."

She cups my cheek tenderly. "And I love you just like that."

I kiss her sweet lips, knowing deep down she's too good for me.

"I don't deserve you," I whisper against her lips.

"I already told you to stop saying stuff like that. You *do* deserve me, Andy. You're worthy of love."

A shiver runs down my spine. I close my eyes, fighting the sudden tightness in my throat and the burning in my eyes. Why can't I be like her, someone who is not afraid to say time and time again she loves me even though I offer nothing in return? *Why am I such a coward?*

"I never thought I'd feel this way about anyone, Jane. But you're my entire world. Even if I'm too fucked up to say the words, I want you to know you're here." I press a fist against my chest. "Forever."

Her beautiful green eyes fill with tears. "That's all I ever wanted. I don't care about words. Your actions say it all."

She rises on her tiptoes and presses her lips against mine. As always, the moment we touch, sparks ignite, and I'm filled with the urge to devour her where she stands. But tonight, I kiss her slowly, savoring her taste as if time stands still. Tingles run down my spine at the same time that my chest overflows with emotion. I pick her up in my arms and take her to bed. Desire is running rampant through my veins, but I'm in no hurry to cross the finish line. Reluctantly, I detangle myself from her and sit on the balls of my feet. Jane is on her back, watching me with hooded eyes. I take my shirt off first, knowing she loves to run her fingers over my abs, and I love her hands on me.

We don't speak. There's no need for words. I help her out of her top, leaving her pink bra in place. The clasp is on the front, which makes me smile. I flick it open, freeing her lovely breasts. The sight of them almost makes me weep. With greedy hands, I cover them both, kneading them softly. She arches her back, letting out a kitten moan.

Unable to resist such an offering, I lean down and suck one of her nipples into my mouth. It turns as hard as a little pebble against my tongue. I take my time playing with it, alternating between flicking and sucking it.

Jane's fingers find my hair, tangling with the strands. She begins to move her hips in a restless manner, and I know where my attention should divert now. Still latched on her tits, I move my left hand south until I'm cupping her pussy. I should have removed her tiny shorts first, but I got too distracted. I can still find her clit through the layers of fabric though, and judging by how Jane's breathing is coming out in bursts now, she's enjoying what I'm doing.

Even so, I'm surprised when she shouts, "Yes, oh God, yes!"

With a chuckle, I let go of her nipple with soft pop and kiss her hard while she rides the orgasm. Only when her body relaxes against the mattress, I stop moving my fingers.

"Wow, that was so damn good," she breathes out.

"I'm here to please." I kiss her cheek.

"Now it's my turn, which means pants off."

"I love that bossy side of you," I say without thought.

Jane's eyebrows shoot up to the heavens, and then grins. "You do, huh?"

I realize then that I said the *L* word and it was the most natural thing in the world. The fear I'll get hurt again is still there, but refusing to say the word out loud is no protection. The truth is, I love this girl whether I confess it or not.

I roll on top of her, resting my elbows on the mattress. "I love every part of you, Jane, with all my heart."

Her eyes widen. "I thought you couldn't say the words."

"I didn't think I could. I guess you fixed me."

She throws her arms around my neck, trapping me as much as I trapped her. "We fixed each other. I was broken too. You made me whole again."

I lean down and rub my nose against hers. "How about we become one now?"

It's a cheesy line, but Jane doesn't call me out on it. Instead, she answers me with one of her scorching kisses and the promise of a sleepless night. Rest is overrated anyway.

MY HEAD IS POUNDING when a blaring sound wakes me from too little sleep. I swear I just closed my eyes. Blindly, I search for the source of the noise—my damn phone. I press the side button, cutting off the annoyance. It starts up the nonsense again a couple of seconds later.

"What the hell." I grab the device and look at the screen with one eye open.

It's not the alarm, it's Coach Clarkson calling. I sit up at once as adrenaline jolts me awake. Coach wouldn't be calling at six in the morning if it wasn't something serious.

"Who is it?" Jane asks softly.

"My coach. Something is wrong."

I press the Answer button. "Hello?"

"Andy Rossi, you'll be the reason I choose to retire early," he grumbles.

"What happened?"

"Did you knock out a student last night?"

I pinch the bridge of my nose. "Yes. He got handsy with my girlfriend."

Jane is now sitting up as well, and looking at me like deer caught in headlights.

"So I heard. It doesn't matter. The dean called me late last night. An official complaint has been made. It seems the guy you punched is related to one of your professors."

"Yeah, I learned that after the fact. What now? Am I in trouble?"

"Yes, son. I'm afraid so. He's being pressured to make an example out of you. You know the school has a zero-tolerance policy for violence, and the fact you're an athlete doesn't bode well."

"How about the school's stance on sexual predators?" Jane asks loudly next to me.

I guess she heard every word Coach said.

"Is that your girlfriend?" he asks.

"Yes."

"Put the call on speaker, please."

I do as he asks. "You're on it."

"Did Derek Norman do anything to you, dear?"

She glances at me briefly and I want to tell her she doesn't need to say anything she's not comfortable with.

But she replies with chin raised high, "Yes, sir. He grabbed my butt. I didn't even see him coming. I'll testify if I need to."

"That's brave of you, Jane, but I don't think it will come to that."

"What's going to happen now?" I ask.

"Professor Norman has asked that you be expelled."

"That son of a bitch. He's as dirty as they come. My father is paying him to make my life hell."

"I'm afraid that without proof, we can't use that argument. I'm calling to let you know we're having a meeting at eight this morning with the dean to discuss this matter. Your presence is required."

"Should I come too?" Jane asks.

"No, dear. You're not a student at Rushmore, so I'm afraid your presence there won't help Andy's case."

I'd rather her not go either.

"I'll be there, sir," I say.

"Good, I'll see you soon. And don't worry, son. I'm not letting an asshat kick one of my best players out of school."

When I end the call, Jane is looking at me with guilt-ridden eyes. "This is all my fault."

"No, it isn't. It's Derek's fault. He shouldn't have touched you."

She drops her eyes to her lap. "I know, but I still feel responsible for the mess you're in now.

I pinch her chin between my thumb and forefinger and bring her face back up. "Hey, stop this nonsense. I'm the one who chose to pound his ass to the ground. It's going to be fine. You heard Coach Clarkson."

"Okay. We'd better get going. I don't want you to be late." She throws her legs over the side of the bed and gets up.

I follow her example, keeping my face a mask of serenity and confidence. In reality, I don't know if Coach Clarkson will be able to save my ass this time. And if he does, I still have no means to pay for my tuition fee next year. Whatever happens today, my future is still looking grim as hell.

41

ANDREAS

MY HEART THUMPS loudly inside of my chest as I stride down the hallway toward the dean's office. I don't regret punching the scumbag who touched Jane. But the possibility that I may get expelled because of it has strengthened the constant anger that simmers in my guts whenever I think about Professor Norman.

I have to keep calm though. Taiyo texted me to say Norman's class was canceled this morning, which means he must be in attendance at this meeting too. I wonder if his nephew will be there as well. Hell, thinking about that bastard brings my blood to the boiling point.

The dean's office looms closer. I have to stop for a moment to take deep breaths. I can't let my emotions take control. My future and Jane's depend on it. She deserves more than a college dropout can give her. I know she's the one. Maybe I've known that for a while, but I was too cowardly to admit it.

With her at the forefront of my mind, I enter the reception area of the dean's office. His assistant lifts her gaze from her computer screen.

"Good morning, Mr. Rossi. They're already waiting for you."

I frown, and glance at the time on my phone. I'm not late. In fact, I'm ten minutes early.

"What time did the meeting start?"

"Oh, about half an hour ago."

"What? Coach Clarkson told me to be here at eight."

The door to the dean's office opens and Coach fills the frame. "Andy, I thought it was you."

"Did the time of the meeting change?"

"No. We wanted to discuss matters before you arrived."

My hands curl into fists. Quickly, the anger swirls up my guts. "Why?"

"Don't worry, son." He steps aside and points inward. "We're ready for you."

My nostrils flare, but I clench my jaw tight and swallow the angry retort in my throat. I have to trust Coach Clarkson.

Keeping my rage in check becomes even harder when I find Norman in the room and his piece-of-shit nephew. A great sense of satisfaction enters my chest when I notice the shiner he's sporting. I know it doesn't make me look good, but I don't fucking care.

"Good morning, sir," I say to the dean, purposely ignoring the douche family.

"Good morning, Mr. Rossi. Please, have a seat." He points at the chair farthest from my accusers.

Coach Clarkson takes the chair next to mine. He's now in between me and the others, probably a safety measure on his part. He knows I have a temper.

"What's going on?" I ask. "Why is that weasel here?"

"Andy...," Coach warns me.

"What? I want to know why he was allowed to come in earlier to this meeting."

"You assaulted my nephew. He doesn't feel safe in your presence. That's why," Norman replies.

"Spare me the victim speech. Your nephew is a perv who thinks it's okay to touch girls without their permission."

"I didn't touch anybody," the rat complains. "You jumped me for no reason."

"That's not the account we have from the event, I'm afraid," the dean interjects.

"Oh, please, sir. You can't take the word of his girlfriend. She's clearly lying," Norman retorts.

I make a motion to stand, but Coach grabs my arm and forces me to stay in place. The dean glances at me briefly, and then turns his attention to Norman and his nephew.

"Miss Alexander's account of the altercation is not the only testimony we have. Miss Vanessa Castro also testified Mr. Derek Norman verbally assaulted her."

"She pushed me!" Derek replies angrily.

The dean twists his face into a scowl. "And we have several eyewitnesses who saw the moment you, Mr. Norman, approached Miss Alexander from behind and touched her inappropriately."

Professor Norman throws his hands up in the air. "They were probably bribed to lie by Andreas and his friends."

"You'd better watch your tongue, Norman. I won't let you smear my players' reputations," Coach grits out.

Norman stands abruptly. "This meeting is absurd. It's clear this school's administration doesn't have any intention of punishing their beloved football players. We're taking this matter elsewhere."

"I suggest you sit back down, Professor Norman," the dean replies sternly.

His eyes flash with cold fury and I doubt his reaction is caused solely by my issue with his nephew.

"We're pressing charges," Norman continues.

His declaration makes Derek's face turn pale. "Uh, I'm not sure if that's nec—"

"Sure, go ahead," the dean interrupts, leaning against his chair in a relaxed manner. "I'm sure the authorities would love to see what our internal investigation uncovered."

Now it's Norman's turn to look like he's seen a ghost. I sit straighter in my chair. This just got interesting.

"What are you talking about?" he asks.

"You know exactly what I'm talking about. I suggest you rethink your strategy here."

Norman swallows hard, and then turns his hateful gaze in my direction. If looks could kill, I'd be dead. He forgets about his nephew and walks out of the office.

"Uncle?" the idiot finally stands, but he seems unsure if he should follow Norman or not.

"I'm not done with you yet, Mr. Norman," the dean says.

The idiot sits back down and grips the sides of his chair in a vise grip. "Wh-what do you mean, sir?" he asks.

"Mr. Norman, your conduct at a social gathering on campus grounds was appalling, to say the least. Even though Mr. Rossi shouldn't have reacted in the way he did, we must take into account the circumstances. We can't punish him for protecting the victim. You, however, not only violated our code of student conduct, but you tried to cover up your misbehavior with lies."

"It wasn't my idea to press charges against Andreas. My uncle made me do it."

I knew it. That son of a bitch.

"That doesn't excuse your behavior. We're placing you on academic probation."

"What? No! Sir, you can't do that. My parents will kill me."

"Consider yourself lucky that you're only getting probation. I was more than ready to expel you. You can go now, Mr. Norman."

"Yes, sir." He jumps out of his chair as if he were electrocuted, and pretty much runs out of the office.

As soon as he's gone, I ask, "What's going to happen with

Norman? You heard his nephew. He's been gunning for me ever since I switched my major. My father put him up to it."

"Coach Clarkson already filled me in on your situation."

I glance at Coach. I haven't told him yet about my change in financial status.

Guessing my train of thought, he says, "Troy told me about what happened between you and your father."

"When?"

"When he called me about last night's incident."

"I don't want you to worry about your tuition fee next year, Mr. Rossi. We'll sort it out. All I want you to worry about for now are your grades," the dean says.

"And football," Coach Clarkson adds.

"Wow, I don't know what to say."

"Let's start with thank you and a promise to stay out of fights from now on," the dean replies.

"Yes, sir. You have my word."

"Good."

"What's going to happen to Professor Norman? He's probably going to fail me in his class out of spite."

"That's an administration issue now. I'm afraid I can't discuss it with you. But rest assured, we know what he's been up to and we'll take the appropriate measures."

Coach Clarkson stands, giving me the cue to the same. The dean has just dismissed us.

I follow Coach out of the office, and when we're in the hallway, I remark, "That went better than I expected."

"It did. We got lucky so many witnesses came forward to support your story."

"I was surprised about that."

"I think you have your teammates to thank for that too. Troy, Danny, and Paris tracked down everyone who was in the room when the incident happened."

The news stuns me. I'm tight with them, but I still didn't expect that.

Coach laughs. "Don't look so shocked, Andy. No one on the team wants to see you gone. We actually like your sorry ass."

"Thanks." I chuckle.

He claps me on the shoulder. "Now, try to stay out of trouble. Got it?"

"Yes, Coach."

"You'd better hit the gym soon. You're looking a little small."

I flex my arm. "What are you talking about? I'm in my best shape."

"Yeah, yeah. We'll see about that during pre-season training."

He walks away, whistling. *Shit.* I don't think I've ever seen Coach in such a great mood. It can't be because he saved my ass from expulsion. Something is up with him. I laugh, shaking my head, and then pull my cell phone out. I need to tell Jane the good news.

42

ANDREAS – A week later

DANNY LET me borrow his car today. It's a pain that I have to depend on my friends to go places, but until I find a job, I have to suck it up. Jane moved in with her father a couple of days ago, and I miss her more than anything. I loved playing house with her, even with Danny around. I'd ask her to move in with me for good, but since I won't be staying in my apartment for much longer, I can't do that yet.

From not being able to say I love you to wanting to shack up. My life sure as hell has done a one-eighty on me.

I'm on my way to the interview at Sugar Loaf Cupcakes. Ophelia finally came through and scored me an interview with the hiring manager. It's for a paid internship, which is perfect for me.

My mood couldn't be better today. We learned this morning that Norman resigned. Taiyo suspects he was forced to leave, but either way, the fact he's gone is good enough for me. I'm curious, of course, to know what transgressions the dean hinted at, but I will probably never know.

I'm singing along with the radio as loud as I can when Lorenzo calls me. It's midmorning; he should be in school.

"Hey, buddy? What's up?"

"Andy, I don't feel well," he croaks.

My relaxed posture becomes rigid in a flash. "What's going on?"

"I think I have a fever."

"Where's Crystal?"

No point asking where our father is. He wouldn't be home at this hour.

"She's at a spa in Santa Monica. She won't be back until Sunday. Dad is away for business."

Son of a bitch.

"How about the housekeeper?"

"I don't know. I haven't heard her at all today. I think Crystal gave her a few days off."

"Are you saying that viper left you alone in the house?"

"Yeah, it's not the first time. I'm used to it."

I press a closed fist against my forehead. "I don't fucking believe this. Don't worry, buddy. I'm on my way."

"Okay."

Shit. Lorenzo sounded awful. I make a U-turn, and then I call my contact at Sugar Loaf to try to reschedule my interview. Unfortunately, I get his voicemail. *Hell.* I leave him a voice message, hoping he won't be completely put off by me and cancel the interview altogether.

The sign for a drugstore looms in the horizon. I signal to turn. I'm betting there isn't a single dose of cold medicine in my father's house.

I shoot Jane a text before I head into the store. She's in the middle of class, so she probably won't see it until later.

Not knowing what's wrong with Lorenzo, I buy every imaginable medicine I can find. The cashier gives me a funny look during check out, but doesn't offer a comment.

It's a forty-five-minute drive to Malibu, and I'm lucky that traffic is not heavy at the moment, or it could take much longer. I call Lorenzo again to keep tabs on him. He should probably drink water if he has a fever. He doesn't answer the phone this time and that fills me worry. My foot becomes lead on the gas pedal. Danny's car is an old Subaru, but it has juice.

I never thought I'd feel relief to be pulling up in front of my father's mansion. My heart is stuck in my throat when I burst through the front door. I kept the spare key even though I'm cut off from anything he owns. But Lorenzo lives here, and that asshole can't ever take my brother away from me.

"Hello?" I call out, just in case Lorenzo was mistaken and the housekeeper is working today.

My greeting is met by silence. *Goddamn it.* How can my father be so fucking careless as to leave Lorenzo in the care of such a selfish bitch? Who am I kidding? The man cares about nothing but himself.

I make a beeline for my brother's bedroom. He's in bed, passed out. I run to his side, and one touch is enough to tell me he's burning up.

"Lorenzo, wake up."

Whimpering, he blinks his eyes open. "Andy?"

"It's me, buddy. Let's get you out of these clothes. You need a cold shower."

"Why?"

I fish the thermometer from the shopping bag and take his temperature. One hundred three degrees. *Jesus.* He needs medication STAT.

"Because you have a high fever." I rummage inside the shopping again, until I find the Tylenol. "But first, you need to swallow these. Open your mouth."

He does as I say without a fight. Things weren't this easy when he was younger. Crystal always disappeared whenever Lorenzo got sick. Most of the time, the housekeeper would tend to him while I was in school. But at night, I was the one on duty.

"I feel like roadkill," he complains.

"I know. You'll get better soon. I promise."

I help him out of bed, and then I drag him to the bathroom.

"Shower or bath?" I ask him.

"If it's going to be cold, shower."

I turn on the water for him. When I face him again, he's struggling to get his shirt off. It's stuck to his back, thanks to the sweating. I help him out of it.

"There you go. Can you manage your pants now?"

"Yeah, I think so. But you might need to hold my arm."

I steady him and wait. Distracted, I glance at the mirror, and stop breathing. Lorenzo's back is a patchwork of bruises. Some deep purple and fresh. Others are older and already yellowing out.

"What happened to you?" I ask in a tight voice.

Lorenzo tenses in my arm. "Nothing. I fell."

Bullshit. I force him to stand straighter and look into my eyes. "Did Father do this you?"

Lorenzo's eyes swell with tears. He nods, keeping his jaw locked tight.

My own eyes prickle. I'm overwhelmed with too many emotions to even know which one is the strongest. I'm enraged that the son of a bitch hurt my brother. Furious at myself that I didn't follow up on my suspicion and get the truth sooner. But most of all, the guilt that pierces my chest leaves me weak.

I pull him into a bear hug. "I'm so sorry. I should have known."

"It's not your fault."

"How long has this been going on?"

"Not long. A month maybe."

Long enough. Bile pools in my mouth. His answer breaks me. I failed my brother. I should have spent more time with him. I naively believed that just because our father never laid a hand on him when I was around, Lorenzo was safe. I should have known that monster would turn on my brother. It can't be a coincidence that it started when I switched majors. God. I'm such a fucking idiot.

"Let's get you cleaned up and under the covers. You need to rest." I try to keep my voice steady for his benefit, but I'm screaming inside.

"What are you going to do, Andy?"

"I don't know yet. But one thing I promise you: you won't live under this asshole's roof any longer."

"But he cut you off. No judge will let you become my guardian."

"Don't worry about any of that. What we need now is to get you better."

The shower and the meds work to get Lorenzo's temperature down. I also found him chicken soup in a can that I'm sure was not meant for my father or Crystal. He's sleeping now, which means I'm all alone with my remorse. I can't look at him without seeing those awful marks on his back. I feel like crying, screaming, breaking things.

I walk out of his room and make a beeline for the bar in the living room. My father keeps it well stocked with the most expensive shit. The first bottle I find is of his preferred whiskey. It's brand new. I open the sucker and pour it all down the drain. Then I find a bottle of tequila. He doesn't drink it, but he likes to have top-shelf spirits for his guests.

Without bothering to look for a glass, I remove the cap and take large gulps straight from the bottle. The premium brand goes down my throat smoothly. I keep drinking until it numbs the pain swirling in my chest.

I stagger to the couch nearby and drop like a potato sack. I'm not drunk yet; it's the sense of failure that's dragging me down. I take another large sip, not caring that the tequila is hitting my hollow stomach. My head is getting fuzzy. I'd better take it easy. I can't pass out in a drunken stupor. Lorenzo's fever might return.

I sense a vibration in my pocket, but my clumsy fingers can't fish my phone out fast enough and I miss Jane's call. It's better that way. I don't want her to hear my pitiful voice. I text her saying that I'm going to spend the night here since Lorenzo is alone.

Instead of replying to my text, she calls again.

Hell, I can't ignore her call twice in a row. *Suck it up, man.*

"Hey, babe."

"Hi. How's Lorenzo?"

"Sleeping now. His fever has gone down." I hiccup.

"Andy, are you drunk?"

"Me? Nah. I just had a shot to get rid of the edge."

The lie rolls off my tongue easily, but it still leaves a bitter taste behind.

"It's hard being at your father's house after everything he's done to you, isn't it?"

Hell, she has no idea. If I tell her what I found out, she's going to reach the same conclusion I did. How could I possibly have not known my father was abusing Lorenzo?

"Yeah," I say.

"Do you want me to come over? I can spend the night."

"There's no need, babe. Besides, you have bootcamp tomorrow."

"Are you sure?"

"I'm sure. I want you rested. If you get injured because you're tired, I'll feel responsible."

"That's stupid thinking."

I wince. She has no idea how true that is. I was fucking stupid. I saw the signs something was off at Lorenzo's kart race and I didn't do anything besides ask him about it. He'd never tell me the truth. That's what victims of abuse do. We hide it at all costs.

"Truly. I'm fine," I insist.

"Okay then. But if Lorenzo gets worse, please call me."

"Sure, babe. I will."

I HISS IN PLEASURE. Jane's mouth is wrapped around my cock, sucking me into oblivion. I curl my hands into fists and start to help her out, fucking her mouth.

She laughs. "That's it, Andy darling. Come for me."

My body tenses immediately. That's not Jane's voice. It's Crystal's. This is not a dream, it's a nightmare. My head is fuzzy as hell when I open my eyes. My vision is blurry, but I see her white-blonde head bobbing up and down, my cock in her mouth. My heart is hammering inside of my chest as I watch frozen what's she doing to me. Again.

"Andy?" Jane's strangled voice calls me from near the front door.

She's staring at the scene with big round eyes and jaw slack.

The sight of her is like a jolt of electricity running through my body. I push Crystal off me and jump from the couch. But I drank more than I should have, and the room begins to spin.

"I can't believe this," Jane says before she turns around and runs out of the house.

"Jane. Wait!" I follow her but end up tripping on my two feet and falling to my knees.

Behind me, Crystal cackles. "Oh, how fickle young love is. She didn't even stay to hear your explanation. But then again, actions speak louder than words."

I look at her, ready to commit murder. "What the hell did you do, bitch?"

She flicks her hair over her shoulder. "I didn't do anything.

You were the one who texted Jane and invited her to come over. It's too bad your cock missed my tongue so very much. All it took was one lick and you were mine again."

I get back on my feet slowly, breathing hard. "You set me up?"

She raises an eyebrow. "What if I did? You need to understand, darling. I was your first, and I'll be your last. Everyone knows no one forgets their first and true love."

"You're not my true love!" I take a step forward with fists ready to punch.

"Hmm, all that rage. Go ahead, babe. Hit me. You know I like it hard." She runs her hands over her breasts, as if that sight did anything for me.

It does actually. A bout of nausea hits me, and I end puking all over my father's Persian rug.

"Oh, babe. That's probably going to stain. Don't worry. I'll tell your father the housekeeper did it."

"No, you won't," Lorenzo says. "I like Fatima."

Hell, when did he get out of bed? And how much has he heard of this disgusting exchange?

Crystal gets up from the couch, not bothering to adjust her skintight skirt.

"Whatever. I'm exhausted. The spa was a bust. I'm going to bed."

I watch her leave, bracing my hands on my knees. Lorenzo walks over, looking worried.

"Did you catch a cold too?"

"No, buddy. How are you feeling?"

"A bit better."

"Good. We're getting out of here."

43

JANE

MY EYES ARE BLURRY, and I can't see shit in front of me. But even if my vision hadn't been compromised, all I can see is Andy's stepmom giving him a blowjob. My stomach is twisted in knots and I want to throw up, but that means stopping the car and I won't do that. I have to put as much distance as possible between that house and me.

I feel like a fool. Now her presence in Andy's apartment makes sense. How long has he been fucking his stepmom?

Bile rises up my throat and I know I won't be able to keep my food down. I swerve to the side of the road and stop the car. I almost don't open the door in time. My throat and eyes burn as I expel the contents of my stomach. When the dry heaves stop, ugly sobs replace them. I close the door again, but I don't drive off right away. I'm too brokenhearted to do anything but cry my eyes out.

My phone rings, and the car's dashboard shows it's Andy calling. I reject the call and turn my phone off for good measure. Fear that he might have followed me spurs me into action. I have to get out of here. I put the car in Drive and return to the freeway.

The tears are still rolling down my cheeks as I blow past my father's house. I don't know where I'm going until I find myself suddenly in Troy's neighborhood. By some miracle, I manage to get a prime parking spot in front of his house. I stumble out of my car at the same time that the front door opens and Troy walks out.

"Jane, what are you doing here?" he asks.

I break into a run and collide into his arms. He engulfs me in a tight hug, and I hide my face against his chest.

"You're scaring me, Jane. What happened?"

"Oh God, Troy. It's Andy. It was awful."

His body tenses against mine. "What did he do?" he asks in a tight voice.

The sound of tires screeching make me tense. Immediately, I know that Andreas has followed me here.

"Jane!" he yells.

I untangle myself from Troy's arm and face him. "Go away! I don't want to hear it. I've seen enough."

"What have you seen, Jane?" Troy glances at me, fury sparkling in his eyes.

"Jane, please, it's not what you think." Andy is closer now.

Troy steps forward and stands in front of me like a human shield. "You gave me your word you wouldn't hurt Jane. And now she's in pieces. You'd better get the hell out of here before I break your face."

"I'm not leaving until I can explain."

"What's to explain?" I say as step from behind Troy. As destroyed as I am, I'm not going to let him fight my battles for me. "I found your stepmother sucking your dick. That's pretty fucking clear to me."

"You did what?" Troy asks in shock. Then he turns to Andreas. "You son of a bitch."

He pulls his arm back and punches Andy square in the face. He never stood a chance. He staggers back, fighting to keep his balance. It's in vain. He falls flat on his ass, and almost immediately, blood begins to drip from his busted nose.

"Andy!" Lorenzo screams from the curb.

I didn't see him until now. Why would Andreas bring his brother here to witness this?

He leans on his elbows and touches his bleeding nose before looking at me with such a pitiful stare, it almost makes me cry again. But I bite the inside of my cheek and fight the tears.

From the corner of my eye, I see someone running toward the house. When the porch light catches his frame, I see Danny's blond curls. He stops short when he sees Andy on the ground and Troy's aggressive stance.

"Fuck. What happened?"

"What do you think? Troy sucker punched me," Andreas gets back on his feet.

"What are you doing here, Danny?" Troy asks in an aggressive tone.

"I called him." Andreas pulls his T-shirt up and wipes off the blood from his face.

With wide eyes, Danny glances from him to us. Then he says, "Everybody needs to calm down."

"There's no calming down as long as this asshole is here," Troy spits with venom.

"It was a setup!" Andreas shouts.

"What?" I ask in a high-pitched tone.

"What you saw. Crystal set me up. I got drunk and she found me passed out on the couch. She's the one who texted you and waited until the she heard your car outside to do what you saw her doing."

"Come on. Do you seriously believe Jane will buy that half-baked excuse? Why would Crystal do that?" Troy asks.

"Because she's a fucking psycho!" Andreas pulls his hair back and starts to pace.

"You need to tell them the whole thing, Andy," Danny chimes in.

He gives him such a tortured look that it twists my heart even more. I hug my middle, afraid to know truth. Whatever it is, I know it will be ugly. Andy said he was damaged, unworthy of me. Maybe his feelings are not only related to the abuse he suffered at his father's hand.

"I need to speak to Jane privately first."

"Over my de—" Troy starts, but I cut him off.

"It's okay. I'll hear him out."

"Jane, are you sure?"

"Yeah. I'm sure. Is Charlie home?"

"No, she's visiting Ben."

"Do you mind waiting outside then?"

Troy glances at Andreas and clenches his jaw. "You have five minutes."

Andy glances at his roommate. "Danny, could you please take Lorenzo back to the car? He shouldn't be up and about."

"Yeah, sure." He steps closer to Andy's brother and steers him away from the house. "Come on, buddy."

Lorenzo throws Andreas a confused glance before going with Danny. He's not himself or he would have already pieced things together.

I head inside, and sense Andreas close behind me. He closes the door, but I keep walking until there's a good distance between us. I can barely look at him after what I saw. That scene will be imprinted on my mind forever.

"You heard Troy. You have five minutes," I tell him.

"Crystal was the first woman I slept with. I was fourteen, she was twenty-eight and Lorenzo's nanny."

Andy's admission that he slept with his stepmother is like a punch to my stomach. Everyone has a past, but that one is too cruel.

"I was naïve and thought I was in love with her. I didn't know she was only using me to get to the top prize, my father. When I caught her in bed with him, it destroyed me. I never felt more betrayed in my life. Then she married the asshole."

"Did you continue to sleep with her after she married him?"

"No. She wanted to, but I couldn't do it. I wouldn't share her with a man I hated so much."

"Are you still in love with her?" I ask in a small voice.

"No, God no. Jane, babe. I have no feelings toward that viper besides loathing. I didn't know what true love was until I fell for you. I'm in love with you."

I let out a ragged breath, my shoulders sagging. "Why did she do that to you?"

"Because she's a jealous bitch. She couldn't accept someone else had taken her place. Little did she know, you didn't take her place. She never had my heart. It has only belonged to one person. You."

He moves closer slowly as if he's afraid I'm going to run away. I won't though, because as crazy as the story sounds, I believe him. I replay all the tender moments we've had, and everything Andy has done for me, and I know in my heart that this man loves me.

I take a step forward. "I wish you had told me that story sooner."

"I couldn't. I never planned for you to know because I'm so ashamed of what I did."

"What you did? Andy, you were fourteen. She was the perv who seduced you. You did nothing wrong, she did. She should be in jail."

"It doesn't matter. I'll carry this stain in my soul forever."

I stop in front of him and punch his arm.

"Hey. What was that for?"

"That's for being such a dumbass. You're not tainted."

His eyes widen, followed by the lopsided curl of his lips. "What's up with you and your brother physically harming me?"

Ah hell. He has blood all over his face, and here I am, giving him a hard time. "I'm sorry. Do you think it's broken?"

"No, it's not broken. But you know what could make it better?"

He snakes his arms around my waist and pulls me flush against his body.

"What?"

"A kiss from you."

I lean forward, but stop short of pressing my lips to his. "She didn't kiss you on the mouth, did she?

He grimaces. "To be honest, I don't know. I was passed out."

"I swear to God that I will kick that skank's ass the next time I see her."

"Hopefully we won't have to suffer her presence ever again. But how about my kiss? I'm still in pain here."

I rise on my tiptoes, but only have the chance to brush my lips against his before Troy comes barging through the door.

"My five minutes aren't up yet, Troy," Andy says without looking in his direction.

"Something happened, Andy," he replies in a sad voice.

Andy turns around, noticing the change in my brother's demeanor. "What now?"

Lorenzo comes in with Danny by his side. He looks like he's in shock, his eyes bugged out and his skin definitely paler.

"It's your father," Danny replies. "He's dead."

44

ANDREAS

My father is dead, and my biggest regret is that I didn't get to punish him with my bare hands for what he did to Lorenzo. The asshole died of a heart attack while in bed with a hooker and the tabloids had a field day. Crystal played the victim role, milking it to the max. Several gossip magazines booked interviews with the "grieving, wronged widow."

The funeral was yesterday. I would have gone for Lorenzo's sake, but he was the first to announce he didn't wish to attend. It saved me from seeing Crystal face-to-face after the stunt she pulled in front of the cameras, but avoiding her is impossible. She was married to my father, and until all the red tape regarding his estate is over, I'm forced to deal with her.

Today, it's the reading of my father's will. I told Jane she didn't need to come, but she insisted on being by my side. She can't come into the meeting, though. The reading is only for the beneficiaries and their lawyers.

Troy and Danny came as well, plus Jack Morris, Ophelia's boyfriend who is a retired attorney and offered to help. I don't know what's in store for me, or if my father had a chance to cut me out of his will like he said. I don't care about the money though. My biggest concern is Lorenzo. I'll fight tooth and nail to become his guardian. It's a blessing that Crystal never wanted to adopt him, but I wouldn't put it past the bitch to want him if there's financial gain for her.

We arrived at the lawyer's office before the viper, but I know the exact moment she steps into the lavish reception area even though my back is to the door. Jane stiffens next to me and her gaze hardens. I follow her line of sight and see Crystal standing on the other side of the room wearing, for once, a dress that doesn't scream gold digger. She's still playing the demure widow for the cameras. I bet she's hired a paparazzo to follow her around and sell her images to the tabloids.

She doesn't remove her sunglasses, but I can feel her gaze on me. Her red lips curl into a smirk as she steps forward, veering in our direction. My skin crawls, remembering her unwanted touch. I brace for what's going to come out of her mouth. I can't be a hothead here. Jane jumps from her seat and strides ahead before I can stop her.

"Jane," Troy calls.

Fuck. I can't let her cause a scene here, even though she has every right to bitch-slap Crystal. I stand as well and follow her, ready jump in between them. The tension in the air becomes a live entity. This could turn ugly at a moment's notice. But Jane stops before she reaches Crystal, and I realize she wanted to block the snake's path to us. The shy girl I met three years ago has turned into a fierce lioness. Pride and love fill my chest, pushing back the anxiety that has riddled me ever since I found out about my father's death.

I stay a step behind, knowing that whatever Jane wants to do or say, she doesn't need me.

"You'd better think twice before you get any closer to Andy and Lorenzo," she warns Crystal in a defiant tone.

"Really? What are you going to do if I don't?"

Jane snorts. "It would be so easy to let your reporter friends know about your sex predator past. Statutory rape applies to both genders, in case you didn't know."

Crystal's lawyer widens his eyes as he glances at his client. I bet she didn't tell him about her dirty secret.

I told Jane I would only press charges against Crystal if it meant getting Lorenzo's guardianship. Does she deserve to be punished? Yes. But I don't want to subject our family to further scrutiny. I don't begrudge Jane for putting a little fear into that bitch's heart though. I used to be so ashamed of my past with Crystal. I feared people would look differently at me if they knew. But the secret lost its stigma and hold on me once Jane knew the truth. She didn't look at me in repugnance like I feared. On the contrary, I've never felt more loved by her, more connected.

The muscles around Crystal's mouth tense. She doesn't know Jane is bluffing. She harrumphs—the only sound she makes—and turns around to take the farthest seat away from us.

I'm fighting a grin when Jane spins around. It dies completely as I meet Jane's steely gaze. Yeah, she's still furious about the disgraceful trap Crystal set up for us. I can't blame her. I'd be enraged too if the situation had been reversed. I might have actually committed murder.

Both Troy and Danny are glowering in Crystal's direction when we return to our chairs. Lorenzo doesn't know about what went down that night, and I prefer that he never finds out. He has no lost love for the woman though. She embraced the wicked stepmom stereotype to a T.

She doesn't glance in our direction until we're called into the lawyer's office. I lean closer to Jane and kiss her on the lips.

"Thanks for having my back, babe."

"Always."

I get encouraging nods from Troy and Danny. Their support means a lot. They have no idea how much I need the encouragement. I honestly couldn't have survived the past week without them. I'm faking confidence here for Lorenzo's sake, but I'm way out of my depth.

I squeeze my brother's shoulder. "Ready?"

"Yeah. Let's get this over with."

Our father's lawyer is an ancient-looking man, frail in appearance, but his eyes are sharp behind his thick glasses. He's one of the top lawyers in the country, and smart as hell. It's hard not to feel intimidated by him. I keep my confident mask on because I can't show weakness in front of him or Crystal.

Once everyone is seated, he breaks the seal of the envelope to my father's will and begins to read from the document.

It's all filler to me until it comes down to listing the division of assets. Crystal leans forward, clutching her designer bag with a death grip. I can't help the sneer that crosses my face.

When the lawyer announces that Daddy Dearest left his entire fortune to Lorenzo and me, I'm stunned into silence.

Crystal shrieks. "What? That can't be right. I deserve half of it."

"Actually, according to your prenuptial agreement, you were only entitled to five hundred thousand dollars per year of marriage provided that you remained faithful. We have proof that wasn't the case, therefore your prenuptial agreement is void."

She turns to her lawyer and continues yapping like a banshee, but I tune her out, keeping my attention on the man behind the massive mahogany desk.

"What about Lorenzo? Does the will mention anything about him?"

"Your lawyer already made me aware that you wish to request guardianship of your brother. Since you have no close kin, and the will doesn't provide guidance regarding this issue, it's all a matter of following protocol now."

Jack pats me on the shoulder. "I'll take care of everything, son."

Crystal rises from her chair in a huff and turns her ire on me. "If you think I'm going to let that bullshit will stand, you're sorely mistaken. I'm coming for every fucking penny."

She marches out of the office, blowing smoke through her nose. Her lawyer trails after her in a much calmer fashion. He's probably loving this setback. It means more billable hours. Scumbag.

"Can she get in the way of my guardianship request?" I ask both Jack and my father's lawyer.

"I'm sure her lawyer will try every venue to guarantee she gets some of your dad's money," Jack replies.

"He can try, but he won't succeed. I drafted that contract. It's solid, just like the evidence she had several lovers throughout their marriage."

"So Dad knew she was cheating on him?" Lorenzo asks.

"Yes, he's known from the beginning."

"I don't get it. Why didn't he just divorce her? She was awful."

The older man shakes his head. "I can't answer that, kid."

I'm still dazed from the surprising developments when I walk out of his office. Troy, Danny, and Jane are deep in conversation. I don't need to guess the topic. They abruptly stop talking and glance at me just as I loosen the tie around my neck.

Jane gets up and walks over. "How was it? That awful woman left the office spitting fire from her mouth."

"She got nothing."

Jane's eyebrows shoot up to the heavens. "Really?"

"She cheated," Lorenzo pipes up. "That voided her prenup."

"Does that mean you got everything?" Danny asks my brother.

Lorenzo shakes his head. "No. Andy and I did."

"What? For real?" Troy looks at me, surprised. "I thought your father cut you off."

"So did I. Maybe he didn't have time to change the will. But it doesn't matter. All I care about now is making sure I become Lorenzo's guardian."

"Still. That's huge. Now you don't have to worry anymore about how to pay for your tuition next year," Danny chimes in.

"Honestly, if I had the luxury of not touching his money, I would." I pull the tie off my neck and shove it in my jacket pocket. Everything I'm wearing feels so damn constricting.

Jane steps into me, looping her arms around my waist. "I know you won't need his money soon. You'll make your own way."

Her embrace disperses some of the darkness swirling in my chest. Despite the outcome of today's meeting, I know the war is far from over. Crystal will be back to torment us.

But a lazy smile blossoms on my lips, and a peaceful warmth spreads through my chest. I don't know what I did to deserve this beautiful woman, but I'm so fucking glad that she chose me. I capture her face between my hands and bring her lips close to mine.

"I love you," I say before I kiss her deeply in front of everyone.

In the background, I hear Troy complain. But he'd better get used to it. If I have my way, Jane and I will be one of those annoying couples who can't keep their hands off each other. I've wasted too much time stuck in the void. Jane is my sun, and I'm never letting her go.

45

JANE

THE ENTIRE WEEK after the death of Andy's father was a whirl-wind. I spent every single moment I could with him and was barely home. My father was too busy with work to notice my absence.

I had to skip school in order to attend the meeting with Andy this morning, but unfortunately, I have a test next week that I must prepare for. So I come home, intent on putting a few hours of studying under my belt. I also made plans to meet with Alicia later to practice. I need to take my mind off of upsetting things.

My father's car is parked in front of the house, which surprises me. The sight doesn't fill me with anxiety like it used to whenever I came home and noticed Mom's car in the garage.

I've been meaning to talk to him alone, and this might be my best chance. The door to his office is open, and from the entryway, I hear his voice. He's on the phone. If I try to wait until he's done, he'll probably get into another call. I step toward his office, but a pile of thick envelopes on the dining room table catches my attention. The top one has Stanford's logo on the corner.

Shit. It's thick, which means it must be my acceptance letter. I wonder if that Dad was the one who left those for me or if it was his housekeeper.

There's a sudden lump in my throat as I change course and veer for the table. I don't care about Stanford—I knew I'd be accepted. The other envelopes in the pile are what interest me. I push Stanford's to the side. My breath catches when I see John Rushmore's logo on the next one. It's also a thick envelope.

Impatiently, I rip the paper and pull everything out. The letter on top is what I care about. I scan through the document in a flash, looking for one word: Congratulations.

My heart jolts forward. I read the same line a few times to make sure I'm not seeing things. But it's there. I've been accepted.

"Yes!" I shout, my outburst echoing in the room.

I read the entire letter more slowly now, but not calmer. My hands are shaking, and the thumping inside of my chest seems to intensify.

I'm in. I'm in.

My father finds me while I'm sporting the biggest grin on my face.

"Is that Stanford's letter?" he asks.

His question erases my smile. Grimacing, I lift my face from the letter.

"No. It's Rushmore's." I show him the paper with the school's logo.

He stares at me in silence for several beats. My mind is spinning like a top, working on all the arguments I have collected in the past month to convince him I don't belong at Stanford.

"Are you sure that's where you want to be?" he asks finally.

"Yes, Dad. I'm sure."

He sighs, glancing away. "If that's what you want, I'm not going to stand in your way."

His statement stuns me. I can't believe he's simply giving up after two years of relentless pressure.

"Wait? Really?"

"Your brother came to my office last week. We had a serious conversation about not only you, but our family. I'm not a good parent, I know that. My number one priority has always been my business." He passes a hand over his face and looks at me. "I had no idea what your mother was doing to you, Jane. And I'm so sorry for that."

I drop my eyes to the floor as an old feeling of failure sweeps over me. I've tried my hardest to not think about Mom since I moved out. She's selfish and cruel, and yet a small part of me still wants to make her love me. It's fucking stupid.

"Okay," I say.

Dad comes closer. "Jane, look at me."

I lift my face, fighting to remain calm and not crumble into a mess of tears. I've been doing so well for the past weeks. *Why do I feel like a weak little girl now?*

"I can't go back in time and fix my mistakes, but I promise to make up for them if you let me."

"Is that why you're not going to force me to attend Stanford?"

"In part. But I also realized I was projecting my dreams onto you and that wasn't fair. I was doing the same thing Elaine was doing to you."

"Okay, but what does that mean? Are you going to spend more time in LA from now on?"

"Yes, to start. I also want to get to know you. I have no idea what your likes and dislikes are. You also need to bring Andreas here for an official meet the parent dinner."

"Dad, you know Andy."

"I know him as Troy's friend. I don't know him as your boyfriend." He gives me a meaningful glance.

My cheeks become warmer. He must know I've been spending a lot of time in Andy's apartment.

"All right. I'm not sure when we can make it happen though. He's still dealing with the aftermath of his father's death."

"My assistant is keeping me updated on that. If he needs any support with anything, you can always ask me."

"Thanks, Dad. You have no idea how much this means to me."

He nods once and seems to run out of things to say. An awkward silence follows. We have a long way to go before we can create some kind of rapport. He took the first step, and now it's my turn to the take the second. I give him a hug, which feels weird. I don't remember ever hugging him, not even as a child. He stiffens at first, but then he throws his arms around my back.

I ease off after a brief moment, and then decide now is the time to tell him about roller derby.

"You said you wanted to know more about me. Are you free three weeks from now?"

"I'll have to check my schedule. Why?"

"I'd like you to come to an event. A sports event."

He raises his eyebrows. "Are you into sports too?"

"Not any sport. Are you familiar with roller derby?"

I expect many reactions from my father, not the goofy grin that splits his face. "Yeah, I'm familiar."

I watch him through narrowed eyes and point at his face. "What's that?"

He shakes his head. "What's what?"

"That dreamy smile."

His face becomes his usual impartial mask. "Nothing. I don't know what you're talking about. Make sure to let my assistant know the date and put a ticket aside for me. I'll be there."

He spins around, sticking his hands into his pockets, and walks back to his office with a new lightness to his steps.

It occurs me that I also don't know much about my father, and I might have unveiled a side of him I had no idea he possessed. Roller derby seems to have been the trigger. Now I have more reasons to look forward to the first game of the season.

46

ANDREAS – Three weeks later

I'm on pins and needles today, waiting for my damn phone to ring with good news. Lorenzo is sitting on the couch facing the TV, playing a video game with Danny. Jack managed to get temporary permission for Lorenzo to stay with me while we wait on the finalization of my guardianship request. He's supposed to call me today about that, hence why I keep maniacally checking my phone.

I wish Jane were here to keep me calm, but today is her debut roller derby game and she's at the gym with her teammates. She's been my rock during the past few weeks, the only one who managed to keep my head from spiraling into a dark abyss of pessimism.

Crystal and her lawyer haven't gone away. As we predicted, she's fighting the will, and as a last resort, requested to be Lorenzo's guardian as well. Jack guaranteed me she doesn't have a leg to stand on, but there's always the possibility that things could go her way.

I told Jack to use our trump card if necessary. I will disclose how she seduced me when I was a teen if it comes down to it. I'm not playing around. There's no chance in hell I'll let that snake take Lorenzo away from me.

When the phone finally rings, I jolt in my seat. That's how wound tight I am. It's Jack. I reach for the device in a hurry, almost dropping it to the floor.

"Jack, please tell me you have good news."

"You can pop that champagne, son. The judge has just signed the papers. You're officially Lorenzo's guardian."

I punch the air. "Yes!"

Danny and my brother pause the game and look at me.

"Did you get it?" Lorenzo asks, eyes filled with hope.

"Yes, bro. You're not going anywhere."

He smiles from ear to ear. "Awesome."

"Now we need to find a new place to live."

His grin wilts a fraction. "Why? I love living here. I can't wait to meet some hot college babes."

Danny snorts. "You have a little growing up to do, buddy."

"No way. Girls love a tragic story. They won't be able to resist consoling poor little orphan me." He bats his eyelashes in an exaggerated way as he presses his palm to his chest.

I twist my face into a scowl. "Yeah, yeah. That story will still work when you're out of diapers. You'd better stick to the hot babes in your age group."

Lorenzo rolls his eyes. "Fine. I won't go after any girls from Rushmore, but that doesn't mean I have to stick to the annoying girls in my class."

"Why don't you just concentrate on your studies for now?" I tell him sternly, not sure if I'm pulling it off.

His entire life I was the fun older brother who didn't hesitate to break the rules. Now, I have an entirely different role. I can't let him get away with shit anymore.

"What about karting?" He turns serious. "Am I not allowed to compete anymore?"

"Do you want to?"

I'm surprised by his question. I thought he'd want nothing to do with the sport that reminds him of our father.

He nods decisively. "Yeah. My interest might have started because of Dad, but I actually love to race."

"Well, if that's the case, of course you can compete."

"Great. I can't wait to go back to the tracks." He switches his attention back to the TV and unpauses the game.

I watch him play for a bit, noticing that he's definitely more relaxed now, even though I didn't think he was nervous before. He's better at hiding things than me.

My phone pings, announcing an incoming message from Jane.

Hᴇʏ, any news?

Yeah. I got it. I'm officially Lorenzo's guardian.

That's amazing, babe. I'm so happy for you.

I'm so relieved. I can't wait to celebrate it later with you.

Me too. If I survive the game. I have to go. I'll see you later. Love you.

I ᴄʜᴜᴄᴋʟᴇ as I type my reply.

I ᴋɴᴏᴡ.

You're an ass, but I still love you.

"Wʜᴀᴛ's sᴏ ғᴜɴɴʏ?" Danny asks.

"Nothing, man. I just happen to have the fucking best girlfriend in the world."

JANE – A few hours later

Tonight, it's my first game in the roller derby league. From inside the locker room, we can hear the wild clamor from the crowd. It's a full house and the knowledge is wreaking havoc with my nerves. Adrenaline is pumping in my veins as I absorb the rush of excitement that's floating in the air.

I'm still pinching myself to prove that this is real. After four gruesome weeks of intense training, the moment has finally arrived. I'm equal measures excited and terrified. Alicia waits next to me, sporting her game face. This is a special moment, more significant for her than for me. She's keeping the memory of her mother alive. Unlike me, who is trying to forget mine.

I won't think about her tonight. I'm not the daughter she wanted, and hence, she's not the mother I deserve. I haven't heard from her since I moved out, but Grandma told me she's traveling with her new boytoy.

At least Dad is trying to make up for his years of neglect. He promised he'd be here tonight. I got him a ticket and judging by how excited he was this morning when I left the house, I know he's out there.

I told Andy to look for him in the crowd and maybe they could sit together. The expression of sheer horror he gave me was priceless. I wish I had caught it on camera. We still haven't had the official boyfriend dinner, and Andy seems petrified of the idea.

"All right, ladies. Are you ready to kick some ass?" Katja shouts enthusiastically.

"Hell yeah!" we all reply in unison.

"Put it in." She shoots her arm forward, and we all stack our hands, ending our team huddle with a war cry.

Then we're putting our mouthguards on, checking the

straps on our helmets, and for me, trying not to puke. I'm so nervous, I'm not sure if I know how to skate anymore. I let everyone go ahead of me, but Alicia notices I'm stalling and throws her arm over my shoulders.

"Come on, girlie. This is going to be awesome."

She drags me with her, and when we emerge from the locker room and I see the crowd filling the entire gym, I balk.

"Oh my God. I think I'm going to pass out."

"No, you're not. Come on, they're going to announce us."

We skate faster to join our teammates. I purposely don't glance at the stands, fearing that if I see a familiar face, it will make me even more nervous.

Stop freaking out, Jane. You got this.

The announcer says our team's name, and then I really have to get over my pre-game jitters. I hop onto the banked track for the greet-the-crowd round. I can't avoid looking at the stands now, and the first thing I spot is a homemade sign with hearts, roller skates, and Jane Blaze in big glittery letters. My heart somersaults to my throat when I see who is holding the sign. Andy.

The butterflies in my stomach fly away as sudden calm washes over me. Seeing the love of my life there supporting me has that effect.

I barely notice my other supporters next to him. My eyes remain glued to Andy as I blow past him. I'm in the middle of the pack, so I can't skate closer to the railing, but I blow him a kiss.

We finish our lap and then wait for our adversaries to do the same. We're playing against Bay Hurricane, Scary Samantha's team, which is the strongest in the league. We might lose tonight. I'll probably get a lot of bruises. But I wouldn't trade this moment for anything in the world. This is where I belong.

ANDREAS

I have lost my voice. I never screamed so much in my entire life. Or yanked my hair back so often. I probably lost a good chunk of it. Lorenzo and Danny had to restrain Troy and me on several occasions when Jane got roughed up on the track. It'll take time to get used seeing her get hurt. It never occurred to me she probably felt the same way when Troy got sacked on the field, or I collided with an opponent.

Second Time Around Divas lost the game, but it was close. After they run their final lap, Jane veers straight to where we're standing, sporting the biggest smile on her face.

I reach over the railing and pull her to me for a scorching kiss. I don't care that Troy and her grandma are standing right next to me. The crowd near us goes crazy, wolf-whistling and shouting.

When I pull back, Jane's face is redder than before.

"What was that for?" she asks out of breath.

"Can't I congratulate my girlfriend?"

"We lost." She laughs.

"Not in my book." I grin from ear to ear.

I won't tell her my second reason for kissing her like that. I want all those baboons ogling her to know she's taken.

"It was an amazing game, dear. I'm so proud of you," Ophelia pipes up.

"Thanks, Grandma." She turns to Troy. "Have you seen Dad?"

"No. I'm sure he will find you outside."

"Jane, come on!" Alicia waves her over.

"I'm coming." She looks at me. "I have to go. Meet you out front in fifteen minutes?"

"I'll be there."

I watch her skate away and join her teammates Alicia and

Katja, who hug her from both sides. Someone elbows me hard on my arm.

"Get your shit together, man. You're drooling," Troy says.

"I wasn't, jackass."

Charlie shakes her head. "Don't mind him, Andy. He still can't handle seeing you all chummy with Jane."

Troy crosses his arms. "I'll never get used to that."

The crowd begins to shift toward the exit, and we do the same. It takes at least ten minutes to get out of the stands since we were closest to the railing. The majority of people are hanging outside the building where a few food trucks are serving morsels that make my stomach growl.

"I'm hungry," Lorenzo pipes up. "Can we see what they have?"

"Uh...."

I want to linger close to the exit, so I don't miss when Jane walks out.

Sensing my hesitation, Danny offers, "I'll go. I'm starving too."

"Hey, look. It's Fred and Sylvana," Charlie says.

I follow her line of sight, and sure as shit, the tall blond dude who had the hots for Jane is standing not too far from us, talking to his cousin.

Charlie waves and calls his name. I scowl. *Fucking great.*

"Try not to murder the guy," Troy tells me under his breath.

"As long as he stays away from Jane, I won't."

The duo walks over and take turns hugging Charlie. Troy—the traitor—shakes hand with him. I shove my hands in my pockets and try not glower... *too much.*

Fred briefly glances at me, but does nothing to acknowledge my presence, not even a nod. Whatever. Not like I'll ever be buddies with him.

Someone sneaks up from behind me and covers my eyes. It only takes me a second to recognize Jane's perfume.

"Guess who?" she asks in a different voice.

"Harley Quinn," I joke, and she pinches my arm.

I spin her around and trap her in my embrace, blocking her view of Fred on purpose.

"Were you testing me, babe?" I ask.

Her eyes dance with mischief. "Maybe."

"Hi Jane. Great game," a girl says.

She breaks free from my arms and looks over my shoulder. "Hey, Sylvana. I didn't see you there. Hi, Fred."

I step aside and let Jane talk to them for a moment. I'm jealous, but letting it show would give the blond too much power. It'd let him know I'm afraid to lose Jane to him, which is not true, at least not exactly.

I *am* afraid to lose her, but not to another guy. If that happens it'll be because I fucked up, which means I have to bring my A game to this relationship. Jane doesn't need another watchdog. She already has Troy. She needs a man who will support her decisions and let her grow as an individual. I will spend the rest of my days being that person for her.

She keeps her conversation with Fred and Sylvana brief, and then we go after Danny and Lorenzo. Before we locate them, another person finds us. Jane's father.

Hell and damn. I was hoping to avoid the man tonight. Wishful thinking.

"Dad, you came." Jane drops my hand to hug him.

He kisses the top of her head, the most affectionate gesture I've seen him do around people. I always had the impression he was a robot without a soul. I guess he's getting better, which makes me happy for Jane and Troy. They deserve a parent who cares. Like I had Mom.

"Why are you surprised? I said I would."

"Nice to see you, Jonathan," Ophelia greets him.

"Likewise." He nods, and then he switches his attention to me.

I try not to squirm under his scrutinizing gaze.

"Andreas Rossi, finally we meet again."

He offers me his hand, which I shake in an automatic reaction. I don't know why I'm freaking out, but I am.

"Sir."

"Sir? You can keep calling me Jonathan."

"Oh, okay. Sure."

"How about we pencil in that dinner we've been meaning to have?"

I swallow hard, but when Troy chuckles next to me, I forget my nervousness for a second to give him a death glare.

"What's so funny?"

He shakes his head, grinning. "Oh, nothing."

"How about tomorrow? Does that work for everyone?"

"It depends who you're including in your invitation," Ophelia chimes in.

Embarrassment seems to wash over the man's face. I suspect he forgot the feisty lady was nearby.

"Er... all of you, naturally," he replies.

She nods. "Good. Jack and Louis are dying to visit your house."

Troy groans and now it's my turn to laugh.

"Shut up," he says.

"I didn't say anything."

Glowering, he replies, "I know what you were thinking."

I snort. "Sure, you're a Vulcan now."

"I can't believe you know what a Vulcan is," Charlie pipes up.

Jane steps next to me and loops her arms around my waist. "Andy is secretly a nerd."

I wrinkle my nose. "Not quite. I just know my pop culture references."

"Well, I'll let you know the time tomorrow," Jonathan continues.

"We were planning on going somewhere to celebrate my game and the fact Andy got guardianship of his brother. You're more than welcome to come."

The man glances into the distance briefly, almost as if he's searching for someone in the crowd, and then back at Jane. He seems torn.

"I'd love to come, honey, but I have a prior commitment."

"Oh, okay. We'll see you tomorrow then."

"Perfect."

He kisses her forehead, says goodbye to the rest of us, and then strides away. He's definitely in a hurry.

"If we're heading somewhere, we'd better go now. These old bones can't handle too much excitement," Ophelia says.

"I need to find Lorenzo and Danny. Do you know where we're going?" I ask.

"Yeah, I'll text you the address. Go find them and meet me there. I have to get Grandma in the car," Troy replies.

"All right."

Jane drops her arms from around me, making me miss her warmth in an instant. I lace our fingers together and bring our joined hands to my lips to kiss her knuckles.

"Where do you think they went?" she asks.

I look over the sea of people to check out the assortment of food offerings. "Hmm, if I were to guess, I'd say they went for hotdogs."

"Really?"

"Oh yeah. Lorenzo doesn't care for experimental cuisine, and Danny loves all-American junk food."

"Oh yeah. Pringles Boy."

"You know about that nickname?"

"Charlie told me."

I find the diner food truck and make a beeline for it, while I gather the courage to broach a subject that's been nagging me since Jack told me I was Lorenzo's guardian. I never asked Jane how she felt about it. It's a lot of responsibility, and maybe she wants no part in it.

"Andy, you're squeezing my hand."

"Oops, sorry."

She stops, forcing me to do the same. "What's up? You got tense suddenly."

Damn. My girl is too observant. I can't really hide anything from her.

"You know that now that I'm Lorenzo's guardian, my life will be very different."

"Yeah, so?"

"So? I'm pretty much a parent now. And you're with me, which means.... Hell, I don't know. I never asked you if you wanted that kind of responsibility."

Jane's lips make a perfect *O.*

"Andy, I'm with you for better or for worse. Lorenzo is your brother. There's no doubt if I want to be part of his life or not. It's a hell yeah. He's my family now too."

I can't help the tears that well up in my eyes, or how my chest feels that much lighter. I pull her to me and kiss her soundly for as long as she lets me. When we finally break apart, we're both short of breath.

"Do you feel better now?" she asks.

"Yeah, babe. Much."

"Good. To be honest, I thought you were going to say something about Fred."

I frown. "Why? I was on my best behavior."

"I know. And that surprised me."

"I won't deny it, jealousy reared its ugly head for a moment. I'm not perfect, babe, but I'm trying to be the man you deserve."

She cups my cheek tenderly. "You *are* the man I deserve."

"If you say so, but I think one can always become better."

Narrowing her eyes to slits, she asks, "What are you saying, Andy? Is that a hint that I need to improve?"

I chuckle, reaching for her face to rub my fingers over her lips. "No, my sweet Jane. You are perfect."

She wrinkles her tiny nose. "No one is perfect."

"You are to me."

I lean closer to kiss her again, but an oversized ice cream cone appears between our faces.

"Andy, look what Danny bought me."

I step back, wiping the bit of whipped cream from the tip of my nose. The white stuff is all over Lorenzo's face.

"What the hell did you get him?" I ask. "That thing is bigger than his face."

He shrugs. "He wanted it. What was I supposed to say? No?"

"Yeah. We're going out to dinner and that much sugar is going to put him in a coma."

Jane chuckles next to me. "He's twelve, Andy, not five."

"You laugh now, but you'll wait and see."

She rises on her tiptoes and kisses me on the cheek. "You'll be a wonderful father. I can't wait to see it."

"Skipping the early years and going straight to pre-teen. Piece of cake." I laugh.

"And you love cake." She smiles.

"Not as much as I love you."

"I know."

*** **THE END** ***

HEART STARTER

My plans were simple. Graduate from college, get a job, and not worry anymore if I can make next month's rent.

It turns out I might have a shot of getting drafted to play in the NFL, and nothing will distract me from that goal.

I didn't count on Sadie Clarkson wrecking my plans. Our first meeting was explosive, to say the least. Now I can't stop thinking about her sassy attitude or sexy mouth.

On top of being a distraction I don't need, she's also the coach's daughter and off-limits.

But forbidden fruit always tastes better. She might cost me everything I've worked for, and yet I'm willing to risk it all.

My sanity.
My heart.
My world.

PRE-ORDER HEART STARTER

ALSO BY MICHELLE HERCULES

Paranormal Romance:

Dark Prince (Blueblood Vampires #1)

Wild Thing (Blueblood Vampires #2)

Forgotten Heir (Blueblood Vampires #3)

Reckless Times (Gifted Academy #5)

Contemporary Romance:

Wonderwall (Love Me, I'm Famous #1)

Sugar, We're Going Down (Love Me, I'm Famous #2)

Wreck of the Day (Love Me, I'm Famous #3)

Devils Don't Fly (Love Me, I'm Famous #4)

Love Me Like You Do (Love Me, I'm Famous #5)

Catch You (Love Me, I'm Famous #6)

All The Right Moves

Heart Stopper (Rebels of Rushmore #1)

Heart Breaker (Rebels of Rushmore #2)

Heart Starter (Rebels of Rushmore #3)

Reverse Harem Romance:

Wicked Gods (Gifted Academy #1)

Ruthless Idols (Gifted Academy #2)

Hateful Heroes (Gifted Academy #3)

Broken Knights (Gifted Academy #4)

Lost Horizon (Oz in Space #1)

Magic Void (Oz in Space #2)

Red's Alphas (Wolves of Crimson Hollow #1)

Wolf's Calling (Wolves of Crimson Hollow #2)

Pack's Queen (Wolves of Crimson Hollow #3)

Mother of Wolves (Wolves of Crimson Hollow #4)

ABOUT THE AUTHOR

USA Today Bestselling Author Michelle Hercules always knew creative arts were her calling but not in a million years did she think she would become an author. With a background in fashion design she thought she would follow that path. But one day, out of the blue, she had an idea for a book. One page turned into ten pages, ten pages turned into a hundred, and before she knew, her first novel, The Prophecy of Arcadia, was born.

Michelle Hercules resides in Florida with her husband and daughter. She is currently working on the *Blueblood Vampires* series and the *Rebels of Rushmore* series.

Join Michelle Hercules' Readers Group:
https://www.facebook.com/groups/mhsoars

Connect with Michelle Hercules:
www.michellehercules.com
books@mhsoars.com